The two pira
half-drowned
deck of the *Isabela*

The vice admiral smiled and turned to the governor. "You wanted Black Richard Neville. Well, here he is."

The governor stared at the man lying spread-eagled on the deck, half-conscious. He barely noticed the other, a half-dead cabin boy. And as the hurricane raged, there was little to be done about them. Crates of priceless treasure broke loose from their moorings, crushing crewmen and passengers alike. The foremast snapped and fell, raining down tackle and rigging. The ship spun around, caught on a reef, and men jumped overboard, clutching their valuables.

Of the five survivors, none knew the fate of the vice admiral or the governor of Cuba, but one survivor's account remained. He insisted till his dying day that he saw the dashing buccaneer Black Richard Neville and the young cabin boy lying forgotten on the deck; then, with the coming of another crashing wave, they simply disappeared, vanishing shortly before the *Isabela* succumbed to her own tragic fate.

Dear Reader,

If January puts ideas of "getting away from it all" into your mind, our Superromance authors can help.

Lynn Erickson's adventurous and very twentieth-century heroine, Tess Bonney, finds herself face-to-face with *The Last Buccaneer* when she is transported through time to the Spanish Main.

Out on the west coast, Nora Carmichael's ordered life is suddenly thrown into chaos when her apartment is invaded by *The Dog from Rodeo Drive*. Author Risa Kirk gives Lane Kincaid, her wonderful hero, the formidable task of convincing Nora that both he and the puppy are perfect for her.

In Boston, Stephanie Webb and her boss, Ben Strother, reluctantly join forces to bring their parents together, but their parents, it seems, have plans of their own. They arrange a vacation in Hilton Head so that their stubborn children will give in to the inevitable—*their* mutual attraction. *The Parent Plan* is a must for Judith Arnold fans!

Media personality Patrice Sullivan returns to North Carolina for her zany daughter's wedding and finds her "ex" as sexy and infuriating as ever. Peg Sutherland's *Simply Irresistible* is just that—a touching and lighthearted romp that stitches together a relationship clearly never meant to end.

In the coming months, in addition to more great books by some of your favorite authors, we've got some new talents to showcase. There's lots of excitement planned for 1994, so go ahead and get away from it all—and then come back and join us for all the fun!

Marsha Zinberg
Senior Editor

Lynn Erickson

THE LAST BUCCANEER

Harlequin Books

TORONTO • NEW YORK • LONDON
AMSTERDAM • PARIS • SYDNEY • HAMBURG
STOCKHOLM • ATHENS • TOKYO • MILAN
MADRID • WARSAW • BUDAPEST • AUCKLAND

This book is dedicated to Brian Henry
It was all his idea

ISBN 0-373-70578-6

THE LAST BUCCANEER

Copyright © 1994 by Carla Peltonen & Molly Swanton.

ABOUT THE AUTHOR

Carla Peltonen and Molly Swanton, better known to romance fans as Lynn Erickson, are history buffs. They put their interest to good use in their contemporary novels, drawing on the past to make the present more vivid and creating some exciting time-travel romances. Their first time-travel romance, *West of the Sun*, won a *Romantic Times* award for best time travel of 1990. *The Last Buccaneer* is equally compelling. Set in the Florida Keys, which have always held great fascination for Molly as well as for treasure hunters, the book has a special place in their hearts.

Carla and Molly live in Aspen, Colorado, and have been writing as a team for more than fifteen years.

Books by Lynn Erickson

HARLEQUIN SUPERROMANCE
298—FOOL'S GOLD
320—FIRECLOUD
347—SHADOW IN THE SUN
370—IN FROM THE COLD
404—WEST OF THE SUN
439—THE NORTHERN LIGHT
482—SILVER LADY
520—A WING AND A PRAYER
549—PARADOX

Don't miss any of our special offers. Write to us at the following address for information on our newest releases.

Harlequin Reader Service
P.O. Box 1397, Buffalo, NY 14240
Canadian address: P.O. Box 603,
Fort Erie, Ont. L2A 5X3

Historical Note

Since the defeat of the Spanish Armada by England in 1588, Spain was losing its monopoly on the New World. England and Holland and France were the new sea dogs, hungry for a taste of the fabled treasures of the West Indies and the Pacific, which were personified by the Manila galleons from the Philippines and the great bullion fleets that set sail from Mexico and Havana to Spain.

England's King James I winked at privateers who were issued letters of marque, allowing them to attack and plunder Spanish treasure ships with impunity.

By the 1620s, the English, Dutch and French all had island strongholds in the Caribbean. The Dutch also ran the black slave trade and had colonized New Amsterdam in modern New York state. The English had settled Jamestown, Virginia, and the Massachusetts Bay Colony. The French controlled the fur trade in Canada. All of these holdings contributed to Spain's weakening grasp on the New World.

The West Indies were ripe for the buccaneer, the man of no country, who took what he wanted where he wanted, with the entire Western hemisphere as high stakes in the game.

The hurricane of September 6, 1622, is fact; the Spanish fleet caught in the storm is also fact, as is the subsequent demise of Spanish power due to the loss of that fleet and its treasure-laden galleons.

And it is fact today that men still search the Caribbean for those lost treasures.

PROLOGUE

The Florida Straits
Dawn: Tuesday, September 6, 1622

THE SPANISH GALLEON *Isabela* had struggled against the hurricane for a full twenty-four hours. The chief pilot on board this, the largest treasure ship in the convoy, had not slept for a day, shouting orders to the crew, seeking sea room to maneuver the unwieldy vessel through the narrow straits.

It was hurricane season, as everyone knew, but when the convoy had left Havana harbor two days ago, the sea had been serene, and the vice admiral of the fleet had thought to make it through these treacherous waters without trouble. He could not have waited any longer despite the unusual lateness of this return trip to Cadiz, because word had come directly from young King Philip's ministers—the treasury was empty. The New World wealth *must* be delivered this season.

From the aft cabin high over the galleon's ornate transom, the vice admiral tried to calm his nervous but very important passenger, the governor of the colony of Cuba. He was only too aware of the danger they were in, although he did not let on to the governor, and he kept checking the storm's progress through the whorled glass of the small-paned window. The storm topsails bellied out tautly from the wind, gamely carrying the weight of the heavily laden ship. The ropes took the strain, groaning. The sea swelled above them, crashed down on the deck and ran out, frothing and hissing through the scuppers.

"Let this accursed wind get no worse," muttered the admiral, "and we'll make deeper waters."

He had to succeed. His fleet consisted of thirty vessels, two towering, fat-sided galleons, the *Isabela* and the *Madonna,* many smaller ships and a number of well-armed warships for protection from the English and French and Dutch pirates. *May the devil torture the thieves without mercy,* the vice admiral added silently, as always.

His fleet was now scattered for fifty miles along the treacherous Florida coast and its dangerous *cayos* or keys, those small islands dotting the straits like teeth that could impale and savage a ship, and where there was not a visible key, the captain knew only too well that there were shallows upon which to run aground.

But the pilot was experienced. He'd sailed these waters before and knew every current, every shoal, every reef. *Sí,* but not in a foul storm such as this one. The admiral saw the pilot shouting at the crewmen to tighten the rigging, to swing a yardarm. Then the pilot turned back to the exhausted, sodden sailor who was fighting the wheel and helped him hold it steady. Spray frothed over the deck and soaked everyone again—and again.

The vice admiral automatically steadied himself with a hand on the bolted-down table and turned away from the mayhem on the deck. He *had* to get the *Isabela* safely back to Spain. His career, his future, his very life depended on it. The *Isabela* carried the wealth of the New World crammed into her four decks, into her holds and storerooms, lashed onto every square inch of free deck space, jammed into chests and crates, filling the holds so that she wallowed in the water like a pregnant sow. Silver coins minted in Peru and Mexico, gold ingots, coins, reals and doubloons and ducats, a fortune from the black slave trade, pesos, bars of copper, bales of indigo, tobacco and hundreds upon hundreds of silver ingots, each one stamped with a serial number, a code noting its refinery and its exact weight. Each ingot was stamped and tested and carefully listed on the ship's manifest. Precious cargo, an untold fortune traded and stolen and scraped from the rich, hot earth of Spain's New World colonies, bound for the empty coffers of young King Philip the Fourth.

Throughout the *Isabela,* in passengers' staterooms and mess halls, in the crew's quarters, men were kneeling and praying, pulling out their jeweled crucifixes, praying to their most holy Catholic God or to his mother Mary for deliverance from this satan-whelped storm. Crewmen fought doggedly, climbing the rigging to untangle lines, hanging out over the roiling sea, bare feet clinging to slippery perches. If the *Isabela* could make open water where there was room to maneuver, they'd survive, but this deadly, narrow passage had to be negotiated first.

"¡Dios!" cried the governor as the vessel heeled violently. "Can we continue to take this beating?"

"Of course," the admiral replied soothingly. "This ship is built to withstand anything the ocean sends us. Do not worry. My men are experienced." It wasn't the high seas he was afraid of; it was the damned hidden shallows and the wind, the endless, howling wind.

Through the window of the cabin, the vice admiral saw the men on deck suddenly turn their attention to the port side. *My God,* he thought, *not a reef,* por favor, *not a reef.* He strained his eyes to see through the quickening light and spray and slanting rain. What were they all looking at? Faintly, over the noise of the tempest, he heard the bow lookout shouting, waving, pointing.

A ship. Yes, out there in the wild waters, bearing down on them, a three-masted frigate, not one of their own, her hull painted black, her sails black, a demon ship. She was much too close in this wind, in these seas. A madman was sailing her, using the wind to race, plunging, right toward them.

"¡Madre de Dios!" the admiral gasped.

The governor came to stand beside him, straining to see through the window. "What? What is it? Are we...?" He fell silent, seeing the black ship flying toward them.

The admiral cursed harshly. He now recognized that ship. Oh, *sí,* there was no mistaking it. Only one like it existed on the whole of the Spanish Main. It was a private ship, and its captain was the infamous Richard Neville, bastard of an Englishman but man of no country now, as black a devil as these waters had ever spawned. He'd killed and plundered and stolen from the Spanish until mothers frightened their children with his name and the name of his ship, *Marauder.*

Now. Here. An ungodly vessel in an ungodly storm. Was Black Richard as insane as he was evil?

"It is him, is it not?" the governor was asking. "Neville, the pirate."

"*Sí,* it is him," the admiral said tightly.

The *Marauder* wallowed in the seas, hidden for a moment by a monstrous wave, then appeared closer. The two Spaniards could see the pirate crew now, clustered on the rails, waiting to close with the *Isabela.* They were grinning ferociously, long hair streaming wetly, bare feet splayed on the plunging deck, cutlasses thrust in gaudy sashes.

"They'll never be able to catch us in this," the admiral said.

"The man is *absolutamente loco,*" the governor said, paling even more. "It is as his brother said. Evil and demented."

The admiral sent a cabin boy out with orders, but there was little that could be done. The ship was pitching and rolling too much to aim the cannons; the powder was too wet for the soldiers' muskets to fire. The Spanish pilot could not even turn his ship broadside or run before the wind. The *Isabela* could only go where the wind took her and hope that the pirate ship was in as much trouble as was the galleon.

"There," the governor said in a hushed voice, "there he is. I see him!"

The man called Black Richard, *Ricardo Negro,* by every Spaniard in the West Indies, was standing on the quarterdeck, directing his crew. His hair was whipping in his face, his white shirt clung wetly to him, a sword was in his hand. Yes, it was he. One could not mistake the black patch over his eye.

"Damn his soul to perdition," the admiral muttered.

The *Marauder* loomed closer, her sleek black hull glistening, her pointed bow diving down, down into the sea, then slicing up, the entire ship shaking off the water as if she were a dog, racing on, closing with the *Isabela*. And then she was nearly upon them—her black bowsprit seeming to transfix the *Isabela*. The governor recoiled inadvertently, imagining that Black Richard searched him out, saw him, grinned evilly at him for the bargain the governor had struck with Neville's brother. God, would that the bargain had been kept!

But the *Marauder* was fighting the accursed storm, too, and with the next battering wave, she was pushed away from the galleon. Broadside momentarily, she was assaulted by a wall of water, and then the governor could see it happen—two of the pirate crew were washed overboard by a wave, two tiny, helpless figures in the immensity of green-gray frothing ocean.

Despite the conditions, the laws of God and humanity held. Orders were given, even as the black-hulled frigate fell off, fighting to approach but losing the battle, and ropes were lowered to the two bobbing sailors drowning in the water. By the act of an all-merciful Savior, the two pirates were hauled, dripping and half-drowned, onto the heaving deck of the *Isabela*.

The vice admiral smiled and turned to the governor, forgetting for a moment the danger the ship was in. "You wanted Black Richard Neville, did you not, Governor? Well, there he is."

The governor in wide-eyed awe stared. It was a miracle! There he lay, spread-eagled on the deck, half-conscious, his crew and ship and weapons gone, coughing seawater out of his lungs. The governor barely noticed the other pirate, a half-dead cabin boy of puny size. "Hang him," the governor ordered, clutching the table to support himself. "Hang the blackguard! Now!"

"But, Governor, could we not wait until the storm is past? Even take him to Spain? The king—" the admiral began to plead.

"No. He has already escaped me for two years, and I want him hung now."

The noose was readied—a thick rope fastened to a yardarm right on the main deck. It swung wildly with the careening of the vessel as the ship crashed into the deep trenches of the sea. The *Marauder* was gone, swallowed up in the storm, fighting for her own survival.

At this point, accounts from the handful of survivors of the *Isabela* that morning of September the sixth, 1622, became sketchy. It was said later that the hurricane that tore through the Straits of Florida gathered strength as if propelled by the devil's breath. The other ships of the fleet were scattered, each fighting desperately for her own life. There was a firm account of the pilot's desperate warning that the ship was being carried into shallow waters. Sailors struggled to raise the mainsail in an attempt to back off the reef. Sea anchors were dropped in hopes of catching and stopping the ship. All to no avail. The *Isabela* was swept onto the shallows, grinding, shuddering, her hull ripped open.

Bedlam reigned. Crates of priceless treasure broke loose from their moorings crushing crewmen and passengers alike. The foremast snapped and fell, raining down tackle and rigging. The ship spun around and was held fast by the reef. Shoved by the wind she listed badly. Some men jumped overboard, clutching their valuables. Others shrieked in fear or fell to their knees and prayed. Some of the crew tried to keep the galleon afloat while other seamen lowered boats which were immediately dashed to splinters against the side of the *Isabela*. Of the five survivors, none knew the fate of the vice admiral or the governor of Cuba or any of the other men that day, only that of their fellow sailors whom they saw die with their own eyes.

One survivor's account remained, however—that of a cook's helper. Till his dying day many years later, he insisted that he'd seen the dashing buccaneer Black Richard Neville and the young cabin boy on the slanting deck of the doomed *Isabela* where they were forgotten, the Spaniards being concerned only with their own salvation. He held to his story that the two Englishmen were there on the deck one moment and then, with the smashing of another terrible wave over the crippled galleon, they simply disappeared, vanished, shortly before the *Isabela* succumbed to the hurricane and met her own tragic fate.

CHAPTER ONE

The Present

IT WAS MAYBE the dumbest thing Tess Bonney had done in a long time.

She sat squashed in the narrow seat of the commuter plane as it flew south following the long curve of the Florida Keys, and she wanted to go back home to Miami.

"Vacationing in Key West?" the young man next to her asked.

And she was so tired from her trip that day—Seville, Spain, to Miami, Florida—that she spoke without thinking. "I'm going to see a cannon."

"Come again?"

Tess perked up and thought fast. Her brother Paul would kill her if she let the news out prematurely. "Oh," she said lightly, "I'm a teaching assistant at the University of Miami, history, you know, and there's this cannon in a museum I want to see."

"Long way to go to look at a cannon," he remarked, flipping the pages of the airline magazine.

"Oh, well," Tess said, shrugging, "you know what history buffs are like."

Of course he didn't, and she settled back in her window seat and watched the sun set and streak the sky with lavender above the bank of clouds that hovered over the Gulf of Mexico.

It had all begun on a Tuesday, she remembered, on a hot June afternoon in the city that never slept—Seville, Spain. But that had been weeks ago, and her excitement over the discovery in those ancient, dusty Seville archives had dulled. In retrospect the discovery really didn't seem so significant. Anyone could have come across that old document. It had been a fluke because, as anyone who'd ever conducted research in the archives could tell you, nothing, but *nothing,* was in order. What Tess had been researching for her master's thesis was a point in Spanish history in the New World, 1638 to 1645; what she'd come across, misfiled, was a letter written by a survivor of a galleon sunk in 1622, specifically the treasure ship, *Isabela,* purportedly the richest of all treasure ships to have sailed the Spanish Main.

No one else, she guessed, would have given the letter much thought. But it had caught her eye because her brother Paul had been working for some years with Mack Solomon, treasure hunter and salvor extraordinaire, in the waters off Key West. For nearly twenty years, Mack Solomon and his crew had been searching for the fabled ghost galleon *Isabela,* scouring the bottom of the *bajamar,* the shallow sea, that had once been called the Spanish Lake or the Spanish Main.

Tess had read and reread the passage in the faded old document telling of the ship's plight in the Florida Straits during a hurricane. Everyone knew about that. They knew the galleon had gone down in that storm on September 6, 1622. The Spanish themselves, desperate because young King Philip the Fourth was broke, had tried to salvage the ship in 1623. Of course, documentation of that futile effort was unspecific about the galleon's location in case the English, French or Dutch should try to salvage the *Isabela* themselves. But in reading the letter Tess had found that the location was clearly described.

Until now, Mack Solomon had been searching the waters to the east of Key West. Her Spanish wasn't great, but she knew that the Spanish word for east was *este.* In this letter from a survivor, the location of the galleon just before it succumbed to the storm was *oeste,* or west of what was then known as the *cayos*— the modern-day Florida Keys.

She'd called Paul in Key West and he'd been blown right out of his socks.

"West? You mean Mack's been searching in the wrong place for twenty years?"

"Well," Tess had said over the trans-Atlantic cable, "I'm just telling you what the letter says."

"Fax it to us! Can you fax it right this minute?"

"Oh, sure."

Sitting in the plane now, Tess still felt funny about the discovery. She simply did not believe in coincidences. It seemed as if that letter had been *put* in the wrong file just for her to find. But then, that was ridiculous.

She recalled how she'd gotten into Miami this morning, glad to be home at last in her tiny apartment. Along with a couple of messages from her parents there had been an urgent one from Paul. "Get here on the first flight you can, Tess,'' he'd said. ''We found a bronze cannon. It was near the Quicksands, Sis, which is *west* of Key West. You're a hero!'' There'd been a pause, then, ''Oh, and for God's sake, don't tell anyone yet. Mack's verifying the serial numbers even as we speak.''

She'd called Paul's apartment in Key West several times and only gotten through to him at five.

''Can you take an evening flight?'' he'd asked.

''No way. My head's splitting, I've got to start organizing my notes for my thesis, and classes start in eight weeks. My credit card's ready to burst. Paul, I just can't come down.''

''Mack would love you to be here. He's planning a party for the crew tonight and you're the guest of honor.''

''Oh, forget it! I'd be so embarrassed. No way, Paul.''

But here she was flying south, anyway. And she'd even blabbed to the total stranger next to her that she was going to see a cannon.

Tess cringed at the thought as the little plane banked on the approach to Key West, a cluster of lights at the very southern tip of the Florida Keys. Several years ago an anchor had been recovered by the Solomon salvage crew. One of the dredging operators had leaked the news to the press. Even *National Geographic* had sent down a camera team. The anchor, it turned out, had come from a Spanish ship sunk in the late seventeenth century. Mack Solomon, already suffering from too much press after so many years of futile searching for the mother lode, was furious. Not

to mention humiliated. Well, Tess thought as the plane
touched down on the hot tarmac, if the news got out,
it was Paul's fault for telling her about the cannon in
the first place.

THE CELEBRATION WAS in full swing by the time Paul
pulled up to Mack's house in the heart of Key West's
Old Town. Tess got out of the Toyota pickup truck,
straightened her short navy skirt and looked around.
She hadn't made the one-hundred-and-sixty-mile trip
down from Miami in years.

"Hasn't changed at all," Tess observed. "Still as
funky as ever down here."

"Insulting my little island, are you?"

"I'm not sure," she said and followed him up the
walk to Mack Solomon's charming island home.

Any observer would pick up on the brother-sister
relationship as soon as he saw Tess and Paul Bonney
together. Both were dark-headed and even wore their
hair a lot alike—cut short, lying in shining dark caps,
fringed around the ears. Paul pushed his forelock to
one side but Tess had bangs. Their builds tended to be
on the slight side, though Paul was leanly muscled
from his years of undersea work. The shape of their
faces was oval; their eyes were dark. Around those
eyes both brother and sister had indecently long
lashes, making Tess's eyes pretty, her brother's em-
barrassingly so, too.

They both had nice noses, although Tess had a delicate tilt to hers while Paul's was more substantial. Her
mouth was also upturned at the corners, her lower lip

heavier, and she had dimples and very dark eyebrows, one of which often went up in a distinct arch.

Paul was twenty-eight, Tess two years his junior, but both could pass for teenagers in a pinch. Tess even joked she could be a boy with her lean hips and small breasts...a five-feet-four-inch straight-hipped youth. If it weren't for her small hands and feet and those seductively long black eyelashes, Tess wondered if anyone would take her for a woman.

Brother and sister entered Mack Solomon's two-story conch house that sat near the waterfront on Whitehead Street. Tess had learned from previous visits that a "conch" referred to a local, someone born on the island. And a conch house was a distinctive island house, a blend of New England and Bahamian architecture, usually a two-story wooden structure with storm shutters, cool porches, intricate latticework and scrolling. Some had widow's walks; others sported wraparound porches. All fine conch homes had beautifully planted gardens in the rear—lush, large, shaded areas where a sea captain of a century ago could take his rest.

Ernest Hemingway had owned a conch house on the island, complete with dozens of cats. Harry Truman had owned one, too, dubbed the Little White House; it was directly across the street from Mack Solomon's.

"Nice place," Tess whispered into Paul's ear. She need not have whispered; the party out back was in high gear. Tess knew the sort of men and women she was about to meet. They were thrill seekers, adventurers, romantics. Optimists to a fault. They'd have to be, Tess decided, or they'd have given up the hunt years ago. It wasn't as if Mack could pay them much, if at all. What these divers and boat captains, winch operators and dredging crews were really in the quest for was the thrill, the long shot, the once-in-a-lifetime experience of being the first man or woman to touch a treasure that had been lost in the mists of time. Oh, the idea of striking it rich, *really* rich, appealed too. But Tess knew these people. If they weren't scouring the ocean floor for treasure they'd be climbing Mount Everest or dousing oil fires or riding bucking broncos or dog sledding to the South Pole. Her brother was one of them.

Tess, on the other hand, found stimulation in more cerebral ways: following a fascinating trail of historical research, understanding past cultures, writing a little, beginning what she hoped would be a rewarding career of teaching and research. She was a scholar, proud of her hard work and her good mind, deriving great pleasure from the intellectual discoveries she made and the superb sense of order she found in history.

These people were different, though. They thrived on disorder and risk, and sometimes, secretly, fleetingly, Tess envied them, although, God knew, she'd never want to emulate their reckless craziness. Now she stood on the Solomons' back porch and looked at these very revelers gathered to celebrate the finding of the bronze cannon. They drank hugely, fearlessly, daring their heads to pound in the morning. They were an eccentric lot, their ages ranging from their early twenties on up; one of the dredge operators was seventy-five if he was a day. Some of the men wore ponytails hanging down their sun-browned, freckled backs; others sported crew cuts, easier to care for when half their lives were spent underwater. Almost everyone had pierced ears, men and women alike.

Paul squeezed her hand. "They're loud, but they're good people. Don't be put off by the noise," he said.

"I'm not," she replied bravely.

They started down the back porch steps when someone abruptly called out, "Yo! Is that your sister, Paul?"

"This is Tess," he said to the suddenly quiet crew, and she could feel her cheeks grow hot and wished with all her heart no one would make a fuss. Sure, she'd helped steer the salvors in the right direction, but she was hardly the heroine Paul kept calling her.

"Three cheers for Tess Bonney," another voice called, "hip, hip, hooray!" Beer cans and half-empty champagne bottles clinked, and Tess felt the heat and humidity claw at her.

And then he was there, *the* Mack Solomon, the most famous undersea treasure hunter in the world. Heck, *National Geographic* had done articles on his exploits and even a TV special. Salvors from all seven seas emulated his search methods. And even though the *Isabela* was still eluding him, Solomon had found and salvaged three other Spanish ships lost in the Caribbean. It was reported by some that Mack had made three fortunes and squandered them all on the search for the elusive *Isabela,* although, with this cannon, he was fast closing in on the long-sought mother lode.

Then Tess remembered something else: Mack and his wife had lost a son to the quest. The young man had drowned ten years ago in a tragic accident while working for his father. No wonder Solomon had to keep going despite the odds! To quit his search of twenty years after such a great loss would be the ultimate defeat.

"Miss Bonney," Mack was saying as he took both of her damp hands in his, "this is quite a pleasure."

He was a good foot taller than Tess, a big-boned man, gray hair, green eyes, generous nose and a leathery, tanned face. Tess allowed herself a wide smile. "I'm honored to meet you, Mr. Solomon." She prayed he hadn't heard the squeak in her voice.

"Mack."

"And I'm Tess," she got out.

"You realize how indebted the crew is to you, Tess?"

"Well," she said, her hands still in his, "it was really a fluke, finding that letter. The archives in Spain are super, but talk about a file clerk's nightmare."

"A fluke to you," he said, "but a helluva bonus to me. As soon as we find the *Isabela,* I can assure you there'll be a nice reward in it for you."

"You don't have to—" But Tess caught herself. "Sure," she said, "I'd love one of the artifacts. I'd treasure it forever."

"We'll find her soon enough," Solomon said. "Now that we have one of the cannons, she's got to be close."

"Today's the day," Tess said, quoting Mack's famous line that had kept the crew searching for twenty years.

"You bet it is!"

Tess couldn't help liking Mack. His energy and exuberance were infectious. Later, when she met his wife, a surprisingly down-home sort of woman named Kitty, Tess felt herself envying her. At twenty-six Tess had yet to meet a man she truly loved and respected. And now, after meeting Mack Solomon, Tess wished he were twenty years younger and still single. He was every woman's dream, hardheaded yet romantic, a man who'd made her feel comfortable in no time at all, and a man who refused to let go of his dream.

The evening wore on. Some of the crew took off, weaving a little, singing off-key Jimmy Buffett songs. Others stayed, content in their lawn chairs. One of the divers, a real blond "looker", had fallen asleep in a hammock with a girl clad only in a bikini top and skimpy shorts. They were both snoring. Mack's wife had long since gone inside, presumably to bed, but Mack was still talking to one of his ship's captains, Ned something-or-other.

Tess walked over to sit beside her brother. "Where *is* the cannon, anyway?"

"Oh, it's still on board the *Seahunt*. Mack won't unload it and tell the press until those serial numbers have been checked and rechecked."

"Um," Tess said, stifling a yawn. She *was* tired. And hot. As midnight approached, the temperature refused to drop. Overhead, the sky was black and thick with humidity and the air on her bare arms and legs was cloying. She wondered if anyone else noticed it, or maybe she was just too used to air-conditioning. Heck, up in Miami, no one, but *no one,* partied outside in the summer. But then she'd always thought these islanders were a bizarre lot. She was supposed to spend the night at Paul's on his couch. Boy, did she hope he had an air conditioner. And come to think of it, she thought, yawning again, when *was* Paul planning to call it a night?

"I'm glad you're still here," came a voice at her ear.

Tess turned to see Mack. She smiled, though very tiredly now. "Not for long," she said. "I just got in from Spain earlier today."

Mack nodded. "Well then," he said, "you'll probably be too tired to make a dive tomorrow in the spot we found the cannon. Too bad." There was the slightest gleam in his eyes.

Tess looked from Mack to Paul and back. She couldn't believe he'd really let her dive with his crew! Heck, she wasn't even a very experienced scuba diver, much less a treasure hunter. She swallowed. "What if I, you know, get in the way?"

"It would be my pleasure to have you in the way, young lady."

She hesitated only an instant longer. "What time do you want me at the dock?"

ABOVE THE RIPPLING, sunlit surface of the water, an announcement of the finding of the cannon was being made to the eager press who'd been invited out to the *Seahunt.* There was going to be quite a commotion, Paul had told Tess before they'd plunged into the crystal-clear blue waters, with the press challenging Mack's claim until an outside expert could be brought in to verify those numbers on the cannon. Of course, the federal government and the state of Florida would send tax men to Key West to assess the value of the find. The tax battle had been going on for years. Did the state own treasure salvaged off its coast? Should the federal government get a cut? And if so, how much? Mack Solomon had spent years in court trying to defend his finds from the tax man.

"Yes, a lot of commotion," Paul had said, "but our job is to hunt for treasure. Let the lawyers rip each other's hearts out."

Tess followed her brother down, down through the warm sea to the ocean floor. Sunlight filtered through the salty water, a hazy light in places where the sand was stirred up from the huge bottom blower the salvors used to scour the sea floor. Men in wet-suit tops like Tess wore moved along the floor behind the heavy equipment, carefully searching the trenches left by the immense, compressor-operated blowers.

Tess kept Paul in sight, kicking her flippers gently, wondering if she would even recognize an artifact if she were swimming directly above it. Wouldn't anything lying on the sandy bottom for almost four hundred years be completely encrusted, look like a coral formation or something? Probably not gold, though. Gold resisted time and the elements, retaining its gleam through the ages. Still, Paul had told her that the most likely find they'd make before actually spotting the hull where the mother lode would lie would be the iron ballast balls the galleon had carried. It was a safe bet that the main part of her had been swept away on the furious sea until she'd finally sunk some distance from where her hull had first been ripped open. If the salvors could find that trail of debris, part of a mast, hull ribs, ballast balls, anything, they could follow it until the hull was located—the hull and all its treasure.

"But the cannon?" Tess had asked as they'd filled their tanks with air that morning. "Doesn't finding a cannon mean you're close?"

It had been Mack who'd answered her. "I wish," he'd said. "But the cannon could have gone overboard during the storm long before the hull was torn apart."

"So the ship could be just about anywhere," Tess had mused, gazing out at the vast blue sea.

"Hey," Mack had said in answer to her doubtful declaration, "don't you know that today's the day?"

Tess checked the underwater watch Paul had strapped on her wrist before going over the side of the boat. They had twenty minutes of air left, not much, but in the shallow water they were searching at least she didn't have to decompress before surfacing after only one tank of air.

Ahead of them the blower moved along the sandy floor like a giant beast digging grooves in the earth with its breath. Divers followed, combing the bottom methodically. Tess and Paul swam to the right of the main body of searchers. She had to assume he was keeping her away from the direct action in case she bungled something. That was okay, though, because Paul would dive again after this tank of air, and again and again, day after day, month after month, until they found the long lost treasure.

It was Paul who pointed to their right. Forty or so feet away, just visible, was part of the living coral reef that stretched all the way from Key Largo to well beyond Key West, a part of the entity that had formed the Keys themselves millions of years ago. Divers and fishermen and boaters always said things like, "We'll fish inside the reef today," or, "We're going outside the reef, into blue waters." Meaning deep water. Tess knew that Solomon was hoping to find the galleon inside the reef, near the Quicksands. Much easier to salvage. But there were those on his team who believed the *Isabela* had been carried on the swollen sea to much deeper waters. It was an ongoing debate.

Paul nudged Tess's arm and pointed toward the reef again. She realized he meant it was okay for her to swim over and explore. She knew the reef was beautiful; the shallows where they were searching were really quite dull, just sand and rock and more sand, and few fish save for a barracuda or two who stayed well clear of the divers.

Tess nodded, blowing bubbles in a stream out of her regulator, and Paul tapped the face of his watch, then indicated fifteen minutes more. Tess nodded and turned away, kicking more steadily now against the current as she headed toward the reef. Away from the churned-up sand the water was much clearer, the sunlight filtering down in golden shafts to highlight the unique formations of coral, the creatures that themselves comprised the living reef.

Tess moved along the edge of the reef slowly, careful not to disturb the coral in any way. The coral, living or dead, was protected by the federal government, and fines for damaging the reef or taking the coral from the sea were stiff. Whereas most animal life on earth grew to maturity rapidly, coral grew slowly, often taking hundreds of years to reach its potential size. Like earth's rain forests, Tess knew, the living reefs of the planet were fast shrinking or being destroyed.

Nevertheless, a wide variety of colorful fish still flourished on the reef. Tess swam among yellowtail snappers, sergeant majors and parrot fish that had no fear of mankind, coming right up to her mask and peering inside. Barracuda and gray reef sharks were less trusting, staying well clear of a human intruder, and disappearing from Tess's sight completely as she propelled herself over the top of a particularly large mass of brain coral.

She checked her watch. Eight minutes before she'd have to surface. She was on the far side of the reef now, out of sight of the divers, but she knew where she was and, anyway, once she surfaced she'd spot the *Seahunt.*

Seven minutes.

A thought struck Tess as she explored: what if she actually came across a part of the *Isabela,* maybe even the hull itself? The reef could easily be hiding clues to the galleon's whereabouts, though Paul had said they'd taken dozens of aerial photos of the reef and seen nothing unusual. Oh well, she thought, it was just a fantasy.

Four minutes.

She hated to surface. The water was deliciously warm, and it was such a clear day. Frequently the sea was churned up, sandy, making visibility poor. But today was perfect.

Just over three minutes.

Tess began to head back toward the divers, moving over the top of the reef and realizing she'd explored a lot more of the coral formations that she'd intended. The divers were nowhere in sight. A moment of alarm seized her but subsided. She'd surface and see the *Seahunt*. No big deal. She glanced at her watch. Two minutes. And that was when she spotted the object lying in the open sand just beyond the reef.

Her heart quickened. It could be an encrusted iron ball, a ballast ball. It *could* be. Excitement filled her. Flashes of scenes raced through her head: Mack congratulating her again, Paul so proud he'd be popping, that adorable blond diver she'd seen last night trying desperately to get near her as reporters all clamored for the story of how she'd found...

It was round, all right, merely a round hunk of dead coral. Oh, rats.

One minute. She had to surface or... A dull gleam, a flash of something caught her eye ten feet or so to her left, lying on the bottom. It might be... But she had no time.

To heck with it Tess decided in a split second, and she kicked her flippers furiously, aware that her air tank had a slight reserve, but uncertain just how much.

The object *was* shiny, still catching the sunlight that filtered through the salty water. Other than gold, what could possibly gleam so brightly? A beer can? But it wasn't. As her hand brushed away the sand that half hid the object, Tess knew she'd found something extraordinary. Her heart began to pound. Carefully, forgetting her air, she lifted the object from its grave and held it in front of her mask.

Her brain reeled. It was a piece of jewelry, gold jewelry, a long, heavy chain with a square-cut pendant dangling from it. In the pendant were precious gems partially encrusted—they looked like emeralds. Tess studied the artifact in wonder. It was beautiful, absolutely beautiful. And it was old, so old the shapes of the gold links were imperfect as were the cuts of the stones.

Motionless, she held it in front of her, a shaft of sunlight gleaming on the ancient gold links. The water moved gently around her, lulling her, calming her—tons and tons of sea water, warm... It was almost as if she were in a trance, she would realize later, but at the time she merely let the sensation carry her down through layers of reality. The jewel began to feel queer in her hand, as if it were pulsing, and Tess was suddenly overcome by a rush of emotions: love and joy, fear and sorrow, anger. A lifetime of emotions. But not hers. It was as if she were experiencing the emotions of someone else, someone who had lived and died a very long time ago. The owner of the jewel.

With great effort Tess shook herself out of the curious euphoria. She collected her wits and checked the time. Uh-oh, no time whatsoever was left! Instantly she began to kick, forcing herself up, up through the sunlit water. She could see the surface, so she wasn't afraid of running out of air. Heck, she could go for three minutes or more without—

Later Tess would try to remember the chain of events exactly as they occurred; her life would depend on reliving them. But at the moment all she knew was that she'd been caught in some sort of a current, a powerful surge of water that gripped her and dragged her along. The next thing she knew she was spinning, and through a haze of fear she thought she'd been caught in a spout, a whirlpool, a funnel that was sucking at her, wrenching her limbs, a force so violent there was no arguing with it—she could only let herself be carried away.

At some point she knew her air was gone. Strangely it didn't matter because she was going to drown, anyway. Still, she fought. Even as her mask was ripped away, her air tanks and watch, even as the beautiful gold necklace was torn from her fingers, Tess struggled, whirled around and around, the sunlight above her spinning, spinning, and she was choking, reaching up for that light, for precious air. It was so close....

CHAPTER TWO

TESS BLINKED, the sunlight hurting her eyes. Then a racking cough shook her, and she gagged on bitter seawater, retching weakly. She became aware of a hard surface beneath her that had a strange, undulating movement. Her head ached, her chest hurt as though she'd run a marathon, and her stomach was empty and sore. It darted through her mind that she was on a boat—the rolling sensation beneath her persisted—but then a babble of voices interrupted the notion and she realized there were men nearby, but she couldn't understand what they were saying.

She hurt. Every bone and muscle and nerve ending in her body hurt. And those puzzling voices again. Why couldn't she comprehend them? A wave of panic began to well up from deep in her sore belly and she tried to sit up, but everything around her swam unsteadily and all she could manage was a groan.

She felt something hard prod her in the ribs then, and she doubled up instinctively, protectively, in the fetal position. She could hear the men laughing and more of that strange language. As she lay there gasping, deathly sick, she tried to figure out where she was and what had happened to her.

Her memory came back in disoriented flashes. Diving, she'd been diving. The necklace, the gleaming gold chain . . . and then she'd been dragged into a whirlpool . . . drowning . . . Oh, God . . .

"¿Qué es este?" she heard. *Spanish.* They were speaking Spanish. But who? Where was she?

A moment later Tess felt callused hands grab her and haul her to her feet. She blinked again, coughing, trying to push away the rough hands. Men held her— short, dark-haired men, barefooted, with ragged, cut-off trousers and torn, sleeveless shirts or no shirts at all. One of them poked at her wet-suit top, exclaimed something to the others. She felt as if she were still in the whirlpool, spinning, spinning. In a minute she would be sick to her stomach again if they didn't stop pushing her. And there were those words again, more Spanish, almost unintelligible. A dialect. There was a shouted order from behind her . . . a man in a uniform, high boots, a sword and helmet. She shut her eyes and shook her head. She was dreaming, drowning and dreaming. But wasn't your life supposed to flash before your eyes? This wasn't her life!

When she opened her eyes again he was still there, the man in the costume, still shouting orders at the ones who held her. It was then, finally, that Tess registered that she was really on a ship, a sailing ship. White sails bellied out above her head, a polished wooden rail leaned out over the leaping waves, ropes thrummed in the wind, and below her bare feet a scrubbed wooden deck slanted and bucked.

A sailing ship? Wildly, Tess looked around for the *Seahunt,* for Paul, for anyone. There was nothing, only the same sun-drenched, laughing blue ocean in which she'd been submerged. No *Seahunt,* no divers, no buoys, nothing. What had happened? Had these men saved her from drowning? If so, why hadn't they handed her back to Mack or Paul?

"Let me go," Tess managed to croak, trying to shake off the hands that held her. But only coarse laughter greeted her words, and more of the incomprehensible dialect. She glanced around, searching for someone who looked like he could speak English, someone familiar. But all the sun-darkened, shaggy-haired men leered and poked and made remarks she couldn't understand.

Sharp cracking sounds overhead made Tess look up. From the top of the three masts of the vessel, pennants, red and gold with imperial lions and eagles, fluttered out in the wind. At the rear of the ship, aft, was a tall, ornate cabin of gleaming wood decorated with carvings and painted designs and pierced with many-paned windows.

It really was an old-fashioned sailing vessel, it really was. "Look," Tess said, "can anyone speak English here? *¿Inglés? ¿Por favor, habla inglés?*"

They stared at her in amazement and babbled, pawing at her, poking, fingering her wet suit, shaking their heads, grinning gap-toothed lewd grins. *"Inglés,"* they repeated. Okay, so they understood that, at least.

"Yo inglés," she repeated. *"Americana. ¿Comprende?"*

But their reactions were only more of the same, more laughter, more shoving.

Tess felt a tightening in her chest, as if she was ready to break out in a sobbing fit. But she wouldn't, she couldn't, not here, not now. "Okay," she managed to say, "just please take me back to Key West. *Please.*" But it wasn't any use. Either they didn't understand her at all or they just plain weren't listening. She tried another tack. "My throat is killing me. Can I have some water, please? Water. *Agua.*"

Water. At least they understood that. But all they did was laugh, and then they began to drag and push her across the deck to a square opening from which they removed a grate. From the dark hole emerged the low wailing of many voices, an anguished keening noise, and a terrible, gut-churning smell.

"Hey, wait a minute!" Tess cried, but they lowered her by her arms down into the dark hold, and when she was as far as their grasps would allow, they simply dropped her.

Tess hit bottom with a thud, all the air knocked out of her lungs. She was dazed and hurt and terrified, trying to get to her hands and knees, sucking in air that wouldn't fill her lungs. When she finally did get her breath back, another shock hit her—the overpowering stench in the hold. A human stench, rank. She felt her gorge rise.

Tess didn't know how long she stayed there on her hands and knees, sick to her stomach, deathly afraid. But when she finally came to her senses and her eyes adjusted to the gloom, what she could see made her shrink in horror against a bulkhead.

"No," she whispered. "Oh, God, no." Black people, men and women, in rags, chained by their ankles in rows along the bulkhead, sitting, lying in their own filth.

They stared back at her, white-eyed, numb, beyond any curiosity. Tess couldn't move. She couldn't breathe and she felt as if her body were made of wood. She told herself over and over that what she was seeing was still a crazy dream. *This isn't happening,* she thought, *I drowned and this isn't real.*

Tess remained rooted to her spot, wanting to move, wanting to scream and rail at those men on deck, to cry out at the injustice. But she couldn't. If they could treat these poor souls this way, what would they do to her? *Stay calm,* she told herself, *take it easy.*

Paul, she thought a dozen times over the next few hours, Paul would be looking for her. He'd see this ship. He'd check. He couldn't know she'd drowned, so the next logical step would be to check out this ship. Sure. Paul...

But Paul didn't come.

Think, she commanded herself. Forget the squalor and filth and these forlorn people. *Think.* There had to be an explanation for all of this. She just had to figure it out. All right. She was in the hold of a sailing ship. Spanish, yes, because she'd recognized the flags from her research. Imperial Spanish flags from the seventeenth century. Okay, so it was a replica galleon out on a training exercise or participating in a tall ship rally. Everyone was in costume. Fine. Very realistic. Too damn realistic.

But why, *why* were they treating her like this? They should have welcomed her, radioed the coast guard, offered her refreshments, a drink perhaps, had their doctor check her out. Not thrown her into a dungeon!

And these people. *Slaves,* her mind insisted, but there were no slaves anymore. Ridiculous. Then they were refugees, boat people. Poor, sad wretches trying to escape Haiti or some place like that. But why were they chained? Her mind couldn't make any theory work, no matter how it twisted and dodged and explained the facts.

Another hour went by. Maybe two. At last the grate was pulled open over her head and Tess looked up, blinking painfully into the light. The boat people stirred, shrank back in their chains, cried out to one another. Then a strange thing happened. The seamen above them dumped buckets and more buckets of seawater down into the hold, dousing everyone. The cold seawater washed some of the filth down drains and the worst of the dirt off the refugees.

After a time the deluge stopped. And then another equally strange thing took place. Clothes were tossed down into the hold, piles and piles of the roughest garments, full of holes, ripped, threadbare. Shirts, trousers, long skirts—all came raining down. All a uniform, washed-out gray, made from some rough fabric, linen or wool, Tess thought when she touched a pile.

It got even more bizarre. As she huddled in a corner, trying to be inconspicuous, several sailors were lowered down to unchain the men and women so they could dress in the clothes provided them. It was done very quickly and very efficiently, as if these seamen had handled the same situation more than once before. Odd. And all Tess could hope was that they'd leave her alone.

Trying to move as unobtrusively as possible, Tess quietly helped herself to a shirt and a pair of baggy cutoff trousers. For a while she merely clutched them to her chest while trying to melt back in the gloom of her corner. She waited and watched and finally, slowly, pulled on the baggy trousers. No one seemed to be paying any attention to her. Good, she thought, though she wasn't sure why.

Next came the shirt. As awful and scratchy as it was, it was better than the oppressively hot wet-suit jacket she still wore. Cautiously, turning her back to the others, Tess quickly peeled it off and threw the shirt on over her bikini top. She then sat back and tried to look very small, dissolving into the shadows. It occurred to her as she hunkered down between a support timber and the bulkhead that she probably looked like a boy now and that was good, too, because Lord only knew what these oafs might do if they realized she was a woman.

When the others were finished dressing, the sailors rechained them in rows then called to their mates on deck, who lowered down the ropes again. They scurried up, like rats, Tess thought, and the heavy iron grate was replaced. Then, and only then, did Tess realize she'd been holding her breath the whole time. She sat back and drew her knees up to her chest and whistled between her teeth thinking, what next?

Still unable to make any sense of this nightmarish situation, one thing she did know. When she got back to Key West the sailors were all going to pay. You bet.

There was no excuse on earth for the way these men were treating them. "I promise all of you," she whispered, "they won't get away with this."

In the foul hold time crawled by with hideous slowness. The heat was terrible, the air so heavy with odor it was all Tess could do to keep from vomiting again. Sweat soaked her, mingling with the seawater on her skin, making her short dark hair stand out in spikes around her face. The chained blacks began to sing low, rhythmic melodies, clapping softly to the alien, exotic words and rhythms. Despite the terrible predicament, Tess was lulled. She rested her back against a support and her head hung forward. The soft chanting went on, a sad and beautiful refrain. The ship rocked gently. She felt herself dozing off, mercifully dozing....

A BOOMING CRASH shocked her into instant wakefulness. The impact threw her against a bulkhead, stunning her for a moment. The blacks were screaming, holding on to one another. Tess rose groggily to her knees, but the ship listed abruptly and threw her off balance again.

Now what? her tired brain asked. Had the ship run aground, collided with another vessel? Above her head she could hear men tearing across the deck. Orders were shouted; the flap of canvas luffing echoed down into the hold. What was happening? Tess stood under the grate and stared upward as if she could see what was going on through the decking.

She could tell that the galleon was doing some frantic maneuvering because she and the chained blacks were being thrown back and forth. And then there was another bone-jarring crash. She heard the sound of wood splintering, screams, shouts, the report of guns, then the recoil and hollow boom of a cannon.

My God, Tess thought, *a sea battle, a fight. This can't be happening, this can't be...*

The galleon swung violently, throwing her to the floor again. Everyone in the hold was shrieking in terror, a cacophony that beat at her ears. If only she could see what was happening! What if the ship sank? They were trapped down here like rats. They'd go down with it. Oh dear God, there had to be a way out!

The clash of swords could be heard now, men yelling, the thump of feet on the deck, gunshots. It was terrifying to be so helpless, so alone, thrown into this insane world where nothing was real, but every moment was fraught with danger.

"Goddamned poxy Spaniard!" Tess heard a man bellow, and it was a moment before she realized she'd understood the words—they'd been in English!

She stood up so fast she almost hit her head on the curve of the bulkhead. She listened, straining for familiar words. There *were* new voices above her, men who cursed and swore and shouted, and she could understand a word here and there. It was a battle, then, one between the Spanish and the English. And they weren't Americans, either, because she could identify the accents—definitely English.

She heard shouts and screams, the clash of metal, the blacks moaning and wailing around her, the creak of a ship in distress. She smelled the gunpowder and smoke that made her eyes water. Then more smoke. The ship was on fire!

Tess would have prayed if she'd had the presence of mind. She never was quite sure what ran through her head in those next few minutes. She went blank, overcome with horror. The noise got worse. A cannon boomed again, and she cringed, hands covering her ears. She could hear the crash of something heavy on the deck—a mast? Smoke began to seep into the hold, thickening. The wails of the blacks turned to coughing and gasping.

Somewhere inside Tess's head a small, quiet voice said, very clearly, "You're going to die." But she was too numb to panic.

It seemed like hours, but only minutes passed before the hatch was thrown open and faces peered down into the smoky hold. Tess looked up. "Help us," she pleaded, her voice shaking, "please."

"Bloody 'ell," one of the men said, "it speaks the king's English!"

Moments later men shoved ladders into the stinking hold and clambered down. They had keys, the big black iron keys to the leg chains. While keeping up a constant, almost indecipherable flow of speech, most of it foul, they unlocked the blacks and herded everyone up onto the deck.

It was bedlam. The poor, terrified people were coughing and screaming. The brilliant Caribbean sun blinded them while the black billows of smoke choked them. Men were running everywhere. But the boat people and Tess stayed put, huddling pathetically together, their fear and confusion more beastly than anything Tess had known so far in this hellish dream.

Realization struck her abruptly then. She was free. She could make her way to the rail and jump, swim to safety, leave this nightmare behind. But once at the rail, Tess's heart sank. She could see only water. Everywhere water, stretching endlessly. She saw it then as the breeze momentarily lifted the smoke—a sleek black ship that lay alongside the galleon, attached with grappling hooks and lines. A black ship with furled black sails and no flag at all flying from the tall mainmast.

Tess stared openmouthed. Another sailing ship. What *was* this? A movie, it *had* to be a battle scene from a movie. But under her feet the deck was slippery with real blood and real bodies lay everywhere. Aft, on the high poop deck, a very real battle still raged, the Spanish defending, pressed by these other men. A swordsman screamed, fell, another yanked a long curved knife free from his belly. Cutlasses flashed in the sun.

Tess stood utterly motionless and stared in mute wonder and horror as fires licked at the rigging of the galleon and the sails were shredded. The men from the black ship were fierce-looking, bearded, long-haired, wore loose trousers with high boots or bare feet, colorful scarves around their heads, gold hoops in their ears, carried knives and guns and swords in their hands or stuck in their belts.

Pirates. Tess still stared, bludgeoned by the sight of something that couldn't exist. An Errol Flynn movie, a swashbuckling sea tale. Walk the plank, the skull and crossbones, *pirates*. A movie? In which men died in agony?

But she had no more opportunity to watch the fighting. Moments later she and her black companions were led to the rail of the galleon, herded along to the thick ropes that held the ships together. The lines all slanted down to the much lower deck of the black ship, and the Englishmen were shouting and cursing and gesturing for them all to cross over to the other vessel.

"Argh, get yersel' along there," one man was yelling. Another one whistled sharp blasts, as if he were herding cows. "Move along, mates, that's it, step lively, you damned heathens."

Tess stayed with the crowd hidden in its middle, hung onto the ropes, jumped awkwardly to the deck of the black ship. Some of the blacks fell, screaming, into the water between the two vessels. The pirates still on the smaller ship swore and lowered longboats to rescue them. Tess hung over the rail, disbelieving, fascinated, her ear growing accustomed to the strange English dialect.

The ship she was on now was definitely smaller than the galleon, narrower, and it sat lower in the water. She looked around cautiously. It was clean, polished, scrubbed, every rope tied off or coiled neatly, every bit of brass shining, the wood gleaming with polish. The few crewmen left on board were surly, apparently angry at missing the fight, but they handed out to the blacks wooden cups of water dipped from a barrel.

Thankfully, Tess took a cup in turn. Lord, was she thirsty after all those hours in that stinking place! She

drank and drank. "Oh boy, thanks," she said to the
pirate who refilled her cup, and he looked at her oddly.
Quickly, she ducked away. How dumb to single herself out although, really, how was anyone going to
overlook her in this crowd of black folks? And what
on earth was going to happen to them?

The pirates were returning to their ship now, following the last of the blacks over the line from the
galleon. They must have won the battle, because they
were very loud, laughing, brandishing swords, loaded
down with booty from the Spanish ship, hung with
gold chains, carrying hastily stuffed sacks of silver
candlesticks and cups, coins spilling out the sides.
Grinning, running surefooted along the ropes, they
reboarded their own ship. Some had bloody wounds,
but they all laughed and shouted and cursed without
stopping.

Tess kept looking around for cameras even though
a part of her knew there weren't any, there never had
been. Her mind nevertheless kept grasping at straws,
searching for an answer that just wasn't there. She told
herself she must be in the middle of a dream, a scene
from the past, an impossible scene in which pirates
had just captured a Spanish slave ship. Tess kept
watching and grasping at those straws as torches were
lit and thrown by the last few buccaneers off the galleon, and then the grappling hooks were released, the
connecting lines thrown off, the galleon set free to
·float—and burn.

She stayed there at the rail, surrounded by her
scared, huddled black companions, staring at the tall
galleon as flames licked at its masts, as the last few

survivors rushed in panic to lower longboats, clamber down into them and row off from the stricken ship that was now a huge floating pyre, its tarred planking burning furiously.

This couldn't be happening. Tess knew that. But it was. Even as the distance between the ships grew, she could feel the hot blast of the fire and smell the oily smoke. It was real, all right; even though her mind couldn't accept it, her senses were forced to. They felt the heat, smelled the smoke, heard the fluent English swearing, felt the ship roll beneath her, saw the pirate crew race into action, climbing the rigging to unfurl the huge black sails and working in frenzied activity but also in perfect order, so that the ship was soon headed on a southeast tack, her sails bellied out with the west wind, her shining deck tilted as she leaped to life, sprinting toward the horizon, her sails cracking as she left behind the sinking galleon.

Tess leaned on the rail and felt the fresh, hot sea air on her face. She was shaking still, unable to control the little leaping spasms in her nerves. But it wasn't the aftermath of her ordeal or the reality of witnessing the bloody battle. It wasn't hunger or thirst or exhaustion. Rather, Tess was electrified by the knowledge that suddenly seized her. She was living history. Not reading about it, theorizing, but actually living it. There was no film crew, no training exercise on the high seas. These were not boat people.

It was all . . . real.

The sun was sinking off to the west, a red ball resting on the water that looked like hammered gold. The day was ending, this insane day Tess had begun in utter normalcy.

The pirates were passing out food now. Some kind of bread, onions, wizened apples. Food that would keep on a ship on a sea voyage. Tess took a hunk of bread and an apple and chewed on them. She was voraciously hungry—she'd only had a bagel for breakfast. And how long ago had *that* been? The pirate who handed her the food gave her a look and said something she didn't catch. She tried to melt back into the crowd of dark bodies. Best not to be noticed, she thought, until she figured out what was going to happen next.

And, she was aware, as she eyed the motley crew, that maybe she could still pass as a boy with her short hair. She didn't trust the look of these men. They were wild, wilder than anything she could have imagined. It was then that Tess noticed two of the crew, both in the rigging working ropes—they were black. Not slaves that she was with, but real members of the ship's crew. Odd. Black pirates . . .

The man who'd given her the food came back, pushing his way through the blacks, leading another pirate. "Eh, what'd I tell yerself?" he said, pointing at Tess, who paled and tried to hunker down behind a black woman. "See 'im? The lad there?"

The second pirate was a big-barreled man, middle-aged, with grizzled hair, a once-broken nose and a beard over rough features. He studied Tess for a time before he spoke. "So, Jamie, this is the one that spoke English?"

"Must be, Ruby," the first pirate said, nodding.

"Speak, lad," the man called Ruby ordered in a gruff voice. "Give us a word or two."

Tess took a deep breath and stepped out from behind the black woman. "Uh," she said, trying to smile, "well, hello. Uh, sir," she added.

"You speak English?" Ruby asked.

"Yes, I do. Well, American English. You sound more like English English. Where are you from? Where are we?" Tess said hurriedly.

"I'll be," said the first pirate, Jamie.

Ruby looked at Tess curiously "You're on the *Marauder*, that I can tell you. And we're headed for Red Turtle Cay. As for any more questions..." Then Ruby turned and began to scan the deck, as if looking for someone. And Jamie moved aside then, respectfully, as Ruby continued to look around. Finally, his eyes coming to rest, he cupped his hands and shouted, "Eh, Captain, have a look at this one!"

The activity on the deck seemed to grind to a halt. Everyone's gaze moved to the port side of the black ship, searching out the man Ruby addressed—the captain. Tess looked, too. And when she finally saw him, she experienced a sudden, strange twist in the pit of her stomach. The captain. Oh, there was no mistaking this man's authority. He was younger than Ruby, around thirty, Tess guessed. He was taller than most of his men, clean-shaven with dark blond hair caught back in a ponytail. His hands were on his hips; his legs, encased in high leather boots, were apart, braced against the ship's movement. He was laughing when Tess first saw him, his head thrown back, strong cords in his neck, a gold earring glinting in the sun. He sported a loose white shirt open on a sun-bronzed chest. A sword hung at his side and knives were thrust into a red sash. A handsome man, carefree, compelling. A picture from a child's book, too clear, too bright, too pretty. Not at all real.

But there he was, the captain of this pirate ship, radiating daring and command, a buccaneer from another more dangerous time. He had stopped laughing upon hearing Ruby call out to him, but a smile was still curving his mouth as he turned toward Ruby, and Tess saw with surprise that the man wore a patch over one eye and that the other one was a terrifying mineral blue and it was trained on her.

Spellbound, Tess gaped at him. The hush on deck stretched out and he stopped smiling, his attention vigorously on her, the pale sheep in the dark flock. Her blood froze, her knees went weak and shaky. She had drowned. She had nitrogen narcosis. She was dead.

An agonizing moment passed. She felt his single blue eye on her like a burning brand. Assessing, deciding. Her heart dropped like a rock to her feet, her throat closed up. And then slowly, with frightening deliberation, he began to move toward her taking large strides, closing the distance. His men parted. The blacks cowered. Slowly, the man approached—the captain of the buccaneers.

CHAPTER THREE

FOR A TIME Richard Neville sat in his captain's chair and studied the young fellow who stood by the door and watched him silently and warily. Richard was well aware of what his hard, one-eyed stare could do to a person, and he utilized it whenever he felt the need to impress. So he folded his hands over his lean belly, propped a booted foot on his desk and fixed the lad with his one good eye, which served him well enough. Finally, when the boy appeared to be sufficiently cowed, Richard said, "Well, and where be you from, young man?"

There was no answer, merely a flicker in the fine dark eyes.

"Speak up, boy. Have you no tongue? Ruby says you have a semblance of English. Well?"

Still the boy did not speak. An odd one, Richard decided, unable to fit him into any category. And probably useless, as well. Why, there wasn't a muscle to be seen on the lad. He was puny, too soft, with dimples and womanly eyelashes. Gad, what was Richard to do with him? And what in heaven's name had the Spaniards been doing with such a peculiar captive? The only possible use for such a—Richard searched for the word—a *pretty* fellow, aye, would be to serve that pompous governor or perhaps a rich merchant in Havana. Serve them in ways that were unholy but that the Spanish had learned from their Moorish masters. Did the youth realize this? Did he realize how much he owed Richard? Well, Richard would see to it that he did.

"So, lad, you perhaps don't know how to address me, although I thought everyone in these waters knew me." Richard stood, flourished an imaginary hat and made a graceful leg, amusing himself with this curious waif. "I am Captain Richard Neville, at your service." Then he sat himself back in his chair and eyed the boy again, adding, "Black Richard, that is. Do you know me yet?"

The boy shook his head mutely. "All I know is you're a pirate," he finally said.

Richard laughed. "So, you can speak then. And you say I'm a pirate. How do you know I'm not a privateer with a letter of marque all legal-like from our splendid King James?"

The boy looked at him blankly. "I don't know what you mean."

"What, are you daft? A privateer has royal license to do what I do, and therein lies the only difference. Privateers sink ships and plunder and worse, but they face no hangman's noose back in merry old England."

"And you do?" asked the lad carefully.

"Aye, sad as that is to admit. There's a hefty price on my head," he said, grinning broadly.

The boy stared wordlessly.

"Well then, tell me how it is the Spanish had you, boy. Speak up. I grow weary of this game," Richard said brusquely.

At long last the lad cleared his throat. "I—I was lost at sea," he began.

"English? Are you English?" Certainly this language the boy spoke was a kind of English, but what a strange dialect. "Speak up, I say."

"I'm American."

"American?" Richard raised a brow.

"That's right." The boy seemed to be gathering his courage. "I'm from Miami. That's in Florida. And I don't really like the way I've been treated here. You better let me go." Beneath those indecently long lashes the youth's dark eyes fairly sparked, and one of his dark eyebrows had an impudent arch to it.

Richard tossed his head back and laughed. "There is a fire in you! Good! But who are you, a lowly captive of the Spanish, to be complaining of your treatment?"

The boy let out a quavering sigh. "Listen," he said, "just let me go. Put me ashore on Key West."

"Key West..." Richard grinned. "You speak in riddles. Come now, where are you really from and how is it you were on a Spanish slave ship?"

"I'm from Florida, like I told you. Florida, the United States of America. And I was on that ship because I almost drowned and they happened to pick me up," the lad said. "And I'd like to go back." Then he added, "Please."

"Florida is a Spanish colony and there are only a few missions there," Richard said reasonably. "There are no *Americans* in Florida, if by American you mean a member of one of the English colonies." He folded his fingers across his chest and smiled smugly. "And I've never heard them referred to as Americans. They are English by birth."

"Not any more," the boy said, glowering.

"You have some peculiar notions for a young lad," Richard said, humoring him.

"And you have some really weird ideas for a grown man who appears to be relatively intelligent," the youth said.

"You've a tongue on you."

The boy ran a hand over his face, the fingers shaking a little. "I'm sorry. I've been through a lot today. I'm . . . I'm a little confused."

Richard eyed him. Here was a strange one who fit into no category Richard was familiar with. He spoke well but with an odd accent. Was this a bastard son of some nobleman, sent to the colonies to spare the family shame? But Florida?

"Could I, uh, have something to drink? Please. I'm still really thirsty."

Richard reached out for the seabag hung from a peg on the bulkhead. "Here, lad. Drink your fill."

The youth took a long swallow and came up sputtering, breathing fire. "What *is* that?"

"Grog," Richard replied mildly.

"I meant water," breathed the boy.

There was a knock on the door of the cabin. "Come in," Richard said.

It was Ruby Salvador, his first mate. "Well, Ruby, we have caught ourselves a queer fish indeed."

Ruby stood, filling the portal, and gave the boy a long look and shook his grizzled head. "What should we do with him, Captain? If I throw him in with the other slaves the crew will surely ferret him out quick enough. He's a . . . a girlish sort, I'd say, and the tars, well . . ."

"True enough," Richard said as he, too, studied the youth's innocent face, the too-delicate features and those slim hands and feet. A pity. Where in the world would such a boy stand a chance among real men?

"What is your name?" Richard asked him. "Come now, surely you have a name."

"Bonney," he said finally. "I'm, uh, Billy Bonney." And for no reason at all two spots of red flared on his smooth cheeks.

"Well, Billy," Richard said, "I'll wager you realize your predicament. What would you have me do with you?"

"Take me back to Key West," Billy said abruptly. "You can't possibly keep me captive. You have to . . ."

"I know naught of your Key West," Richard said, and he came to his feet, impatient. "And if I did, I'd have no time to be escorting a boy to this place. We head for Red Turtle Cay, my little friend, as the Spanish will be hot on our heels now."

"I demand you take me to—"

"Do not argue the point," Richard said harshly.

Ruby merely rolled his eyes and left while this Billy Bonney stood in the corner of Richard's cabin biting his lip.

Richard was at a loss. He hadn't liberated this boy from the Spaniards only to enslave him himself. And if he took this pretty-faced thing under his protection, allowing him to bed down on a pallet in his own quarters, there would be no end to the jests among the crew. But to return the boy Billy, a white lad, to the slaves' quarters would not do. Nor could Richard put him in among his men. Ruby had a small cabin of his own, but the boy was not Ruby's problem.

Richard paced as he felt his sleek black ship skimming the waves, free on this warm blue sea, free to sail where she would. No man nor woman nor boy of any color should be enslaved or held a captive.

"Gad," he grumbled, stopping abruptly in front of Billy who backed into the wall. He pinned him with a flinty eye. "I have no cabin boy," he said, "and although you are free now to do as you will, I strongly suggest you take the post until I can put you ashore on Red Turtle Cay. It's the best I can do."

"Free," the boy repeated, as if not quite believing Richard.

"Aye, free. I do not hold with the keeping of slaves nor the indenturing of servants. It is deplorable behavior. Many of my crew members were once slaves. My own mother—" But he caught himself. "Never you mind. 'Tis enough that I risk my neck to save *your* hide. Now, what say you to my generous offer? Will you serve as my cabin boy?"

Billy Bonney studied the captain for a long moment. The boy should by rights be afraid of him, but still he did not cower in his corner. At last he said, "All right, I'll be your cabin boy. Whatever. But if you think you can mistreat me, *Captain Neville,* then you're messing with the wrong . . . person."

A slow smile quirked Richard's lips as he stuck his face into Billy's. "Here I free you from the bloody Spanish, take you under my protection, and all I get is your insolence! To hell with the crew, I shall throw you to the fish, Billy Bonney. Aye, maybe I will at that!" He turned on his heel then and left the cabin, his grin devilishly smug. The boy was a twit, a pest, yet, in truth, he could not recall when he'd so enjoyed sparring wits with someone. And a young lad at that! Strange fellow, though, with that peculiar dialect and a choice of words that caused Richard to pause. The boy was either daft or possessed of a miraculous knowledge. Interesting, he decided, and refreshing. And again he pondered where Billy Bonney had said he hailed from. Miami? Key West? If such places existed, which was most doubtful, why had Richard never heard of them? Well, Billy Bonney wouldn't be the first in these waters to lie about his origins, would he?

The *Marauder* fled before the brisk hot wind all that night and the following day, skimming across the silver sea toward her safe haven in the Out Islands, on a spit of land known as Red Turtle Cay, where there was a harbor and a town, where there were no questions asked, and a man with a price on his head was free to seek refuge.

The first night Richard stayed on deck with Ruby, scanning the dark starlit horizon for sight of a ship that might be shadowing them. When they'd attacked the *Santa Luisa* and made their escape, the coast had been clear. But the Spanish, as dastardly a lot as they were, were not stupid. Red Turtle Cay was well-known now, and a daring Spanish captain might approach her harbor if the catch was worth it. Aye, Richard thought as the night slipped away and a red dawn crowned the eastern sky, the Spanish could be following, keeping a safe distance, readying their cannons.

Ruby was by his side at the helm, quietly standing sentry with his captain. A loyal man, Ruby Salvador, a man who detested the arrogant Spaniards perhaps even more than Richard, for Ruby, born in Spain, had been left for dead as a youngster by his countrymen when the Spanish Armada had attacked the English coast some thirty-odd years ago. It was no wonder Ruby now pirated Spanish ships with a vengeance. The Spanish had forsaken him. The English had taken him in. The English had been decent and generous with the foreign sailor, much more so than with one of their own, Richard often thought. Aye, with Richard Neville they'd not been kind at all.

"Rest, Captain," Ruby said when the sun was a ball of fire in the summer sky. "I'll be keeping the watch."

Richard gazed up at the sinister black sails that bellied out staunchly in the wind. He nodded. He was tired. A meal and a few hours' rest and he'd relieve Ruby the watch. "I'll go below," he said. "Take care the Spaniards don't run us aground, my friend."

"Or the English or the French," Ruby said and smiled through his graying beard. "And, Captain," he called after Richard, "put that boy to work or the crew will be having a fine time behind your back."

"Aye," Richard said under his breath as he swung down onto the main deck. "The cabin boy, Billy." In truth, he'd forgotten all about the lad with the too-pretty countenance.

He slept like the dead and awakened with a start in the baking hot cabin as the sun was in the western sky. As always his body and mind automatically registered the movement of his ship beneath him. He could sense a yardarm being swung or feel an errant breath of wind catch the topgallants, making her quiver delicately. The sharp creak of the ribs in her hull, the snap of a sail, the jingle of iron and the groaning strain of rope were as beloved and familiar to him as an oft-times lover's flesh. The moans, the whispers, the soft undulant movements...

Richard's gaze traveled across the cabin to where Billy Bonney sat on the floor with his back to him. The boy was mending one of Richard's shirts. A small task, but Richard had deemed it necessary to give him something to do to earn his keep. Cabin boy, after all, was a position that was earned. This twit of a boy with the strange tongue had done nothing so far to prove his mettle.

He gazed at his new cabin boy for a long time, wondering again how it was the Spaniards had captured him. And where. The heat in the cabin was hellishly oppressive, a wet heat. A bead of sweat ran slowly across Richard's temple, and he could feel the sodden dampness of his white shirt where he lay, hands behind his head, on the hard mattress of his bunk.

"Rats," he heard Billy whisper when the boy pricked his finger on the needle.

"Rats?" Richard cocked a brow and glanced around the cabin. "There are no scurrying creatures about. Not on my ship," he said, annoyed.

"I never said there were." Billy went back to his mending chores.

Useless, Richard decided again. He'd wager Billy didn't know a flying jib from a mizzen staysail, or how to properly tie a good seaman's knot. Useless.

And yet... Richard watched him and had to admit the boy did rather intrigue him. First, of course, he was taken by his extraordinary good looks, the smooth facial skin, those eyelashes, his slimness. The lad must be of a good family, aristocracy, perhaps. No peasant had ever spawned a child of Billy's ilk. In a woman's garb young Billy could almost pass for a female of the species. The hair, of course, something would have to be done with that short, dark mass. A curl or two, perhaps. Richard had seen French women who wore their hair shockingly cropped. Curled around the face, true, but shorter than the length of a man's hair. Aye, he thought, a skirt and a wig and Billy Bonney—

"Gad!" Richard growled suddenly. Had he gone mad, mentally dressing his cabin boy? A woman. He needed a real woman. As soon as they dropped anchor in Red Turtle Cay, he'd remedy the situation. By God, he would most assuredly take care of his needs first thing.

"Fetch me my dinner," Richard commanded gruffly as he swung off his bunk.

"Your dinner." Billy turned to find his captain's one eye planted angrily on him. "Ah, yes," he said, "your dinner. I'll see to it right away." And then he added before racing out of the cabin, *"Master,"* and Richard could have throttled him for his impudence if he could have caught the brat.

Richard had a conference with some of his crew that afternoon in his cabin. Ruby was there, Joseph Bellows the pilot, Jamie Talbot the second mate, old Benjamin the bosun, head gunner Stretch Tilden, and Jacob Thorne the third mate.

They discussed how to divide the spoils of this last voyage, how much to pay Samuel Black, who'd lost a leg in the fight on the *Luisa.* And all the while, Richard was aware of his men surreptitiously studying Billy, who, praises be, had the sense to keep his mouth shut. It aggravated him a bit, the attention Billy attracted. God's teeth, he hoped the boy wasn't going to be a problem.

Ruby rested until midnight and then once again relieved Richard at the helm. It was a familiar pattern, one they'd fallen into when Richard had first taken to pirating over two years ago. It was one thing to trust the *Marauder* to a second mate's hands when they were in safe waters, but quite another when the Spanish could be following just below the horizon.

"We'll make port on the afternoon tide," Ruby said. "It'll be good to be ashore, Captain."

"It will," Richard agreed. "I've been thinking much on that red-haired lass at the Laughing Parrot Tavern. What was her name?"

"Who knows?" Ruby said. "But I'll wager you'll recognize her."

"That I shall," Richard said and headed below to his quarters.

With dawn only a few hours away, Richard again slept soundly, having dropped onto his bunk after giving the cabin boy a cursory glance where he lay curled up on a pallet in a dark corner. In the wee hours Richard dreamed of his mother, picking autumn flowers in the English countryside. The air was cool and moist and his mother's face was peaceful. It was a sweet dream.

Morning came shortly, the first rays of sun spilling through the porthole onto his desk and bunk. It was already steaming hot in his cabin, breathlessly so. He stretched and yawned and lay there a moment recalling the details of his dream before they quickly faded. A sound came from the corner, like the tittering of a mouse, and Richard turned his handsome head. The cabin boy, Billy. He was still fast asleep. Richard smiled at the sounds the lad made in his slumber. Indeed, the boy was a mousy sort.

Richard rose finally, wondering if Billy planned on sleeping away the morning. It mattered not to Richard, really, save for the fact that the crew would be expecting the cabin boy to jump about doing chores.

He pulled on his trousers and strode to the boy's side, giving him a nudge on the rump with his bare foot. "Get up, Billy," he said, "there's work to be done." He nudged him once more, noting the softness of the lad's behind. *Pitiful,* Richard thought. Born a man with a woman's tenderness. "Get up, boy!" Not only was his cabin boy too soft but he was as shy as a fawn. When he finally arose he stood in the big nightshirt Richard had left out for him and did nothing.

"Get dressed," Richard commanded. "I'm hungry and this cabin needs cleaning. Put on your clothes, boy." But still the lad only fumbled with his shirt and trousers and made no move to change into them.

Richard tucked his own shirttails in and put his hands on his hips in disgust. "You're a nuisance. Not only are you dim-witted, but you are utterly useless to me. This afternoon when I put you ashore I'll be happy to see the last of you, boy!"

Billy only sighed. "I'd . . . I'd like to get dressed in private," he finally said.

"Gad," Richard said, shooting him a scathing glance before he headed to fetch his own meal.

The late morning and early afternoon did nothing to answer his questions about this odd boy who'd been held by the Spaniards. Richard had spent a good part of the morning in his quarters, going over charts and writing in his log. Billy had spent his time doing a passable job of cleaning the cabin, straightening, even washing Richard's bed sheet which, frankly, had never been washed since they'd left harbor. But all the while the lad had asked questions, coming up with the strangest notions. For instance, Richard recalled, Billy had asked about the year and the month. Then the cabin boy had ventured to name the monarchs of Europe, and when Richard had said, "Yes, Philip the Fourth is king of Spain," the lad had paled and leaned against the wall for a moment. It was as if he'd been living in a cave. His parents, if he had any, had afforded him no education whatsoever.

But he could read.

He'd picked up books on the shelf above the desk and read the words. He'd read over Richard's shoulder, pointing at the Spanish *cayos* north of the Florida Straits and saying, "That's Key West. There." And then he'd looked at Richard imploringly. "You could take me there if you wanted."

"There? But that *cayo* is worthless. There are only some savages who dwell on it. And I am given to understand they are not friendly."

Billy had studied him for a moment longer, then seemed to give up for the time being. He'd looked back at the map opened on the desk, poring over it until Richard had finally rolled the thing up and put it away.

Then there'd been a chart of the ocean, an excellent Portuguese map Richard had liberated from a Spanish ship. Billy had taken it down without permission, unrolled it, and pointed to land masses and islands, seas, places a lad should never have even heard about much less recognized. Gad, a good navigator should not have done so well!

"How do you come by this knowledge?" Richard had asked.

But Billy Bonney had answered innocently, "Why, at school."

By the noontime meal, Richard was indeed perplexed. The boy was educated and yet completely uneducated. He knew nothing in certain areas, yet he seemed to possess an uncanny sense of history and politics, even venturing bizarre notions about the future of the Spanish colonies, not to mention the English, French and Dutch holdings in the New World.

"The English will eventually hold everything from this point—" Billy showed him on the chart "—to here. And the Spanish will hold everything to the south. Of course, new nations will be formed when the colonists grow tired of being controlled from three thousand miles away, but that won't happen for a couple hundred years."

"Ridiculous," Richard said. "I'll give you a good imagination, Billy, but you are most certainly wrong."

"We'll see," he replied and went about his chores.

It was when Richard was shaving that he heard the commotion. At first he thought the lookout must have spotted the Out Islands, home, but then Billy abruptly came storming in after attempting to empty his scrub bucket. It seemed the bucket had been emptied on the cabin boy—by the crew.

"Those bastards!" Billy cried, standing there like a drowned rat.

"Perhaps it was a jest," Richard offered, hiding a smile.

"They're nothing but animals! Pigs! They stink and their language is disgusting! If one of them so much as touches me again I'll . . . I'll stick him with a knife! I swear it!" And then all the anger seemed to drain out of him and he sagged, his wet shirt and pants hanging on his scrawny limbs. "Oh, God," he sobbed pathetically, "I know I'm dead. I drowned. And this is hell!"

He made such a piteous sight that the black captain's heart went out to him for a moment. He truly was one of the innocents of the world, a lost soul. He was born a boy, yet the Lord had seen fit to endow him with tiny feet and hands, a narrow waist that many a woman would envy and skin that was smooth, un-marred. Not even the first peach fuzz grew on the boy's chin.

He *was* comely, Richard was thinking as he scraped his razor-sharp knife up the side of his left cheek, his head tilted to catch his image in the gold-framed Spanish ladies' mirror. What was to become of Billy, he wondered, when they put ashore? Why, every cut-throat and pirate and scalawag in the whole of the Spanish Main lived on the island. Billy wouldn't last a minute among those scourges of the earth. Perhaps Richard should offer...

He shut the notion down with an iron will. He'd saved him from his fate with the Spanish. Once was enough. The boy had lived this long; he'd survive somehow.

Richard frowned deeply and tore his eyes from the pitiful sight of those slim, womanly shoulders that shook with the boy's sobbing, and went back to his shaving. "You'll manage," Richard growled under his breath.

They dropped anchor late that afternoon in the harbor at Red Turtle Cay and made shore in long-boats. The crew was gleeful, dividing up the coins Richard game them as their share of the take from the *Santa Luisa*. The gold and silver would not last long, however, but a good time would be had by all.

Red Turtle Cay was a free port. There were ships of all flags, stolen ships, privateers, anchored in the har-bor alongside the *Marauder*—Dutch, Spanish, En-glish, French, Portuguese. The town itself was small, consisting of three inns and half a dozen taverns that

also offered rooms. There was a scattering of houses
built in styles that reminded homesick buccaneers of
their native lands. Ruby and his family lived in such a
house. On the island, worldly goods abounded, stolen
by the pirates and on sale for outrageous prices,
though barter for a bed or a woman or a bottle of fine
French brandy was not uncommon. There was tobacco to be had and cured meats, indigo, silk, flour,
gold and silver and enough precious gems to fill the
holds of a plump galleon. And all of the goods on Red
Turtle Cay had been stolen from the Spaniards who
presumed to control the *bajamar* of the West Indies,
the waters so arrogantly called the Spanish Main.

Ruby took to overseeing the release of the slaves
they'd freed from the Spaniards. He gave them each
a gold coin and sent them on their way. In a matter of
hours, every man, woman and child would find employment on this very rich island—employment as a
free person. Some would work at the inns and taverns
and stores, but most would go to sea again as pirates.
It was not a bad life.

"You're really letting them go?" Billy asked at
Richard's side.

"Gad, are you still here?"

The boy flashed him a look with those dark, long-
lashed eyes. "Of course I am. Where do you expect me
to go?"

Richard grumbled something unintelligible. Then,
"I keep my word, Billy, they are free. As, I might add,
are you. Now," he said, "be off with you, lad. But
take care. This is not a fitting place for a boy of... of
your, uh, tender sensibilities. You understand?" He

fixed his eye on Billy sternly. "You understand my meaning?"

"Er, yes," Billy replied, and he cast his gaze about, his peach-colored cheeks turning an ashen hue.

"Try the inns," Richard said. "Surely one of the innkeepers will give you employment and a bed. Now, I've enjoyed meeting you, lad, but I have quite a thirst and, shall we say, other needs that must be attended to. Well met, Master Bonney." He took the boy's hand, opened it and dropped ten gold pieces into the small palm. "Fare thee well." He turned on his heel and made straight for the Laughing Parrot, willfully shutting out the forlorn figure standing behind him on the dock.

CHAPTER FOUR

TESS FELT THE HEAVY gold coins in her hand and couldn't believe it. He was dumping her on the dock like so much garbage. Here she was, stranded nearly four hundred years from her own time, with no means to survive, no way even to get back to Key West, and he just couldn't care less as long as he got his tankard of ale!

Billy Bonney, she thought in derision. The name had flown into her head—the notorious Billy the Kid's real name—when Richard Neville had asked her. But as she watched him swagger away down the harbor thoroughfare, her alter ego Billy was not exactly turning out as she'd hoped. For a time there on the *Marauder,* Tess had almost believed the captain was taking pity on her, *him,* well, the cabin boy. It had been in Richard's eyes, eye, that was, in his silent perusal of her. At least, Tess thought, she'd believed he cared about her welfare. Never for a minute had she thought he'd set her on the dock at Red Turtle Cay and casually say fare thee well.

She thought of running after him, begging him to take her to Key West, because maybe, if she could find that whirlpool again, she could find her way home.

Should she tell him she was Tess, not Billy? Would he help her then?

Tess weighed the pros and cons. If he knew she was a woman, if he saw her in that light, Richard Neville might sympathize with her predicament—though he'd never believe she was from the future—but he might also get other ideas. No, Tess decided, it would be better if he felt sorry for poor little Billy, his cabin boy.

Okay then. But how was she going to talk the captain into sailing her back to Key West? As far as he was concerned, he'd promised to set her safely ashore and he'd done it. If she followed him directly to his tavern he might get mad. Obviously he had plans for his evening and they didn't include a teenage cabin boy.

The captain had disappeared from sight. She took a breath, glanced around and spotted Ruby. He was with a woman, a fair-haired, husky woman dressed in a colorful long skirt and a low-cut white blouse. Her cheeks were red and she was laughing, one small dark-headed child hanging on to her skirt, an infant propped on a full hip. Ruby was giving her a squeeze, chucking the infant on the chin, tousling the boy's hair. It was certainly a homecoming if ever Tess saw one.

Ruby…she thought. He had Richard's ear, seemed almost fatherly toward the one-eyed pirate captain of his. Maybe, Tess mused, maybe Ruby could get his captain's attention more effectively than she could. Maybe Ruby even knew where to find him.

Tess took a deep breath. She had to have some sort of protector in this world she'd landed in, and Black Richard Neville seemed to be her best bet. So she straightened, put a scared, sorrowful expression on her face, which wasn't hard at all, and walked toward Ruby.

"Mr. Salvador," she said. "Um, excuse me."

He looked down at her, surprised. "Well, it's little Billy, isn't it."

"I hate to bother you, and I see you're busy, but I don't know where to go or what to do here. I, uh, thought you could maybe help me," she said, carefully keeping her face averted from Ruby's wife. A man might mistake her for a boy, but another woman could perhaps see through the farce.

"Did not the captain give you some gold pieces, boy?" Ruby was asking.

"Well, yes, but...well, I've never been on my own before, and I'm afraid someone will cheat me or steal them," Tess said forlornly.

"The poor darlin'," his wife said. "Do something, Ruby."

Ruby looked lost. "Edith, love, what would you have me do?"

Edith hitched the dark-eyed child up more securely on her hip. "Where's your family, boy?" she asked Billy.

"All dead, ma'am," Tess replied quickly, her eyes on the ground.

"There's no one?"

Tess shook her head.

"This is Billy Bonney, my dear, the lad we rescued from a Spanish slaver," Ruby explained. "The captain took him on as cabin boy until we got home."

Edith raised her brows in dismay. "Isn't that just like Black Richard? You cannot leave a young lad like this to fend for himself."

"Do you think," Tess began, "do you think the captain could keep me as cabin boy? Or his servant?"

Ruby stroked his beard, frowning. "I cannot answer that question, Billy. It's for the captain to decide."

Tess stood there, glancing up at Ruby, her eyes filling with tears, a feat which again, was not hard to accomplish. "What will I do?" she asked.

"All right," Ruby said, nudged by his wife, "I'll find the captain for you. We'll search him out and ask him. Will that suit you, Billy?" He turned to his wife. "And you, Edith?"

"Oh, yes, thank you," Tess said. "Thank you very much."

"Come along then," Ruby said, and to his wife, "I'll be home presently, love."

Ruby led Tess away from the crowded docks and inns and taverns that lined the busy waterfront. People of all sorts jammed the dirt streets: swaggering soldiers, traders, blacks, Indians, fair ladies with low-necked blouses, ruffians, scarred sailors, men of a dozen countries. The buildings of Red Turtle Cay were copies of those loved best by each nationality. There were flat-fronted, two-story Dutch homes of brick, French chalets in miniature, English cottages, Portuguese tiled courtyards as well as lean-tos and shacks. In the rubbish-filled streets, drunks mingled right alongside bejeweled rich men in all their finery.

What a place, Tess thought, looking around, fascinated and frightened at the same time, hurrying to keep up with Ruby's long strides. "Do you know where he is, the captain, I mean?" Tess asked.

"Aye, he'll be at the Laughing Parrot."

"That's a . . . a bar?"

"A tavern. There's no bars here, lad, except maybe gold ones," Ruby said, and chuckled.

"Right." Tess stuck close to Ruby, dodging a donkey loaded with heavy brassbound chests. With each long stride she took, her fascination grew. History— she was living and breathing and smelling it. The cloying, hot summer air bludgeoning her was the same air breathed by the great seventeenth-century monarchs of Europe, richly appointed courtiers of China, fierce Japanese warriors, and all the peoples dotting the sparsely populated earth who wouldn't be discovered for centuries. A pure air. Unpolluted. They rounded a corner and Tess touched a flowering vine climbing a stone wall and marveled at the sensation of softness, its scent. Her whole being was filled with this living history, and for a few minutes she felt a curious thrill of adventure. Tess, the bookworm—she'd even sailed on a frigate with real life buccaneers!

She moved along, catching up to Ruby. "Uh, Ruby, sir," she began, "how long have you known Captain Neville?"

"Since he came onto the *Sea Lady* as a common sailor when he had but eighteen years. The *Sea Lady,* that's what she was called before he took her and renamed her the *Marauder.*"

"The captain stole that ship?" Tess asked.

"Well, he did that, it's true, but his father owned the ship and had promised it to him when Richard got his captain's papers. But his father died before he could turn it over to him, you see."

"But why did he have to steal it? Couldn't he just wait until he inherited it?" Tess asked.

Ruby sighed, then went on around another corner, past two painted women, then skirted a mud puddle. "Ah, it's a sad story, Billy, and it's why we're all here now. The captain is a bastard son. He couldn't inherit. His half brother Thomas got everything. And Thomas is a knave. He paid the *Sea Lady*'s captain to murder Richard Neville, seeing as Thomas always hated him. But Richard, well, he turned the tables and killed the *Sea Lady*'s captain and took the ship. There be no justice for a bastard son who mutinies, so he became Black Richard the pirate and me along with him. The English put a price on his head, and there's no going back now."

"That's awful," Tess said. "He only killed that captain in self-defense."

"True enough, but who'd listen? Once Edmund Moore, Richard's father, was dead, there was no one."

"What about his mother?" Tess asked.

"A fine woman, Elizabeth. But there was naught she could do. He hasn't heard from her in nigh onto two years, and he daren't return to England. They'd hang him before you could say 'Long Live the King.'"

"Um," Tess said, avoiding a pig rooting in the mud of the street. "And did your captain, Richard, that is, lose his eye in the fight for the *Marauder*? Did that other captain injure him?"

"He did not," Ruby said.

"Then how?"

Ruby seemed to grow uncomfortable. "That would be for Richard Neville to tell you."

"Oh," Tess said, "I get it. You've spilled enough beans already."

"Beans?"

"Never mind."

Ruby stopped in front of a stucco, half-timbered building. The low-linteled door was open, and raucous voices spilled out into the still steaming twilight of Red Turtle Cay. Above the door hung a wooden sign, carved and painted. On it was a green and yellow parrot with its beak open wide. The Laughing Parrot.

"Here it be, Billy, my boy, and I'll wager the captain's inside. I won't ask him if he'll take you on. You'll need to do that yourself."

"Oh, I will, don't worry," Tess assured him. "It's just that I'm glad you're here with me."

Ruby only grumbled something then steered her in the door and across the crowded room. The place, Tess saw immediately, was everything she'd imagined, and worse. It could have been taken right out of a movie—the filthy, odiferous alehouse frequented by a bunch of murdering, thieving pirates, the dregs of the earth. Along one long wall was a bar. In the center of the huge room were massive wooden kegs stacked on their sides, the pile reaching the ceiling. Dozens of scarred wooden trestle tables caked with candle wax filled the available space, and every bench was taken.

Tess's first impression was that there wasn't a sober man—or woman—in sight. Heavy pewter tankards of ale were crashing together in salutes. In a far dark corner two bearded men with bandannas tied on their heads were fighting with long daggers. In another corner a skinny, filthy-looking wench was screaming bloody murder as a man who could have been Long John Silver himself lifted her rag of a skirt and fondled her bare buttocks. Barmaids from the far corners of the earth scurried to and fro carrying ales and bottles of wine and whiskey and brandy and grog.

The place stank of unwashed bodies and stale liquor and heavy tobacco smoke. Tess was sure she could even smell the coppery odor of blood from the stains on the plank flooring. And if she'd thought the structures on Red Turtle Cay told of the many nationalities who inhabited the pirate hideaway, then this place clinched her observation. As she made her way across the floor behind Ruby, half-hidden by his bulk, her ear picked up at least half a dozen languages.

It was loud. A man could be killed at a table next to her and Tess doubted she'd even hear it. She imagined a rotting stack of bodies that had been tossed out back to make more room for the next group of thieves. And this, she thought, shrinking inside, was Richard Neville's hangout. Swell.

They found him at a table near the far wall, two tankards of ale before him, a very well endowed redhead on his lap. He was nuzzling the trollop's neck with his teeth.

"Captain," Ruby said, plunking himself down, "I thought we'd find you hereabouts." He nodded to an open place on the rough-hewn bench across the table. Tess made her way around and sat, her stomach churning.

"Ah, Ruby," Richard began, but then he spotted Tess. "What's this?" He disengaged the woman's arms from around his neck and settled that single, flinty eye on Tess.

"Oh," Ruby said. "Edith took pity on poor Billy here and bade me bring him along." Then Ruby banged the table and cast about for a barmaid. "Ale!" he shouted. "One for me and one for the boy!"

"So you brought the lad here?" Richard inquired through a frown. "He'll not last an hour with this crew, Ruby. That, or he'll be puking his ale on the table, I'll wager you."

"The boy can handle himself, can't you there, Billy?"

"Sure," Tess said, trying to put distance between herself and the thug next to her, a youngish Englishman whose breath was so sour she thought she might faint.

And then Richard pushed the woman all the way off his lap and put a booted foot up on the bench while he continued to study Tess. "I thought you'd be bedded down at an inn by now," he said.

"I don't want to go to an inn. Alone," she added. "I . . . I like working for you, Captain Neville."

He took a swig of ale and wiped his mouth with the back of his hand. "I'm in no need of a servant," he said.

The woman next to him was pouting, but she was also not very drunk, and she was studying Tess with a sharp eye. Tess was growing nervous. The ales came, thankfully, and she took a few sips of the warm, frothy stuff, hiding behind the tankard.

Richard, too, was watching Tess, a brow lifted, and she was starting to think this had been the worst idea of her life. They were sitting here, the handsome young captain and his whore, whom he called Matilda, slowly but surely recognizing Billy Bonney for who "he" really was.

Tess swallowed a lump in her throat. "You know," she said, "maybe you're right. I think I'll just go on over to a hotel and—" She never finished her sentence, however, because at that moment one of the pirates sitting at the table next to theirs came to his feet and pointed right at Tess.

"Would you look at that laddy!" the drunk blubbered. "Now, never have I seen such a fine laddy in me life! Come here, boy, and I'll favor you with a gold crown or two!"

Tess shrank back into her seat.

"Mind yer own business," Ruby shot back. "The boy is with us."

"To hell with that!" the drunk slurred. "He can see a good thing himself. Say, laddy, you tell 'em!"

With all the courage she could muster, Tess said, "I like this company, mister. Now lay off."

"Lay off, is it?" he began, and finally, mercifully, Richard rose to his feet. "And who in hell do you think you..." the drunk started to say, but then suddenly he fell silent. A moment later he mumbled, "Aye, it be Black Richard, himself, I see. I concede the laddy is in good company.'' He sat down with a heavy thud and went back to his drink.

"Phew," Tess got out.

"Phew?" Richard said, sitting back down himself. "Did I not warn you, boy?" He swore under his breath.

For a moment Tess looked at him and tried to make up her mind. He was her only hope. Oh, sure, there had to be other ship captains on this island who could be persuaded to sail her to Key West. But what would the price be?

She took a breath. "Listen," she said and leaned across the table. "I want to work for you. I don't want to stay on this filthy island and rot. I can't . . . trust anyone else here. You can see that. Let me work for you. *Please.*"

He regarded her somberly, soberly it seemed, and said, "No. I have no need to waste my money. No, I say, boy, you're too much trouble. I have enough trouble of my own."

"I'll work for free, then."

"Nay. You'd be no better than a slave and I don't countenance bondage."

"Then pay me in another way." She stared at him in earnest, a bubble of panic forming in her stomach. She wanted to go home, home to the twentieth century, home to her family, her apartment, her job. She didn't even know if she could get home, but she had to try. She couldn't stay *here!*

An image of holding that gold chain with its emerald setting flew into her mind. And then the sense of spinning in the whirlpool, spinning into another time.

Had the whirlpool always existed? Was it there now? Tess didn't know. But if she couldn't get back to those waters, she knew one thing for sure. She'd never have a prayer of getting home. That was where everything converged—the necklace, the whirlpool, the door to this time. And she had to get back there to return to her own time; of that she was positive.

She gave Richard an imploring look. "I'll work for nothing. I won't be any trouble. But in return I want you to take me to that *cayo,* Key West, as soon as you can."

"I can't do it, lad."

"Then take me there whenever you can. I don't care. A month from now, a year. Just when you can."

Tess saw it in his eye then, his answer. It was still no. But at that moment, she would always thank God, providence intervened in the form of Ruby.

"It doesn't seem such a bad bargain," the first mate said above the din at Richard's ear. "The boy is a good sort. He's honest. I'll wager he'll stay out of trouble and do a fair day's work for you, Captain."

Richard mumbled.

"Aye," Ruby went on and gave Tess a wink, "the lad reminds me of another I once knew, someone else who was in need of a protector for a time."

Richard raised that brow again and clasped his hands on the table, shaking his head. "It's blackmail, is it? The boy's gotten to that soft spot in your heart, Ruby Salvador. Or was this Edith's notion?"

Ruby shrugged.

Richard was quiet for a moment, his attention now on Tess. Finally he sat back and said, "You'll not get underfoot, Billy, because at the first sign of trouble I'll have to whip you, lad. You understand?''

Tess nodded quickly.

''And I won't be promising when I'll be passing your Key West with my ship. Is that clear?''

''Yes. Oh, yes. Just if you do, I'd be eternally grateful if you'd get me there somehow.''

''We'll see.''

''Then it's a bargain?''

''Gad, I suppose it is.''

''Shake on it?''

Slowly, hesitantly, Richard Neville, Black Richard the pirate, put out his strong, sun-browned hand and encased hers. The bargain was struck.

TESS'S BARGAIN was struck, all right, but it was a long, miserable night nonetheless. Ruby stayed for a time at the Laughing Parrot but when he deemed himself on the verge of drunkenness he declared that Edith would string him up by the ears if he did not get home straightaway.

''The captain'll look after you now, Billy,'' he told her. ''You'll be in fine hands. See to it you do your chores, though, or he'll end the bargain for sure.''

And so Tess was forced to stay at the tavern while Richard went about charming his trollop right out of her dingy stockings. Half-choking in the foul air, Tess sat with her arms folded stiffly across her chest and studied Richard's technique. She found it really quite crude. He was cocksure of himself and obviously thought he was God's gift to women. He could even flirt with the barmaid while a deft hand was reaching up his whore's skirts. He had a smile on his lips, too, one that Tess was just noticing. It was more like a smirk, she decided, a self-satisfied little grin that lifted one corner of his mouth as the woman in his lap cooed and sighed at his touches.

Disgusting! Tess fumed silently. The woman almost writhed while she sat on his rock-hard thighs. On and on it went. Ale after ale. Sensuous touch after sensuous touch until Tess thought she was going to scream. And then, finally, the wench got up to relieve herself out back in the privy, and Tess let out a breath of relief.

Richard watched the woman go, her backside swaying, with that supercilious grin on his lips.

Tess yawned widely.

He took a long drink then set his tankard down hard. He was drunk. "You know," he said, leaning toward Tess, "you might take a lesson here, boy, on how to court a woman properly."

"I really don't—"

"How old are you, anyway?"

"Twenty-six," Tess said before she realized he'd thought her much younger. Uh-oh.

"Gad! I deemed you fifteen years. No more." He stared at her curiously.

"I look young, I know."

"I should say so. Well, at any rate, you need to hone your manhood, boy. Perhaps you could overcome some of that prettiness."

Tess made an annoyed sound.

"I daresay," Richard went on, "that some female somewhere would take a fancy to you."

"No doubt."

"Bah!" he snorted. "You're making light of a lesson I'm trying to give."

"Why, not at all," Tess said, barely in control of her sarcasm. "It's just that I'm sure no one could come close to your expert methods, Captain."

"Methods! What a term. I shall have to remember that." He focused his bloodshot eye on her. "I do have a way with women, do I not?"

"Oh, you certainly do, Captain. And I must say," Tess added recklessly, "that's what makes me glad I'm not a woman."

The woman Matilda returned then, and Tess was actually glad she did. The conversation was getting sticky. But Richard quickly forgot it, going straight back to his seduction. It was another full hour before he finally rose, gripping his tramp around the waist, and announced, "To the inn. I'm drunk and I'm tired and I'm ready to lay down with you, Matilda. Come along, Billy, there's a pallet in my room. You can rest there." And dutifully, gritting her teeth, Tess followed them out.

The night air, as sultry as it was, refreshed Tess mercifully, and she sucked in lungfuls until she felt dizzy. Richard and his woman walked ahead, both staggering a little, his arm around her shoulders, hugging her to his side.

He was tall, Tess noticed, at least a head taller than his doxy. And he did make a commanding sight as he moved along the street past another tavern, an inn, and yet another tavern. Tess sensed that as drunk as he seemed, he could still take down an attacker on the

street. There was a certain fluidity to his gait, an ath-
letic ability that came as naturally to this seventeenth-
century buccaneer as breathing. In her own time, she
mused, Richard Neville would probably fit right in
with her brother's treasure-hunting buddies—he'd be
just one of the boys.

They finally rounded a corner and entered the
Crow's Nest Inn where Richard kept a room over-
looking the harbor. Downstairs was a taproom with a
few tables and behind that were the kitchens. Men and
women still ate at this late hour and drank their ales
and brandies. A few looked up to acknowledge Richard's entrance, especially the barmaid.

"Hello, Gwenne," he called. "I'm home and
headed to my room. This is Billy behind me. He'll be
fetching my meals."

"Aye," Gwenne said, giving both Billy and the
whore a good looking over. "You just send the boy
down and I'll show him the ropes."

"You're a fine woman, Gwenne," Richard said,
and he gave her a wink, then headed on up the narrow, creaking wooden steps, his hand on his whore's
rump.

Richard's room was large, with high ceilings and a
wide, shuttered window where the breeze from the
ocean flowed in. There was a bed, a chair and table, a
washstand. About a quarter of the room could be
curtained off enclosing a stuffy corner, Tess saw, that
had only a thin straw pad laid over a hard wooden
frame. The pallet, she assumed, her bed. But she was
so tired it hardly mattered. What she couldn't believe, couldn't even bear to think about, was that

Richard and the woman were about to drop on his own bed and engage in sex. And Tess was supposed to... what? Lie on her bed behind that flimsy curtain and sleep?

She tried. There wasn't really a choice. She tugged the curtain across its rope and fell onto the straw mattress, her body exhausted, her head reeling from the smoke and ale at the tavern.

Sleep escaped her. The first noises that came to her were soft little love groans that made her cheeks flame and her belly coil. Oh, God, she thought, squeezing her eyes shut, just make them both pass out. *Please.*

They did not pass out. The groans and whispers turned to moans. The bedsprings creaked, once or twice at first and then with a wild, abandoned rhythm. The woman sobbed and cried and pleaded, and Richard groaned all the right things, sighing deeply.

Tess put her hands over her ears but it did no good. She'd never been so mortified in her life. And then, just as she thought her agony couldn't get worse, the most amazing, despicable thing happened. Tess Bonney, intellectual, thoroughly modern woman, felt a pang deep inside, a sexual acknowledgment of the lovemaking going on only a few feet from her. Her body crawled with the shame and horror of her involuntary response. And no matter how hard she tried to shut out the image of Richard laboring on top of that woman, she couldn't.

She hated him. She hated him for putting her in this unbearable position, and she hated him for his sexuality. And even as their moans and cries finally subsided and the sounds of sleep reached Tess, she still felt an unaccountable anger at Richard as if he, all on his own, had summoned her to this time and place, and methodically, with purpose, was putting her through this hell.

CHAPTER FIVE

IT WASN'T LIKE HIM, Richard thought, to sit and brood like this. He never brooded, always being so occupied he rarely had time to consider anything, much less to think too deeply. But the few times he did, he always fell into a black melancholy.

He lived a wild life, he knew that, a dangerous and an exciting one. Perhaps not one he would have espoused had he been given his choice, certainly not one his father Edmund would have fancied for him. And his mother... Richard tapped his fingers on the scarred table in his quarters over the taproom of the Crow's Nest and frowned. Elizabeth Neville was a woman of fine sensibilities. She'd raised her high-spirited son with a sense of right and wrong—much good it had done him—and was likely to be suffering greatly at her only son's current occupation. It was not what she'd had in mind for him.

Richard stood up abruptly, scraping his chair across the floor, and stomped over to the curtained alcove where the boy, Billy, slept. Yanking the hanging aside, he poked the boy with the toe of his boot.

"Get up, Billy," he said curtly. "Lazy layabed!"

The lad mumbled and moved languorously, still asleep, stretching out a pale, slim arm, his fingers curled, the side of his cheek a perfect, smooth curve flushed with pink.

"Billy!" Richard growled, poking harder.

The boy sat bolt upright, a terrified expression on his sleep-dazed face, his chest rising and falling in panic. "What? Uh, I..." And he rubbed his hands over his face. They were shaking, Richard noted, and he suddenly, unaccountably, felt ashamed of himself. It only fired his irritation.

"I'm hungry, Billy. It's late. Go down to the kitchen and fetch me something. Earn your keep, for God's sake, lad."

"Oh, sorry." The boy took a deep, shaky breath. "I was having a dream, a nightmare."

"Silly twit," Richard said.

"Whew, it was awful. It was back in the slave hold and... Well, I guess you're not really interested." He looked up at Richard, his dark eyes cleared of fright now, the usual gleam of challenge and wit sparkling in them again. That, along with a shuttered wariness that intrigued Richard. As he'd done so often before, he wondered where this lad had come from, what his background was. Billy was lying, of course, with his foolish prattling of America and Miami and being lost at sea. Lying, surely, but why?

Well, many on Red Turtle Cay lied about their pasts. It was no great novelty. Richard shrugged mentally and glowered at Billy. "My breakfast?" he said, his arms folded, his boot tapping impatiently.

"Okay, sure, just give me a minute," Billy said. "Sorry I slept so late."

When the boy had gone down to the kitchen, Richard stalked restlessly from unshuttered window to plank door and back. He hated being landbound. It afforded too much idleness, gave him time to think, to worry. It had been bothering him for months that he'd not heard from his mother. In truth, it had been two years since he'd last had word from her, and many months ago he'd sent a letter to Henry Palliser, the Moore family barrister, his father's friend, whom Richard knew sympathized with him.

It was a dicey matter, sending any letter such a distance across the seas to England, but Richard had to be especially careful. With his reputation, it was no simple task to find a captain willing to carry one for him, and then it was usually a Dutchman who'd deliver it to Rotterdam first and then have to locate a ship sailing for London.

And to get mail back was even worse. He had it all sent to Basseterre on Saint Christopher, to the Palm Tree Inn, where the landlord knew him only as Percy Farthingale, gentleman of leisure, sailing the West Indies for his health.

Assuming his letter had reached Henry Palliser and Henry had dispatched one in return, Richard might receive a reply very soon. There could be a simple reason why Elizabeth had never answered his last epistle. Gad, it could have been lost. But, still, he worried. He needed to know if his mother was safe and happy—well, as happy as a woman could be whose beloved companion of so many years had died. Not her husband, no, but the man whose housekeeper she had been, the man whose lover she had been after his wife had died. The man who was Richard's father, in blood if not in law.

Richard conjured up his mother's face there in that stuffy room on the hot, foreign island called Red Turtle Cay. A calm face, with pale blond hair pulled back neatly in a severe style, serious blue eyes and a serene smile. A beautiful face and a lovely character that had caught Edmund's eye thirty years ago and never lost it until Edmund had died.

And since then... Richard wondered how his mother fared, how she was handling Thomas and Caroline Moore, Edmund's children by his deceased wife, those two dreadful creatures who had caused Richard's childhood to be a hell on earth.

Billy came backing in the door just then, his hands full. There was a mug of ale, a loaf of freshly baked bread, some fruit and a slab of cheese, all piled in a wooden bowl the boy held balanced precariously. He put it down on the table and smiled. "This enough?"

Richard reached for the bread, tearing off a heel. He mumbled something, lost in thought, swallowed some warm, weak ale. He still paced, chewing as he moved back and forth. When he finally looked up, long minutes later, Billy was standing there, watching him.

"Eh? What is it?" Richard asked brusquely.

"Oh, you looked worried," Billy said. "I wondered if something was wrong."

"Wrong? Well, lad, what could be wrong?"

"I don't know. You looked—"

"Just never you mind how I *look*," Richard said. "Tell Gwenne I want a bath, Billy. Go on now, step lively. And tell her to make it more than lukewarm this time.''

"Oh, I'd love a bath," the lad said longingly.

"Go for a swim then."

"No, I mean in real water, not seawater. A real one with shampoo and bubble bath."

There he went again, saying things that made no sense. "Shampoo?" Richard mocked. "Bubbles?" He shook his head. "Billy, you are daft. You're fortunate I'm an indulgent master."

Billy sighed. "Right, real lucky."

"The bath."

"Yes, sir, Captain," Billy said, a little sadly, Richard thought, and he felt sorry for the boy again, with his soulful dark eyes and shell pink, sensuously curved mouth, a sweet, tender mouth, turned down now in disappointment.

Richard relented. Again. "If you fancy a bath, lad..."

"Yes?" Billy said, his expression brighter.

"You're welcome to use mine after I'm done," Richard offered magnanimously.

Richard oversaw the filling of the wooden tub that Billy lugged up the narrow stairs. Aye, he felt a bit of a twinge at the sight of the slim built lad sweating and laboring. Richard could have done it himself with one hand in half the time, but Billy needed training, breaking in, as it were. And the bucket. Hot and cold ones, until Richard put in his fingers and deemed the water just right.

"Come here," he ordered. "My boots." Billy had to be shown what to do and turned around, Richard's foot on his backside. "Brace yourself now and pull," Richard had to tell him, as he pushed with his foot. Billy twisted and looked at him in bewilderment and a touch of temper, then lost his balance as Richard pushed too hard on his rear. "Brace yourself, I said," Richard repeated disgustedly. Then the other boot. Gad, it was easier to do it himself. What good was a cabin boy who didn't even know how to get your boots off?

Richard pulled his shirt over his head and tossed it aside, then reached down and started unbuttoning the flap at the front of his trousers.

"Wait," he heard Billy say in a strangled voice.

He looked up.

"Uh, wait, um, you don't want me in here while you take a bath," Billy said quickly.

Richard continued unbuttoning his trousers. "It's of no account to me. You could tidy up a bit while I bathe. Make the bed and such."

"Uh..." Billy was as tense as a coiled spring, edging toward the door. "I'll, uh, do it later."

Richard stepped out of his trousers, kicking them aside, and as he got into the tub, he was aware of his cabin boy gasping and scooting out of the room, slamming the door behind him.

Strange lad. "Billy!" he shouted through the door. "Bring me some ale, you hear?"

"Aye, aye, sir," came the muffled reply.

Richard soaked in the water and tried to relax. Yet, even while his body settled, his mind still fretted about his mother. There were so many things he'd like to tell her. He wanted, above all, to explain what had happened two years ago when the previous captain of the *Marauder* had tried to kill him, ordered by Thomas, his own half brother turned deadly enemy the moment their father had died. He'd also wanted to be with her after Edmund had passed on, to comfort her, but by the time he'd heard, months had gone by, and then there had been the episode with his captain, a clearly mutinous act, and it had been too late. Now letters were his only tenuous link to his mother, and even that link seemed to have broken.

A knock came on the door. "It's me, Billy. With your ale."

"Well, what are you waiting for, lad? Come in, come in. I'm sweating like a pig. Hurry up with that ale." The door opened. The boy sidled in, holding the tankard, his eyes averted. "Put it down, right there," Richard ordered. "Soap my back, Billy."

What a light touch the lad had. Richard leaned forward, head hanging, and sighed. It was pleasant, he supposed, to have this fellow at his beck and call for duties of this sort, but he still wasn't sure the bother was worth it.

"Can I go now?" Billy asked carefully when he was finished.

"Go? Where do you want to go?"

"Uh, out."

"Fine, go then. But stay close. I'll need you to rinse my hair soon."

The boy scuttled out, and Richard lay there in the water, his mind turned again to his problem. He'd have to risk a trip to Saint Christopher. There was no way around it. Ah, Richard thought, idly rubbing the hard bar of soap on his chest, Ruby would protest. Yes, Ruby would be against it.

And Ruby would doubtless be right. Richard smiled, soaping his hair. Ruby was more a father to him, if truth be told, than Edmund had ever been. A handsome man, yes, but Edmund Moore, beneath the polished veneer, had been a weak man. Richard's mother had been his mainstay for thirty-odd years, even while he indulged his legitimate children, Thomas and Caroline, shamefully. It was true Edmund had loved his bastard son Richard, but he had never been able to take care of Richard the way he'd wanted. Edmund had spoken so often of how he would care for his beloved Richard, how he would leave him a ship or shares in the shipping company or a legacy of gold, but he had never gotten around to doing it. First it had been procrastination, Richard supposed, and then it had been fear of his son Thomas's objections. Poor Edmund, a good enough fellow, but a sadly lacking father.

"Billy!" Richard shouted. "Get in here!"

The door opened a reluctant crack. "Yes?"

"Rinse my hair. There's a tin cup around here somewhere. Oh, there it is. Quick now, the soap's getting in my eye." Billy poured the warm water over Richard's hair, running his fingers through the long, wet tangles to straighten it out. "Ah," Richard sighed, "at least you're good for something. Mayhaps you were a lady's maid, eh, Billy?" And he chuckled wickedly.

"Right, Captain, that's it," Billy muttered darkly, pouring water right on Richard's face, and even while

Richard sat up, sputtering, he knew he'd finally insulted the lad's manhood. About bloody time. "Can I go now?" Billy asked.

"Aye, go, leave. And clean this room up later, or I might regret my bargain, Billy Bonney," he warned.

The door slammed behind Billy again. That boy. He'd need to learn meekness, Richard decided, oh, yes, meekness and humility and his lowly station in life. And Richard was just the man to teach him.

Aye, meekness. Richard was not, had never been meek himself, despite his illegitimacy. He could even feel a touch of sympathy for poor Billy. Richard had had a difficult enough time of it himself as a youth. He must have been a wicked child, a terror for Edmund to deal with. He'd been wild, hot-tempered, too proud. Not easy character traits for a bastard son in a household devoted to the two older legitimate children. He'd always been restless as a child, then a youth, then a young man, until Edmund had let him go to sea as a common sailor. And even then he'd been restless unless sailing or fighting, drinking or whoring, always desperate to see what was over the horizon, running from a society that would not accept him.

His mother understood him. She didn't always agree with his actions, but she never raised her voice, and in her quiet way she could make him feel more ashamed than anyone else ranting at him.

Not trusting Thomas Moore, he'd feared greatly for her safety ever since Edmund had died. His half brother would likely try to dislodge his father's mistress from the London house, even though Elizabeth had been promised a home for life. Edmund had it put in writing and he'd given her a gift of a gold and emerald necklace at the same time, a chain of thick, twisted links, a work of art, also a fortune easily convertible into cash in an emergency, one link at a time.

Well, Richard had waited long enough, and despite Ruby's protests, the *Marauder* would sail to Saint Christopher in the Leeward Islands as soon as she was refitted and supplied.

Richard raised his head, water streaming off his long hair onto his shoulders and back, and grinned. It should prove to be an interesting voyage.

"RECONSIDER," Ruby repeated over a mug of ale in the inn's taproom that afternoon.

"No, not this time, old friend," Richard said. "It has to be done."

Ruby shook his grizzled head.

The boy Billy leaned forward on the table and looked from one to the other. Richard could smell the clean, soapy smell of his hair, the lad was so close.

"Reconsider what?" Billy asked.

"Billy, leave us," Richard said. "This is none of your business."

"Somehow I have a feeling it is," Billy said. "Remember, we have a bargain."

"By all the saints, you have a nerve!" Richard said in a low, angry voice. "Questioning *me*. A cabin boy, questioning the captain! Why do I put up with you?"

Billy sat back on the stool, dark eyes hooded in that way he had, not chastised, not humbled, just waiting for the next opportunity. There seemed to be no fear in the fellow.

"Gad, the Spanish threaten their children with my name, and my own cabin boy defies me," he said bitterly to Ruby.

"Aye, he's a sharp one," Ruby replied, smiling.

"Sharp as a sword," Richard grumbled, "turned on him who wields it."

"Let him be, Captain. He means no harm," Ruby said.

"If we could change the subject?" Richard asked sarcastically.

"Aye, Captain."

"We sail tomorrow morning on the tide, Ruby. Tell the men."

"You are not well advised," Ruby said, stroking his beard.

"A pox on that, Ruby. I am captain and I say we sail for Saint Christopher. Have I ever led you wrong?"

"Not yet."

"Don't go soft on me, man," Richard said. "Not a ship on these waters can catch us."

"But it's on the island that you're vulnerable," Ruby insisted.

"We've done it before and not a thing happened. We go in disguise as always. Me as Percy and you as my manservant."

"Aye, I know that. But the price on your head is bigger now. The English offer one reward and the Spanish offer even more. 'Tis not safe."

"Not safe, ha! What *is* safe? What are my choices, tell me, Ruby? Do I stay here in this cesspool and rot? I tell you, I must find out about my mother!"

Ruby bowed his head, folded his hands. No, he had no answer. They had to sail to Saint Christopher, they had to make the trek across the island to Basseterre as they'd done before, he and Ruby, and they had to collect Richard's mail.

"Wait then. Wait for a time until the furor over the *Luisa* has died down," Ruby cautioned.

Richard fixed his friend with one steely blue eye. "We sail on the morning tide. Give the orders, Ruby."

"Aye, aye, Captain."

When Ruby had left, Richard leaned back against the wall and took a long draft of ale, wiping the froth from his lips with the back of his hand.

"Excuse me," he heard Billy say, "where are we going that's so dangerous?"

Richard turned and graced his cabin boy with the same steely gaze. "Listen, boy, you can end the bargain right now, if you want. Just say the words. I won't hold you."

"Where are we going? Just tell me," Billy said staunchly.

"Saint Christopher in the Leewards. A week's sail south. An English island."

"And why's it dangerous?"

Richard waved an impatient hand. "Ruby's becoming an old lady. We've gone before. I have my letters sent there. I need to collect my mail."

"I see." Billy watched him with an assessing gaze. "Who're you expecting letters from? A sweetheart, a wife?"

"By all that's holy, you know how to try a man's soul. No sweetheart, no wife. What do you think I am, a home-and-hearth sort? I left England free as a bird and I'll stay that way. No, Billy, I await news from my mother. There, does that satisfy you?"

"So, this news is worth risking your life for?" Billy asked, looking down at his small hands.

"Aye, it is."

"Too bad you can't just pick up a phone," Richard heard the boy say to himself.

"What's that, boy?"

"Uh, nothing, Captain, nothing at all."

THE MORNING DAWNED pale and sultry and mother-of-pearl pink. Richard had been up at first light, stalking the quarterdeck, seeing to the last few supplies being stowed on board: fresh fruit to avoid the scurvy, although this was but a short sail, gunpowder, cannonballs, shot, flour, dried meat, barrels of fresh water, onions, rounds of cheese from the Dutch. The crewmen knew their jobs. They moved quickly, swarming across the gangplank, stacking, storing, tying down cargo.

Billy stood in the shelter of the aft companionway to the captain's cabin, staring at the ordered confusion with big eyes, as if seeing it all for the first time. For once, his mouth stayed shut.

The bell for the dawn watch rang and the pilot, Joseph Bellows, turned the hourglass. Richard's practiced eye checked every detail of his ship. The decks were spotless, the hull caulked, all rigging repaired during this layover. All ropes were neatly coiled, all cannon gleaming under a new film of oil. Jacob Thorne, a toothless old-timer, was at the bow on a tiny roped platform, swinging the lead weight, ready to call out the fathoms when the ship began to move.

Richard stood at his quarterdeck, feet apart in an arrogant stance, moving easily with the gentle rocking of his vessel as she lay at anchor in the protected harbor of Red Turtle Cay. He belonged there, always feeling a weight lift from him when he was on the high seas. He loved the sea, he loved ships of all sorts, save perhaps the fat-sided Spanish galleons. He only felt whole and happy with the wind in his face, his eye squinting into storm and sun, his tongue tasting salt, the deck heeled over, the spars and rigging and halyards groaning under the press of canvas that would chortle with joy as the breeze shifted a degree or so. Freedom is what it was.

They were ready. Ruby asked permission to stand on the quarterdeck, for no man stepped on the captain's deck without word given him.

"Permission granted."

"All is ready, Captain."

"Thank you, Mr. Salvador. Stand down now, ready for up anchor."

"Yes, sir."

"Up anchor!" Richard shouted in his captain's voice.

His crew responded, cranking the heavy chains.

"All hands lay to! All sails ho!"

The lovely, orchestrated mayhem of a full-rigged frigate's crew began. Men swarmed into the rigging to free the sails from their yards.

"South by southwest! Steady as she goes!" he yelled.

Slowly, slowly, her anchors up, the *Marauder*'s keel caught the current, her first sails caught the morning breeze, the deck slanted, and Richard felt the delicate shudder his ship gave as she began to move. A sensual shudder, as a woman would give when a man took her.

Richard kept a sharp eye out, but Ruby was a skilled first mate, his pilot was dependable, his crew perfectly trained. Still, she was Richard's ship, his own, promised to him by his father, even though he'd had to kill to have her. She was worth it.

The frigate moved more quickly now, out into open water, more of her sails let out, luffing then catching the wind, as sailors climbed higher and higher. And still, Richard noticed, his cabin boy stood, mesmerized, silent, watching the spectacle unfold, his long-lashed dark eyes wide with wonder, that one eyebrow arched fetchingly.

At last she was under full sail, headed away from Red Turtle Cay, her canvas bellied out by a strong northeast wind, racing to the south, the bit between her teeth as white bow waves creamed to each side, lines shrieking, spars stretched on a larboard tack. Then Richard cried, "All sails ho! Topsails, mainsails, royals and topgallants!" His men let out the ropes, granting her every inch of sail. Then came the snapping report of canvas on the other tack, turning, and "Steady as she goes!" Richard called, every bit of canvas responding to his orders, and he felt the recurring thrill of commanding this beautiful dark lady of his as she leaped, hissing, across the waves.

IT WAS AN UNEVENTFUL voyage save for some choppy seas. Although they kept a sharp lookout, no English ship was sighted and the only Spanish one a small coastal vessel that fled in terror. The boy, Billy, was as sick as a dog for the first two days, as useless a servant as there could be, for Richard had to bring him water and dry crusts and empty his puke bucket.

Richard didn't try to insist she carry out any of her duties. Tess was glad. She couldn't have handled anything because on this trip she'd inexplicably become deathly seasick.

"Aye, it happens," Ruby said, shaking his head, looking down at Tess retching in a bucket.

The humiliation! There she was lying on her pallet, green as the Marquesa Shoals, as Richard remarked with his usual wit, and sick as a dog.

She wouldn't think much about it till later, but during that spell of sickness, Richard actually showed her remarkable kindness. He emptied her bucket for her, brought in food and water, even held her shoulders once while she retched miserably.

She sagged back on her pallet, white-faced, her hair wet spikes. "I'm going to die," she moaned.

"There, there. No one dies from being sick in this fashion, boy."

"How would you know?" she breathed weakly.

"Because I myself was once as sick as you. 'Twas one of my first ocean voyages."

"How did you manage to work?"

"I didn't. In truth, Ruby covered my duties for me. So you see, Billy, I am only paying the favor back in kind."

"A real Boy Scout," she groaned, diving for the bucket while Richard supported her yet again.

On the third day she recovered rapidly and completely. She thanked Richard, embarrassed, and then looked around herself, smelled the fresh salt air, and began to ask a million questions.

"What's that the pilot is doing?" Tess asked. "What's that thing?"

Patiently, Richard explained. "It's an astrolabe. The pilot sights the sun and fixes our latitude, so we know where we are."

"What about longitude? How can you know where you are unless you know both latitude and longitude?"

Richard laughed. "No one can fix longitude. We estimate. How far we've come at such and such speed."

"Oh, my God, you don't really know where you are," Tess said, horrified.

"Of course I do. I've been here before. It's in the log," Richard said, insulted. "Listen, boy, the man who invents a way to fix longitude will own the world."

"I bet," Tess said. "Too bad I can't remember who did it."

"Who did what?"

"Nothing, Captain."

On the evening before they were to reach Saint Christopher, where they'd anchor in a secret cove, Ruby had supper in the captain's cabin, while Tess waited on them both.

"So," Richard said, pulling a leg off a roast chicken, "we know what to do tomorrow, right?" He chewed on a piece of crispy skin. "The crew has been informed?"

"Aye, captain, they'll wait till midnight, no later." Ruby popped a piece of white meat into his mouth. "I'm still worried. It's too soon. Surely word is out everywhere. They'll have posted bills. A man would sell his soul for a dozen pieces of eight. He'd sell you for less."

"No one'll know it's me. Ah, Ruby, you're turning soft and I hate to see it."

"How many men in these waters have one eye, Captain? I tell you, let me go alone."

Richard laughed and tore off a hunk of crusty new bread, wiping it in gravy.

Tess's voice broke the silence. "I have an idea."

Both men turned in tandem at her remark. She stood there holding a platter of fruit, half-afraid to say what she was thinking.

"Well, Billy?" Richard asked, smiling indulgently.

"I'll go. No one knows me."

Richard laughed. Ruby frowned.

"Wait, Captain," the first mate said after a moment, "it's not a bad notion."

"Billy? Go into Basseterre? You jest, Ruby!"

"No one would suspect me," Tess said.

"You silly twit."

"Why not?" Tess asked.

"It's too dangerous."

"It's more dangerous for you," she said stubbornly.

"I thank you for your concern," Richard said with heavy irony.

"You have to be alive to keep your end of the bargain," Tess replied without hesitation.

"Ah, I stand corrected."

"Right," she said, "so let me go."

"Never, and that's the end of it."

"You *want* to go, don't you?" Tess asked. "You'd love to get killed. You wouldn't miss it for the world. You're a thrill junky!"

"A *what?*"

"Oh, never mind," Tess said angrily. "You're just looking for trouble."

Ruby said, "Aye, there's some truth to what he says. There's no need for you to go."

"I have to claim my mail. Have you both forgotten? The landlord won't give it to just anyone. Percy Farthingale has to claim it! Now, will the two of you stop this?"

Ruby frowned again. "Something has come to me. Something to give us an edge."

"I'm going, Ruby, and that's the end of that," Richard said.

"Yes, and I will go, too, as your manservant. And—" Ruby paused and eyed Tess, who was clearing the table of greasy dishes "—he goes, too."

"What? As my son?" Richard asked facetiously.

"No," Ruby said. "As your sister."

Tess paled. As his *sister!* Did Ruby somehow recognize her for a woman? She searched both their faces, but saw nothing suspicious, only a dawning enthusiasm on Richard's.

"They'll never suspect a lass. Perfect! Who would even connect Black Richard to Percy the Fop and his pretty sister. Ah, Ruby, you're a paragon among men," Richard said.

He even opened a sea chest in which he'd stored booty from a Spanish ship he'd captured, a chest he hadn't touched in over a year. He pulled out gold chains and glass jars, beads, a rosary, silver plates, throwing them helter-skelter on the cabin floor.

"Aha!" he finally said, "I knew there was a gown in here. Look, a fine silk gown and a mantilla, too. And slippers. What say you, Billy? Do you fancy the color?" He held up a mauve silk gown with a low-cut bodice that fastened down the front with ribboned lacing, a gathered skirt and an overskirt, long, full sleeves and lace draped around her neck.

Tess looked, trying to make her face unreadable. "Very nice," she said. "Whose was it?" She wanted to draw attention away from herself.

Richard shrugged. "Some Spanish *señorita*. How should I remember?"

"Did you rape and kill her?" Tess challenged, and arched that slim brow.

Richard frowned, dropping the gown. "That warrants no answer. Don't press me, Billy."

"Sorry." Tess walked over and fingered the silk. "How do you know it'll fit me?"

"Try it on."

"Uh, later." Tess held the dress up, shook it out, laid it over the back of a chair and turned away. "I've got to finish cleaning up," was all she said, terrified that they'd see something . . . something female about her.

What would happen when she put on that dress? Tess gazed wistfully at the gown that spilled and frothed over the chair. It was beautiful, absolutely gorgeous. But maybe it wouldn't fit. People were smaller in 1622, women tiny, their waists so small she probably wouldn't be able to squeeze into it, so she wouldn't have to worry. Great idea she'd had—to go to Basseterre! But she hadn't figured on Ruby's clever idea. And it *was* a good idea; it was just that it endangered her role as Billy.

Maybe she could somehow get out of this trip. Maybe she could pretend to be sick again. Maybe she could swagger and talk in a low voice so that the dress wouldn't matter. *Oh sure,* she thought, going about her chores, trying to be as quiet and unobtrusive as a real cabin boy.

"So, Billy," Richard said as he stripped and got into his bunk later that night. "You're not afraid of this excursion on the morrow, are you?"

"Uh, no, Captain."

"Good lad. It'll be uneventful, I wager." Then Richard fixed Tess with his sapphire blue eye and asked, "You have no mind to balk at wearing the gown, do you now?"

Tess swallowed and blew out the oil lamp. "No, not a bit, Captain," she said.

"Aye, that's all right then, Billy. After all, we do have a bargain, don't we, lad?" Richard said pointedly in the darkness.

RICHARD OUGHT NOT to have worried. Billy said nothing in the morning, obediently bringing Richard his bowl of oatcakes, a green banana, and a cup of watered-down grog. Richard ate swiftly then swung himself up the stairs to the quarterdeck where he oversaw the anchoring of the *Marauder* in a hidden cove of Saint Christopher some miles from Basseterre. The sails were furled and fastened, the pilot, good Joseph, was given orders to wait until the midnight tide, no longer, and under no circumstances was anyone to leave the ship. Then he went down to his cabin again where he found Billy washing up over a bucket of water. The boy's narrow back was to him, and Billy jumped as if struck when Richard thrust the door open.

"Hurry," Richard said. "Get that damned gown on. We're off shortly."

Billy was hurriedly dragging on his loose white shirt. Richard opened his own chest and pulled out his Percy garments: a long-waisted, close-fitted gray doublet with dozens of buttons down the front and a pointed belly-piece and high collar. Breeches of fawn color, embroidered hose and low shoes of Spanish leather. Hateful clothing—hot, constricting, uncomfortable. And a hat with a high crown, cocked brim and a feather.

"Uh, Captain," Billy said.

"Aye, what is it?" Richard asked, struggling into the hose.

"If I have to put on that thing, you'll have to leave the cabin."

"I'm leaving in a moment, anyway," Richard said, shrugging into the doublet. "It's too hot in here with these hellish things on." His fingers fumbled with the buttons. "Billy, come here and help me with these devilish buttons."

Billy stood in front of him, his small, deft fingers doing up the buttons easily. All Richard could see was the top of his dark head, the fingers working on the stiff fabric of the doublet. A small, ticklish heat curled in his belly.

"Gads, what takes you so long?" he said, unaccountably irritable, yanking away from the boy. "I'll be topside. Get that gown on, Billy, and be quick about it." He snatched up his cutlass and his walking stick, then shoving his pistol into the waist of his breeches, he ducked out of the cabin, slamming the door a little too hard behind him.

An entire half hour by the glass went by before Billy appeared. While waiting for him, Richard paced impatiently, dressed in his foppish finery, his cocked brim pulled low over his eye patch. Ruby joined him, dressed more soberly in black, but just as hot and uncomfortable. At one point Richard stuck his head down the companionway and shouted to Billy to hurry.

"I'm trying!" Billy yelled back.

At last the boy climbed the steps to the quarter-deck. Richard was pacing, angry, keyed-up, hating the wait. He was seeing to the lowering of the longboat they'd row to shore when behind him Ruby sputtered a muffled exclamation.

Richard straightened from the rail, turned. All he saw was Ruby's broad, black-clothed back.

"What is it?" Richard asked.

Ruby turned, stepped aside, and Richard saw her... him rather. Billy. A slim young lass, a fetching vision in lavender silk and lace, a dark-eyed beauty with a black mantilla over cropped hair. Richard gaped.

"By God and all the saints," Ruby was saying.

Richard had nothing to say, nothing at all. A kind of shock filled him, turned him hot and cold and hot again. There came a strange tumbling in his gut.

"Will I pass?" Billy was asking, and even his voice seemed feminine—husky, familiar—but a woman's voice.

With great difficulty, Richard cleared his throat. "Aye, you'll pass," he said brusquely. He frowned, puzzled and revolted by his own reaction. *Get ahold of yourself, man,* he thought. *It's only your troublesome cabin boy.*

But Billy, cheeky lad, gave him a bright, winsome smile and twirled around, making the silk skirt rustle and sway out. Ruby muttered something that Richard didn't hear.

The ladder down to the longboat posed a problem. Billy struggled with the billowing skirts of the unfamiliar gown while trying to climb down. Ruby was below him, waiting in the boat in case he fell, Richard above, handing him down. It seemed to take forever.

Finally, Richard swung himself down past Billy into the longboat and gave a yank on one of Billy's legs, causing the boy to cry out, lose his grip on the ladder and almost fall. And Richard had to steady him then, his hands around the narrow, silken waist, so that Billy would not fall in the water and ruin their plan. He let go as soon as he could, so quickly that Billy sat down hard on one of the longboat thwarts.

"Easy," Ruby admonished, "the lad is doing his best."

It must have been the danger they were going into, Richard thought, that made him so edgy. It must have been the worry about his mother or some sort of instinct for trouble that heightened his awareness. He was about to jump out of his skin with impatience by the time Billy was settled in a froth of mauve in the bottom of the boat, breathlessly saying he was sorry.

It must have been the uncomfortable clothes that made Richard so jumpy—or maybe it was the heat and the tedious work of pulling on the oars to shore. Or maybe it was that damned Billy, taking his role entirely too seriously, mincing and smiling shyly, all softness and prettiness and rustling silk exuding the aroma of lavender.

CHAPTER SIX

"GAD," RICHARD GRUMBLED, "can't you keep pace, boy?"

"I'm trying," Billy said, struggling along behind them, a sheen of sweat on his hairless upper lip.

"Well, lift those skirts then." Richard stopped along the rutted road and waited for his cabin boy. He was scowling, staring at Billy's trim ankles and those absurdly delicate feet in the leather slippers. Irritation pricked him. No boy should possess such remarkable prettiness. It was indecent, an affront to manhood. And what had previously seemed an ingenious idea was turning Richard's mood sour.

"It's not his fault," Ruby said at his captain's side. "I'll wager Billy would rather have been born a strapping man."

Richard only gave a disgusted grunt.

They reached the outskirts of Basseterre in no great hurry due to Billy's slowness. Still, Richard was forced to admit, the cover of a female walking along with them did tend to draw attention away from himself and Ruby. In fact, the cabin boy seemed to be a smashing hit. As they passed a small sugarcane plantation on the hilly edge of town, two of the field hands stopped their harvesting to gawk at the trim-waisted female with the swishing skirts and delicate lace mantilla. Richard imagined they'd even gotten a whiff of Billy's lavender sachet.

Basseterre had grown considerably over the last year. So much so that Richard and Ruby were taken aback. Whereas before only the harbor along Old Road had been sprinkled with houses and inns and taverns and government buildings, now several more roads had been carved out of the jungle, and farmhouses had sprung up along them like mushrooms.

It was decidedly an English settlement, most of the structures being built of brick and native stone. Flowers bloomed in window boxes and gardens abounded. Civilization had arrived, Richard could see, and he wondered just how long it would be before one of the colony-bent nations would cast an eye on Red Turtle Cay, deeming it time to clean up the island and rid the West Indies of pirates. A sadness settled over him as he walked on, occasionally tipping his plumed hat to a passerby.

If Billy had been able to fool the field hands, the boy was nothing short of a complete success with the townsfolk. Women bristled, noting Billy's fine dress and downcast, long-lashed dark eyes. And men invariably tipped their hats to her—*him*, Richard reminded himself with a spurt of unreasonable anger. And then, taking the game to its limit, Billy even tucked his arm in Richard's and shot him a smile that made Richard's heart explode in his breast. So angry was he that he squeezed the boy's forearm until the smile turned to a grimace of pain. Still, as they walked and bid good-day to folk, Richard could not help but notice every detail of his erstwhile cabin boy, right down to the feminine sway of the skirts and the slim, smooth feel of his mauve-clad arm. Gad, he could almost believe . . .

Enough! he commanded himself, working to keep his brain on the task at hand. There was danger here, he kept telling himself, lurking around every corner. Despite his efforts at disguise, his face was known far and wide, and Lord only knew how many gold crowns were now offered for word of his whereabouts. Soldiers and sailors leaned against the walls of the taverns and inns, strode the quay not far away, and Richard's hat, though cocked rakishly, did not entirely cover the patch over his eye. He moved more quickly, his senses sharpened with a growing feeling of impending trouble.

"It's a nice town," Billy said coyly, returning a nod from a gentleman in a passing carriage. "A whole lot nicer than Red Turtle." The boy dipped his lace-covered head fetchingly at yet another admirer.

Richard plastered a congenial smile on his lips and leaned close. "No one bade you speak, boy. Just play your game, but for Lord's sake, keep quiet."

"Am I bothering you?"

He didn't grace the cabin boy with a reply, merely tightened the hold on his arm until his own fingers were white. The whole game was becoming wearisome, and it infuriated Richard that, like so many of the townsmen, he couldn't help the effect Billy's overpowering femininity was having on him.

It *was* vile, immoral, and it was all the boy's fault for taking his role too seriously. By God, Richard seethed inwardly, he was not like many a sailor who, having been too long at sea, could barely distinguish between a pretty lad and a female. Never! The very notion of such unholiness made his blood boil. Not him, he thought again, half dragging Billy along now.

Striding on the other side of Billy, Ruby whispered, "I don't like it, Captain. I've got a bad feeling."

Even Billy seemed tense as they moved toward the heart of the town. There were too many soldiers, sailors, customs officials milling about. Too damned many. And what if someone spotted Billy for the fellow he was?

Richard gave him a quick, sidelong glance. But no, he could see Billy was not the problem, playing his role to the hilt, his fresh, heady scent trailing behind them. The eyes of the sailors and militia turned to the boy, not to Richard or Ruby.

They made the Palm Tree Inn without incident, and all three breathed sighs of relief. Fortunately the proprietor was there, greeting Richard as he would any acquaintance, playing his role well, too.

"Ah, there is a letter come for you, Master Farthingale, sir," he said to Richard. "I'll just go into my office and fetch it. May I offer you refreshment? The heat is terrible this day."

"Nothing, thank you," Richard said, eyeing him. The man had usually been less effusive, sullen and worried that Richard would be spotted and his own head would roll. But today was different. He seemed confident. Probably he was going to double his price for this service.

"The lady, perhaps?"

"The lady is not thirsty," Richard said stiffly.

"Ah, then, I'll just be a moment." He ducked away to fetch the letter.

"I don't like it," Ruby said, standing near the door, keeping a close eye on the street.

"Don't worry," Richard said. "We'll be gone soon. I am just glad there is a letter."

The man returned and handed Richard a weighty packet. It was indeed from Henry Palliser, the London barrister, and there would most definitely be word of Elizabeth Neville, if not a letter from her included. Richard took the packet and handed the landlord his usual gold piece. He paused a moment then, waiting for the man to demand more. But the landlord never uttered a word, merely bit the coin to test its genuineness, smiled and tucked it in his purse. And that was when Richard knew in his heart the man was going to betray them. It was in his eyes, in the too-ready smile.

"Let's go," Ruby was saying as he stared out the door cautiously.

And even Billy was anxious. "Come on, we better get going. Come on, Richard." The cabin boy tugged on his arm.

Richard shot the proprietor a last hard look, thinking he should probably kill him then and there, but finally he turned, relenting and, tucking the packet safely inside his doublet, he followed Ruby and Billy out.

If Richard had been on edge during the trip into town he was doubly so now. Each block that they walked had grown longer. Every glance in their direction was sinister. The three of them moved more quickly, barely even stopping when Billy stumbled. "Come," Richard said gruffly, pulling on Billy's arm, glancing to each side of them, casting a look behind.

They could see the outskirts of Basseterre now, the last two-story brick home with its peaceful flower boxes. A dog raced up to them, barking fitfully, drawing attention, but Ruby gave it a boot and it slunk off.

"We'll be in the clear soon," Billy said.

"Don't tell me you're nervous, boy." Richard marched on steadily.

"It's not me," he replied. "It's you. Something happened back at the inn. Your friend—"

"He's no friend. He's paid well for his small service."

"But you got all uptight."

Richard waved off her incomprehensible words. "We'll be safely on the *Marauder* in an hour. Stop sniveling."

And then Billy mumbled, "I don't care what you say, macho-man, you *are* uptight."

Richard was about to reply, maybe even give the quick-tongued boy a good shaking, when the men came out of nowhere.

There were four of them, the king's own soldiers from the government house, and they meant business.

"Halt!" one of them shouted. "Halt or you'll be stopped forcibly!"

It took Richard only a moment to decide on a plan, but in that moment he played the entire upcoming scene out in his mind. Oddly, surprising him, his very first concern was for Billy, so defenseless, so vulnerable.

Slowly, deliberately, he pushed the cabin boy behind him. His eye never left the biggest of the soldiers whose hand gripped the pommel of his sword, ready to draw it.

"It's not the woman we want, Richard Neville," another one of them said, "it's you, you murdering blackguard."

A slow, dangerous smile curved Richard's lips. At his side, Ruby drew his sword and moved back a pace, ready. "If you want me," Richard said, elegantly tossing aside his hat, "then here I stand. I await your pleasure, gentlemen." He felt for Billy at his back, snagged the cabin boy's arm and, with a sudden move, cast him away where he safely, unceremoniously, landed on his silk-clad behind in a bush.

"Oh!" was all Richard heard from the boy and then all four soldiers were upon them.

Richard thrust his walking stick at the man on his left, buying a few seconds, then his cutlass came singing from his scabbard, sticking the other advancing soldier in the gut so quickly the man never saw it. Ruby engaged the larger of the men, feinting, parrying, swinging his sword as if it weighed nothing in his experienced hand. But Richard barely noticed his friend's battle; he was too busy with his own, the remaining two soldiers trying to corner him against a stone wall, forcing him to leap aside before he was trapped.

Sweat broke from every pore in Richard's body as the clang of swords echoed on the street. The soldiers were good; they'd fought real battles before. Still, Richard never doubted his ability to best them, though it flashed through his mind that he might shed some of his own blood in the process.

At some point, as he ducked and parried and came up slashing with his sword, he heard Billy cry out, "No! Richard, watch out!" But the frightened words were meaningless.

He advanced, keeping the two soldiers at bay. He retreated when they came at him both at once.

"Stick him!" one of them cried. "Now!"

The deadly slash of a rapier came inches from his head, and Richard threw himself to the dusty ground, rolled once, then sprang to his feet in a single fluid motion, his sword swinging, glinting in the fierce sun. He caught one of the men in the thigh, opening up a wide gash that poured blood immediately. The man dropped. But as he did so the other lunged forward, and before Richard could counter he took the point of the soldier's blade in his own thigh and staggered momentarily.

"Oh, God!" Billy's high-pitched voice reached him.

And then Ruby, whose attacker was on his way down, warned, "Captain! Watch your side!"

The soldier was coming at him again; one stick to Richard's thigh was not enough. But Richard's blood was hot—if they took him, if he died, he'd never read the letter....

He came out of a defensive crouch with the speed of a jungle cat, his sword lifting up from the ground where it was pointed, catching the shocked man in the ribs, felling him. The next moments were a haze. Ruby was yelling at him to run. Billy was on his feet, clutching his skirts, hurrying toward Richard. Two of the four fallen soldiers were crying out in mortal pain, and all Richard knew was that they had to get out of there fast.

"The swamp!" he shouted, grabbing Billy and pushing him down the road. "Head for the mangroves!"

They ran. The three of them ran along the hilly road as if the devil himself were in pursuit. Richard kept hold of Billy, dragging him when he stumbled, flinging panting insults at his awkwardness.

Ruby led the way, well aware that the protection of the swamp was still some distance ahead. Sweat poured from all three, soaking their hot, heavy clothing, but they had to keep going—a troop of soldiers would be hot on their heels by now. The packet from England still stuck safely in Richard's doublet, he gritted his teeth against the flaming pain in his leg and cursed the proprietor of the inn. It could have been no other man, Richard knew, who had given them away to the soldiers. Damn his bloody soul to hell!

The mangrove swamp lay ahead now, running from the rocky beach up into a ravine that made its way to the base of the verdant volcano. It would be bad in that cover, Richard knew, wet and fraught with a variety of stinging insects. And hot. Hot as Hades in there. But what choice did they have? To lead the soldiers to the *Marauder* would be disastrous. Later, when the soldiers gave up their search, they would go the last mile to the cove. He could only hope they reached the ship in time or he and Ruby and Billy would be abandoned. Richard prayed the hunt would keep to land; if the English sent ships to search the coast, it would be a battle like no other before. His beautiful black ship might well find Davy's locker.

His leg was paining him. The hurt was brutal, running in knifelike thrusts up to his abdomen. Spots danced before Richard's eye and he fought to put one foot before the other.

"Oh, God," Billy kept saying at his side, and in truth, it was more the cabin boy hauling the captain along now. Hating his weakness, Richard put his weight on Billy's shoulder as Ruby began to cut a path into the fetid swamp.

"Malaria," Billy breathed, his knees threatening to collapse under Richard's weight. "We don't have to worry about the soldiers. The mosquitos will get us, anyway."

"We must not drink the water then," Ruby said in front of them. "The fever is in this stuff."

But Billy stopped short where his skirts dragged in the dark water. "Trust me on this one, boys," he said. "It's the mosquitos. Maybe if we rub mud on us..."

They were barely a quarter of a mile into the mangroves when Billy did make them stop and rub the stinking mud onto their exposed flesh. Richard was furious; the soldiers were going to catch them. But Billy was so angry and insistent, refusing to go another foot, that Richard went along with the boy's whim. When they were done, their hands and faces blackened and caked, they moved on, deeper into the twisted thickness. And despite the pounding ache in his leg, Richard had to admit to himself that the sting of insect bites was at least lessened. He leaned on Billy and gave him a speculative look.

They stopped, finally, on a dry spit of land in the midst of the mangroves. On all sides of them the trees thrust their gnarled roots into the black waters, feeding in the muck. Ruby cleared a spot for them to rest, and Richard and Billy sank onto the ground, panting, sweating, exhausted.

"Oh, God," Billy said for the hundredth time. "Your leg, Richard. We better take a—"

"Leave it be," he got out between clenched teeth, rudely shoving the delicate hand away.

"Okay. So die. See if I give a hoot."

Still panting, Richard planted a hard look on the boy's mud-caked face. "I said leave me be. I'll see to the wound when we're on board, safely asea."

Ruby finally sank down himself, rubbing absently at the mud on his forearms. "High tide's at midnight, Captain. We best wait till dark before moving."

"Aye," Richard said, warding off the pain as well as he could. "The soldiers won't crawl around in this stinking swamp after the sun sets. On that I'll stake my life."

They quieted down at last, the three of them resting, calming their rapidly beating hearts. At times Richard felt himself slipping, dragged down by the fierce ache in his body, his brain fighting to stay awake and alert. Still, his leg wound oozed blood slowly, and he pressed a hand to the hole, grimacing in pain as he did so.

The swamp resounded with noises of all kinds—a cacophony of insects buzzing and birds calling, peli-

cans flapping huge wings—strange sounds to Richard's ear as he listened for a footfall, the breaking of
a branch, any human noises. Thankfully there weren't
any, only the constant buzzing and whining and click-
ing of tiny creatures and the soft breathing of Billy
who rested next to him.

Richard looked over at the boy. Their gazes met and
held for an uncomfortable moment before Billy
glanced away. Still, Richard stared at the small, mud-
streaked face. Late light touched the tiny facial hairs,
barely a fuzz on his cheeks. And again, Richard
thought how womanly the skin on this fellow looked.
He'd never grow a beard. And then there was the long
column of neck where no sinews or muscle showed,
only pure, soft flesh.

His head ached and he felt a dizziness that held him
in its insidious grip, making his thoughts wander and
settle on the absurd, considering their predicament.

"It's quiet," Ruby said after a time. "Too quiet."

"It is," Richard agreed, his gaze still on Billy, and
he forgot Ruby and the soldiers, his mind searching
while he studied the cabin boy, searching as if there
was something he'd forgotten, something missing in
his knowledge. It bothered Richard endlessly. He realized that ever since he'd taken Billy Bonney from the
Spanish he'd felt the same way, as if a piece of a puzzle was lost. He must have finally drifted off, Richard
realized later, because when he awoke, Billy's fingers
were on his leg, barely perceptible, too careful. "What
are you up to?" he growled, his lips dry.

Billy withdrew his touch. "I wish you'd let me look
at it."

"No."

"It should be cleaned out, at least."

"No. There's nothing to clean it with at any rate."

"I guess you're right."

"Of course I am."

"Does it . . . does it hurt much?"

"No."

"Liar," Billy said.

They were all suffering from the oppressive heat of the swamp. Their sweat ran so freely that Billy kept scooping up handfuls of mud and insisting on rubbing more on himself, Richard and Ruby, no matter how much they protested. "You haven't been bitten, have you?" Billy said as he dipped his fingers into the black ooze in his other hand and spread it on Richard's cheeks and neck.

He hated the boy's touch; it sickened him. It crossed his weary brain that he might indeed sail this accursed boy to his Key West and dump him on the *cayo* just to be rid of him. A hellish bargain he'd made that night in the tavern on Red Turtle. He must have been drunk as the devil.

And yet . . . Richard groaned and stretched out his leg, bearing the stab of pain that shot through him. Yet he had to be honest with himself—Billy had made life quite stimulating on board the ship. He was always coming up with the strangest notions. And his language. He used words that had never passed Richard's ears before. He was a lively thing, this cabin boy, who Richard swore was keeping something secret from all of them. How in heaven's name the Spanish had gotten him continued to perplex Richard. The boy might as well have sprung up from some unknown place in this world. Curious, indeed.

The sun set on the English island of Saint Christopher, and the sky took on a lavender hue—a hue nearly the color of Billy's ruined gown. Richard knew it was time to go. Whether or not he had the strength to make the ship was quite another matter altogether.

"We best move along," Ruby said, and Richard did allow his trusted first mate to help him to his feet, though he shied away from Billy's attention at his other side.

The trek out of the swamp was hell. Thirst and lack of food and the weakness of Richard's spirits were taking their toll. He had to lean on Ruby now for support, one leg keeping him upright, the other numb, useless. "One eye," Richard said through his teeth, "and now, perhaps, one leg."

"You'll be fine, Captain," Ruby told him.

But Richard was beginning to wonder. A wound like that could fester so easily. He himself had seen men die, screaming in agony, from a lesser cut. And how many more clumped around on one leg?

The going was rough and slow and they were all soaked again in swamp water before they reached dry land and the road. But darkness had fallen, and there was only a sliver of a moon, and if there were soldiers about they were not in sight. Richard was well aware of the burden he presented as they made their way to the cove and the waiting longboat. He wasn't sure of the time, but it must be close to midnight. He prayed the *Marauder* was still there, waiting. If they were too late, they'd be abandoned, marooned, left to their fate. And he'd made Joseph the pilot swear to leave with the tide, no matter what. He cursed his own orders, even while knowing they were correct.

Be there, he thought, as he dragged his useless leg through the heat and the dark. *Be there.*

Thank the good Lord, she was still there, lying silently on the smooth water, a black shadow on the black sea, touched by moonlight. Richard heaved a sigh of relief, felt a smile curl the side of his mouth. "Good old Joseph," he growled.

And the longboat was there, too, right where they'd left it that morning. Richard lay supine in the boat, powerless, while Ruby pushed them offshore and Billy manned the rudder.

It was hell, too, getting on board. The crew had to pull him up on ropes. He cursed, his weakness a humiliation in front of his men. And then two of his loyal sailors helped him to his cabin, laid him on his bed and took orders to set sail on the tide. "Watch for the English," Richard told them. "I'll wager they're about on the sea."

"Aye, aye, Captain," they chorused and then left him there, and finally, after these many months, Richard was able to pull the packet from his breast pocket and hold it. He thought warmly of his mother, savoring the moment he'd open the letters.

For now, however, Richard put the packet aside and looked down at the ruined, fawn-colored breeches. For now he'd best attend this accursed hole in his leg. He positioned himself on the bed, gritting his teeth, and removed the embroidered hose. He thought to remove the breeches entirely, but the notion of so much movement and pain put him off, so he tore open the material on his thigh instead, and viewed the puncture.

It hurt. His breeches were stuck to the wound, and he reached for the jug of whiskey, thinking there was no better time than the present to pour a bit on the hole in his leg. But first, Richard decided as he felt his ship shudder and spring to life, first some whiskey in his belly.

The jug was at his lips when Billy, face and hands washed, came into the cabin. "What are you *doing?*" the cabin boy demanded, and he marched straightaway to Richard and took hold of the jug.

"Give me that," Richard said, affronted.

"No. If you want to pour it in that wound of yours, then fine, go ahead and—" Billy's gaze fixed on the bloody hole in Richard's leg. "Oh, my God," he whispered, his free hand going to his mouth.

Richard snatched the jug back and took a long, hot swig, the liquor burning down his throat all the way to his belly. He kept his eye fixed on Billy, though, in case he tried to retake the jug. "Ah," he said, wiping his mouth with his soiled cuff, letting his head loll back while the liquor soothed him.

"Your leg," Billy was whispering. "I had no idea it was so deep."

Richard looked back at him. "I see the sight of blood disturbs you, boy."

"No, it's just that—"

"Bah!" Richard sneered. "You are ready to vomit. Gad, is there no man in you at all?" he taunted and then put the jug to his lips again.

CHAPTER SEVEN

TESS JUST LOOKED AT HIM. Why on earth was he so mad at her? Nothing she said was right; nothing she did was right. She was exhausted, hot, filthy, worried sick about Richard's leg—and he snapped at her every time she turned around.

She sat down on her straw pallet, her back against the ship's bulkhead, her ripped and strained mauve dress in ruins around her, the darling leather slippers and lace mantilla gone, mud plastered on her skin, dry now and flaking off, and she sulked.

There was Richard, as dirty as she was, his fancy gray doublet ripped open, his leg slick with blood, his face pale and glistening with sweat under the mud, sitting up in bed now with his jug of whiskey. She could help him, but she knew he wouldn't let her. He was being as mean as a snake, nasty to a fault. And why?

Oh, she'd like to ask him but it'd only make him angrier. She couldn't do anything, just sit there in the dim, flickering light of the hanging oil lantern over Richard's table. It was still dark out, but the *Marauder* was under way, moving swiftly and silently away from Saint Christopher.

Heck, she'd gone along with his crazy scheme in Basseterre. She'd put on the dress, which was hot and tight and uncomfortable, and done what he wanted. It hadn't been *her* idea to go as a woman, after all. It had almost worked, too, and it hadn't been *her* fault that that man had sold Richard out. Well, they were safe now, but he was still in a foul mood.

"Are you hungry?" he asked grudgingly, putting the jug down.

"Starved," she said.

"Well, there's some hardtack and salt beef." He gestured. "There'll be nothing more till the morrow." Then he took another swig of the whiskey.

Tess stood up and got herself some food. It was awful stuff, but she was so hungry it didn't matter. She went back to her pallet and chewed, watching Richard in the wavering light. She'd just seen a sword fight, men killed. She'd run for her life, hidden in a swamp, been dragged and pushed, been bitten by all kinds of insects. She probably had malaria or yellow fever. And all she'd been doing was trying to help him. He could at least have said thank-you.

Tess chewed and sulked, hugged her knees and wished desperately she could go home. She wondered, with a sinking heart, if Richard would truly live up to his side of the bargain and take her back to Key West. And if he did, if he took her there and she found the spot where she'd been diving, even if she found the whirlpool... Would it whisk her back to her own time? Was there a permanent time warp in that place, a doorway between past and present, or had her experience been a fluke? Maybe she would never get back home. Maybe the doorway was shut, never to open again. Maybe the whirlpool had moved or was gone completely.

Oh, God, then she was stuck here forever, Richard Neville's cabin boy.

No, she'd never accept that. She'd come to this time because of the *Isabela* and its treasure, because of that necklace she'd found. There was some connection, she was sure of it. If she returned to that spot, the whirlpool would be there; it had to be. Otherwise, it was too coincidental—her popping into the very world the *Isabela* was from. And a history major soon learned that there were rarely coincidences; there was always cause and effect.

She had to have faith that she'd get back. She had to!

Richard was swearing again, pouring more whiskey on the hole in his leg. He winced and turned paler, and despite his nastiness, Tess took pity on him. "Can I do anything?" she asked.

"Not a bloody thing," Richard snarled.

She pressed her lips together and bit back a comment. Looking down she took a bite of hardtack and chewed patiently, crossing her legs Indian-fashion under the long skirts. *History,* she thought. *Maybe it's better to read about it.*

She looked up then and caught Richard staring at her. Abruptly he gave an ill-tempered curse and an angry sapphire flash from his single blue eye and jerked his gaze away. *So angry,* she thought. It was as if she'd done something awful, affronted him personally. What had made him so mad at her?

Tess shifted her position, upset, confused, wondering how she was going to stay here with Richard, how she was going to manage in this brutal time. The dry but ruined dress rustled around her, and she pushed the silk impatiently out of her way, noting that Richard moved restlessly and swore again, and then the reason came to her with a sense of dawning wonder.

The gown. It was the gown. Billy the cabin boy was wearing a lady's gown, looking totally female. Richard thought she was a boy, but she looked like a girl now and... Tess felt the blood leave her face. Black Richard the pirate was finding his cabin boy a little too attractive.

Quickly Tess ducked her head and tried to figure out how to deal with this new knowledge. She suddenly felt hot all over, her skin too sensitive, as if Richard were seeing through the layers and layers of mauve silk to her body underneath. She crouched there on her pallet, afraid to move or look up or breathe, and her mind worked feverishly. "Richard," she started to say, but he only grunted an acknowledgment, and she paused, her mind recoiling from confessing everything to him. "Nothing," she said under her breath, chewing busily, her head down.

She could tell him the truth right now, admit her subterfuge, but then... God knew what kind of danger she'd be in, a woman alone and unprotected on a pirate ship. Of course Richard wouldn't allow any harm to come to her—at least she didn't *think* he would. But he'd put her ashore. And then what would she do, where would she go? Panic fluttered in her breast but she fought it down. First things first, she thought. She had to get out of that damn dress!

Richard mumbled something and bent over, trying to tie a strip of cloth around his thigh. He threw a sideways glance at her. "Can't you take that accursed gown off, Billy?" he muttered. "You look like a dockside trollop."

"Uh, yes, sure. I'll get it right off," Tess said. Oh, how Richard resented his cabin boy in lady's finery! A fleeting moment of regret touched Tess as she began working on the buttons, her back turned to Richard. She'd like to tell him the truth. She'd like to be a woman again.

The lantern swung, casting strange, leaping shadows on the cabin walls as the *Marauder* took a new tack. Tess dared a peek at Richard, her heart thudding, but he was intent on the wound on his leg. She saw him wince with pain as he pulled the strip of cloth tight. She saw the cords in his strong neck bulge. He grimaced, and sweat popped out on his forehead. His eye patch faced her, and Tess wondered again what terrible accident had caused him to lose an eye. She had been bothered at first by Richard's patch, but now it seemed so much a part of him, part of his dashing, fairy-tale looks. But still, she was curious. Maybe someday she'd ask him about it.

He was terribly good-looking, all right, with a mouth that was either curling in mockery or laughing ironically and lips sculpted sensually. His nose had an imperious curve to it while his eyes—eye—was a deep cobalt blue under straight dark brows. His jaw was strong, square, covered now with a day's growth of beard. His hair was long and thick and dark blond, pulled back and tied with a strip of cloth. And in his left ear was the gold hoop he always wore.

A pirate. Tess put her hand over her eyes and took a deep breath. The insanity of her predicament washed over her, and she felt a bubble of hysterical laughter in her chest. It went quickly, replaced by the sting of tears in her eyes. *Too much emotion,* Tess told herself, *too much danger and fear.* She did not belong here in this time; she couldn't bear it.

Tess worked at undoing all the fastenings of the gown—the buttons, the ties, the underskirt, the lace around her neck—her fingers fumbling. She pulled it over her head, struggling and sweating in the hot cabin, and somehow managed to put on her old loose shirt while under the muddy silk skirts. Then she tugged on her tattered trousers, knotting the rope around her waist as usual. She dropped the gown, pushed it to one side with her bare foot and, relieved, turned to Richard, Billy the cabin boy once more.

"Do you want some help with that bandage?" she asked, bolder now.

"Damned thing," he muttered, and she took that to mean yes.

He braced his foot on the floor, his fawn breeches ripped open, caked with blood. Tess pushed aside the strip of cloth Richard had been using and, fighting down the nausea that rose in her throat, studied his wound. It was clean now, angry-looking, probably deep. He needed a tetanus shot, stitches, maybe antibiotics. He wasn't going to get any of those, though.

She eyed the whiskey jug. "I think we should bathe the wound with alcohol," she said, "before it gets infected."

"Bah," he grunted. "Later."

"Well, let's put it this way. *I'll* do it. Right now."

"You will not."

But before he could utter another word, Tess picked up the jug and dumped whiskey directly onto the wound.

Richard yelped, the blood draining from his face. "Gad, you are fairly killing me, boy!" he shouted.

"Just the opposite, Captain," Tess replied. "I think we can bandage it now. All right?"

He gritted his teeth and glared at her, muttering, swearing.

He didn't make a sound, though, as she wrapped the cloth around his thigh, around the strong muscle and over the scattered golden hairs on his skin. She breathed slowly and deeply, her head bent, concentrating, trying not to hurt him. It was probably only moments that her fingers were on his flesh, but it seemed a lifetime. She felt his warmth and hardness, and a heaviness settled in the bottom of her heart. She licked suddenly dry lips and felt his gaze on her. Her fingers began to tremble then as she started to tear the ends of the cloth lengthwise in order to secure the bandage. Still, Richard never made a move or a sound, and with the air so still and close in the cabin, it was difficult to breathe. She could hear the beating of their hearts, too loud, too strong. Her fingers worked and her thoughts flitted nervously as she pulled on both ends of the bandage, tightening it.

Then, and only then, did Richard draw in a sharp breath.

Her gaze flew to his. "Sorry if I hurt you," she said gruffly.

"It's all right. I've had worse," he said, his blue eye on her face, and Tess's hands stilled where they were, resting on his bare thigh.

"I'm sorry, captain," she said, "but it has to be done."

"Go on, finish with it," Richard said harshly, reaching for his jug.

When she was done he leaned back breathing deeply, his skin ashen and slick with sweat, his eye closed. She stood in front of him, not sure what to do. What if the wound got infected? What if Richard got gangrene, what if he died? Her heart constricted in her chest, and she took an inadvertent step closer to him.

He opened his eye then and looked at her. "Well, what are you doing standing there like a fool?"

"Nothing, sorry," she said and retreated to her corner.

Richard straightened and reached for the packet of letters, the precious letters he'd risked his life for, his and Tess's. She watched him carefully, watched him unfasten the strings, the cloth covering, the wax seal. He turned one of the envelopes over in his hands twice, reading the address on it intently. Tess wanted to ask him if it was from his mother; she was dying to know.

He opened the envelope, pulled out several pages of stiffly folded paper covered with black script and began to read.

Tess chewed on the salt beef and studied Richard. Her breath caught in her throat when she saw his face drain of color and twist in pain. She wanted to go to him and put a hand on his shoulder in comfort, to ask him what news the letter contained, but she couldn't. She was Billy, a lowly cabin boy, and it would be out of character, presumptuous, fatally wrong.

So she sat there, suffering with Richard, feeling every nuance of emotion as he read on, his expression set now, hard but for the fleeting pain when he read something particularly hurtful.

Finally, an eternity later, he dropped the pages and stared straight ahead for a moment. Tess had never seen agony such as she now saw etched on Richard's features. In the face of it, she bowed her head and remained still and silent. His torment was more than anyone should see, too much to share. What god-awful news had that letter contained?

Then he broke and buried his face in his hands, his shoulders sagging.

Tess rose, unable to bear it any longer. Slowly, afraid but full of sympathy, she went to Richard and stood over his bowed head. "Richard?" she said softly, reaching out and touching his hair. "What is it?"

Muffled, his voice came to her. "She's dead," he said raggedly. "Thomas has killed my mother."

Shock grasped Tess in a cold grip, then pity overwhelmed her. She was going to offer a sympathetic word, but Richard straightened abruptly and she snatched her hand back. He reached for the jug and took a long swallow, his throat working, then he slammed the jug down, and Tess shrank back, afraid to speak.

"Thomas killed her," Richard repeated harshly.

"What happened?" she whispered, but he didn't hear. He drank instead, steadily, purposefully, then he thrust the empty jug at her and ordered her to fetch more.

His head was slumped down when she returned, but he roused himself, fixing her with a bleary eye, and took the jug from her. "To my mother, Billy," he said, holding the jug aloft. "To Elizabeth Neville, may God rest her soul." And he drank deeply once again.

Should she go get Ruby? Tess wondered. Did Richard need help?

He picked up the pages of the letter again, peering at them, but he obviously couldn't focus. "It's all in here," he said.

"What's in there?" Tess asked. "You can tell me."

"He turned her out, took everything from her, even the emerald necklace Edmund gave her. Everything. And I wasn't there." He drank again. "God-cursed Thomas."

"Are you sure, Richard? Maybe there's some mistake...."

"There's no damned mistake! Palliser found her. He found her, and she was dying, and it was too late." Anguish twisted Richard's features, and his head lolled. "She was alone on the streets all winter. And I wasn't there."

A long moment passed, and Richard seemed lost in it. Tess looked at the pages of the letter lying on the table. Cautiously, wondering if he would even notice, she picked one up and read the beautiful, flowing script of the London barrister, Henry Palliser.

Images assailed her, descriptions she'd read about, the horror and squalor on the streets of seventeenth-century London. Palliser, though obviously trying to ease Richard's pain, wrote in enough detail that Tess could understand Elizabeth Neville's plight.

Thomas Moore had turned the aging woman out of her home without a penny. "Causing your father's most detailed instructions to be ignored in totality, with a hard heart and despite her most earnest entreaties, Thomas sent your mother away," the letter read. Penniless, she'd looked for employment for months. And then winter had settled over London, a damp, bone-chilling winter that had sapped the homeless woman of whatever strength she'd had left.

Were there shelters for the homeless then? *Now,* Tess corrected herself. Maybe a soup kitchen...maybe not.

Elizabeth had huddled in alleys and in doorways, reduced to begging. She'd gotten sick. She would have...TB, bronchitis, pneumonia? It must have been horrible, the woman living in her clothes, dirty, hungry, freezing...

But she hadn't died alone, because Henry Palliser wrote that he'd found her after "many inquiries and a lengthy search of the most dismal neighborhoods." He'd found her, sick and half-dead, and he'd taken her to his own home to nurse. However, Elizabeth had been too far gone and after begging Palliser to help Richard in any way he could and entreating him to "send greetings and everlasting love to her good and dutiful son, Richard Neville," she'd died.

Tess put the pages carefully back on the table. Her heart heavy in her chest, she was unable to fathom what Richard must be feeling. "I'm so sorry," she whispered. "Richard, you must be..." But she could say no more.

He struggled to his feet then, holding the jug, hobbling around the table. He was very unsteady, and Tess stood by, ready to grab him if he fell. But he stopped and looked at her. He looked, he spoke, but Tess knew he really wasn't seeing her.

And then the inevitable explosion came. Abruptly he swept the table clean with an arm, scattering papers and mugs, and he roared, "It wasn't enough that he took my eye! He had to have everything! He had to kill her, too. That sodding bastard!" Richard roared.

"Your eye?" Tess breathed.

"Aye, he went for it straightaway. We fought—he was older, bigger. He did it." Richard reached up with his free hand and touched his eye patch. He rocked on his one good leg, and Tess sprang forward to support him, but he put a hand out to the wall and waved her off, raising the jug to his lips again. "Yes," he mumbled, "my eye and my mother."

"Richard, will you lie down?" Tess suggested. "I think you better..."

But he paid no attention. He was turned inward, suffering, drowning in his suffering, and she had no way to reach him, no way to help. She could only stand there and watch him, her heart in her throat.

Richard was a fearsome sight, with his one eye and the mud and blood all over him, weaving in the wavering light of the lantern, his long hair coming loose, his clothes torn to pieces. He turned his bloodshot stare on Tess and swore softly and mercilessly and absolutely soberly, "If it takes till my dying day, I vow to kill Thomas Moore for what he did."

Tess was thankful when he staggered to his bunk and fell asleep shortly after that. She sat and watched him for a time, her heart breaking. He looked young and defenseless as he lay there asleep. A handsome man and a brave one. He'd treated her fairly, even though he thought she was a nobody. He was a heroic figure, and his men loved him. They'd follow him to hell itself, she knew, and apparently they had often enough these past two years. Richard Neville, bastard, his entire family dead now. A man from a time almost four centuries removed from hers. She toyed with the thought, the fantasy, that Richard could escape this world that had no place for him, and come back to her time—when she found the whirlpool again. But Richard could never fit into the twentieth century; the notion was ridiculous. No more than she fitted into his time. No more than she *wanted* to fit in.

The ship rose and plunged, the lantern swinging, the bells for the night watch coming faintly to Tess's ears. She was getting drowsy, sitting there watching over him, and she wondered if she was beginning to feel responsible for her captain, the way a real cabin boy would.

Richard mumbled something in his sleep and shifted his position. How was it that her fate had become linked to this man's? Tess wondered, rising and laying a calming hand on his brow and looking down at him. He wasn't a great bargain, being a criminal, a man with no place in his own world, a man hunted and pursued, entirely alone except for Ruby, unjustly outlawed and with no apparent recourse to justice. There was nothing for Richard Neville but a dead end, which meant the same thing for Tess, too.

And yet . . . he was so vibrantly alive, so romantic, every woman's fantasy, right down to his vulnerability. Tess ran a hand down his face, trailing her fingers over his lips, down his jaw to his neck. She felt the pulse beat under his warm skin, then laid her palm flat on his bare chest, feeling his heart beat strongly, steadily. And then, somehow reassured, she went to her own pallet, curled up and fell instantly asleep.

IN THE MORNING Ruby knocked on the cabin door. He came in as Tess was stirring sleepily and took a long look at the empty jug on the table and the scattered pages of the letter.

"Billy, step lively there and get some gruel for the captain," Ruby said quietly, "and a mug of grog."

"That's all he needs," Tess said sleepily. Then she remembered; it all came flooding back. She sat up and was about to tell Ruby what was in the letter, but he was already shaking Richard awake.

"Ruby, his leg, will you see how it is?" she asked, worried anew.

"You've your orders, Billy," Ruby said.

"Aye, aye, Mr. Salvador." She sat up and straightened her shirt and scrubbed hands through her short hair—her morning toilette, a very easy one when you slept in the same clothes that you wore every day. At the cabin door she stopped and said softly, "Take it easy on the captain, Ruby. He's had very bad news."

Ruby looked at her, frowned, looked at the letters on the floor. She nodded.

When she returned, balancing the wooden bowl and the mug, having made her way up and down companionways, steadying herself against the ship's roll, Tess opened the cabin door quietly and went in.

Richard sat up in his bunk. Ruby was in a chair at the table, his head bowed. They were both silent, but the air in the cabin reverberated with a terrible finality. She looked from one to the other and back again. Richard's face was pale but calm, expressionless.

Ruby looked up then, and Tess could see how badly the news had hit him. "Shall we sail for England then, Captain?" he asked quietly.

Richard shook his head and gave a short, bitter laugh. "The irony of it is that Thomas is on his way to me. My brother, it seems, was bent on sailing on the very ship that carried this letter, so Henry Palliser writes, and he is stopping at every English port in the West Indies to search me out."

Ruby's head rose abruptly.

Richard nodded. "Aye, he's here in the Indies now, the devil."

"He's come to take the ship back, and he means no good to you, my friend," Ruby said.

"So it would seem."

The calmness in their words frightened Tess. If they'd yelled in rage, ranted, threatened, she would have felt better. But there had been a frightening acceptance in the conversation, a shared knowledge that left her out completely. It was as if they both knew what had to be done so clearly there was no need to discuss it.

Quietly Tess gave Richard his breakfast. He grimaced at the bowl of gruel but took a long swig of the weak grog.

Tess gathered her courage. "How's your leg this morning?" she asked.

He saw her then, as if for the first time, and held her with that hard blue eye. "Rather the worse for wear, but I'll live. My head is worse, if truth be told. Now clear out, Billy. Ruby and I have plans to make."

THEY SAILED INTO the harbor of Red Turtle Cay five days later, having encountered a brisk wind and calm seas, although there had been torrential downpours every afternoon.

Tess was worried about Richard. Against her will, telling herself he wasn't her responsibility, she nevertheless watched him anxiously. He was subdued. No longer the laughing, bold pirate he'd been, but a quiet, grim, scheming man—too quiet. She guessed he was planning something dangerous, an attempt to find Thomas, waylay him, kill him. She knew, too, he'd put his whole ship in danger if he had to, her included. Richard was awash in pain and hate, and nothing could deter him from his revenge.

There was good news and bad news in the situation. The good was that Richard paid little attention to Tess, his anger gone, his interest gone. He simply didn't care any longer about Billy the cabin boy. He barely even looked at Tess these days. The bad news was that if, *when,* Richard went chasing around the Caribbean to find his brother, she'd be that much farther from getting back to Key West.

And worse—if Richard were killed or captured by Thomas, which sure as heck could happen, what would become of her? Would the English hang her along with all the other pirates on the *Marauder?* Or the Spanish—would they sink the *Marauder* and turn Black Richard's buccaneers over to the Inquisition, which is what Tess had learned the Catholic Spanish did with all Protestant heretics.

She'd moved back into Richard's quarters over the inn, back to her musty pallet in the curtained alcove. Sleeping there at night, she heard Richard toss and turn, mumble in his sleep, cry out. At least, she thought, lying there in her grubby clothes, it was better than listening to him romping with that whore. No women now, no flirting, no wild parties or carousing in the Laughing Parrot. There were only long secret talks with Ruby, quiet days flexing his wounded leg and poring over maps. Sometimes strange men went in and out of Richard's room, whispering in his ear and taking a coin from him when they were through.

Oh, something was brewing, all right, and Tess was scared.

One day she found Ruby eating a noontime joint of beef below, and plumping herself down across from him, she came straight out and put it to him. "What's going on?"

He evaded her question.

Frustrated, Tess tried another tack. "Thomas Moore and Richard certainly hate each other," she said. "Did they always? I mean, he did have something to do with Richard's eye."

"Ah, he told you about that?"

"Yes," she lied. "But I'd like to know more. I mean, did Thomas really do it on purpose?"

Ruby cocked his grizzled head. "'Tis not a pretty tale."

"Would you tell me? Richard did, but I'm unclear about the details," she ventured.

And, finally, as if Ruby was drifting back over the years, the story unfolded.

IT WAS A BEAUTIFUL, warm summer's day in the heart of London. Flowers bloomed in the garden that ran from behind the Moores' Tudor-style town house down to the Thames River. There were sculpted hedges and a springy, grassy lawn. Richard was twelve, Thomas sixteen. The French fencing master had just left, the boys' weekly lesson over. Crickets chirped, birds sang. The boys continued to practice a particularly difficult new stroke, but now they had no adult eye to supervise, short of the kitchen maid who stepped outside only momentarily to inform them that their tea was ready.

Neither boy heard. They continued their sparring, rapiers flashing in the sun.

It was a boy's game—at first. They moved down toward the river, ducking into well-tended shrubbery and behind spreading trees on the narrow lawn. Thomas feinted here, Richard parried there. The minutes passed. Sweat broke out on both boys' brows and dampened their backs. They were intent on their usual rivalry—Thomas a knight of the realm, Richard the villain as usual.

No one ever knew exactly when the game turned serious... and ugly. Thomas would tell of Richard pushing him. Richard would tell of Thomas knocking him down, Richard being the smaller of the two. What *did* happen was that Thomas stood over his younger brother just as the maid gave them a second call to tea. Thomas was panting and crying, his ego bruised by the bastard son's prowess, and with utter malice in his heart, Thomas simply jabbed the point of his rapier into his brother Richard's eye.

Tess sat back on the bench and stared at Ruby. "That's... horrible."

"Aye," Ruby replied. "Thomas Moore is as evil as they come. And now he's killed the captain's mother."

After hearing this shocking tale, Tess was even more scared than ever. And not long after, one stifling, close morning without the whisper of a breeze, a morning so still the palm fronds hung dispiritedly, Tess rose early, damp with sweat already, restless. Richard still slept, so she left the room quietly and went down the narrow rickety stairs to wash herself at the pump behind the outdoor kitchen shed.

After she finished she went into the kitchen to face the ill-tempered cook, with whom she had an argument whenever she went to fetch Richard's meals. She grabbed some freshly baked bread for herself and a leftover chicken leg from the night before and ate, as

she gathered Richard's breakfast together. She'd surprise him and have it there before he woke up and
maybe this morning he'd smile at her, say a kind word,
anything other than his cold, aloof self-absorption.

But Richard was still asleep. She stood over him,
holding his breakfast and studying him, feeling an
oddly mixed rush of emotions: pity and affection and
a strange yearning. She could understand his need for
revenge, but she was terrified that he'd risk his life, all
their lives, to achieve that end. She imagined, as she
stood over him, what he must have felt when he'd read
in a letter that his half brother had sent his mother
away to die...that Thomas had taken everything from
her, even the necklace Edmund had given her.

Edmund must have loved Elizabeth Neville very
much, Tess thought. Despite his mistakes, his over-
sights, he must have really loved Richard's mother to
have given her that emerald necklace—Tess froze. An
emerald necklace...the scene flew into her head
without a bridging thought: the warm, shimmering
water, the mottled white sand, the sound of her regulator in her ears, bubbles and bright fish and watery
sunlight...and the glimmer of old gold. Tess could feel
the gold chain in her hand, the raw emotions that
surged through it, could see the glint of green stones.

And then the water, sucking, dragging, no air and
the roar in her ears, terror and the fearful panic of
empty lungs and then...oblivion.

CHAPTER EIGHT

RICHARD'S DARK MOOD was contagious. Even the weather seemed to have caught it, turning cool and blustery that week. A gray, grainy sky hung low over the island and the sea was dark and frothy.

Tess climbed the steps at the Crow's Nest carrying the usual breakfast tray and wondered how long he could go on like this before he snapped. It was as if the only thing holding him together was his hatred for his half brother. But worse, with Richard so consumed with the need for revenge, she knew now with certainty she was never going to get him to sail her to Key West.

"Your breakfast," she said cheerfully, pushing his door open with her foot.

He was half-dressed, in breeches, standing by the unshuttered window, the wind on his face and drops of rain spilling in. "I have no appetite." He shifted his weight to his good leg.

"I believe you. But eat, anyway." She picked up a piece of bread and chewed on it, still standing, watching him.

"It would make me sick," was all he'd say.

Anger fought with his sorrow. It played across his face, tightening the muscles. At moments Tess thought the wind had gone forever out of his sails, but then he'd come alive, bark at her or throw something across the room. He was not fit to be in decent company. Even Ruby could do nothing. As for the men who occasionally came to the room bearing news of Thomas Moore's whereabouts, they fled quickly. But Tess was stuck with him—stuck picking up after him, stuck trying to get him to eat, stuck with his oppressive, melancholy mood when he'd stand at his window for hours, staring out at the turbulent sea, alternately grieving and seething.

She got him to bathe on their fourth day back on the island. She didn't even leave when he stripped out of his trousers and shirt and, naked, stepped into the small iron tub. She didn't exactly look, either, but Tess did catch a glimpse of strong, firm thighs and buttocks, well-rounded calves. In spite of herself, her heart thudded. He was a well-built man with rock-hard muscles. Brown curling hair spread across his chest and down in a line to disappear from view in the bathwater. His back was smooth, a few freckles from the sun showing across his broad shoulders. His hair was thick, waving slightly now because he'd allowed her to trim it yesterday.

She was trying...trying to hold him together, her reasons mainly selfish. But Tess was coming to realize she'd grown used to the gruff sea captain, Black Richard Neville.

She soaped his back, her slim fingers kneading his tense neck muscles. "You ought to see a masseuse," she said. "Or maybe a chiropractor."

"What nonsense," he replied. "You baffle me, Billy."

"You'd like it where I come from," Tess told him, leaving out the *when*. "It's a beautiful world. Your problems wouldn't exist there."

"I would that such a place could exist. But in this world there is no room for a bastard."

"In my world there is. No one gives a hoot." She poured warm water over his hair. He relaxed a little, uncomplaining for once about her feminine touch.

"A *hoot*. Where do you really come from, Billy Bonney?"

"I've told you a dozen times, Florida."

"Ah, your Florida again."

She thought a moment before venturing, "You *are* still going to take me to Key West when you can?"

"I said I would. But first..." His voice trailed away.

"Okay. Just checking."

She liked touching him. Oh, she had to be careful, but she'd grown used to the feel of his skin when he allowed her to shave him. She was even getting used to doing his laundry, the scent of him becoming familiar as she'd lift his shirt to her nose for a moment before dropping it into the washtub. Though most times he'd call her names, detesting her feminine ways, she saw right through him now—Richard Neville had grown fond of his cabin boy. He'd become protective and gentle with Billy even when he pretended to insult and ignore him.

Yes, Tess thought as he stepped out of the tub and she allowed herself to stand there close to him, look-ing at him, her heart beating a heavy rhythm in her breast, yes, by hook or by crook she would use him to get her back to Key West, but she was also coming to care for him. If only, she thought, as she had more often of late, he could somehow leave all this ugliness and injustice behind, start over in her world. Ridiculous! He'd be a fish out of water, just as she was here.

If only she could find her own way back. There had to be a way. The necklace, if it really was Elizabeth Neville's, was the key, but how was she going to get her hands on it?

She looked at Richard again. His back was to her, and she saw the white ridges of old scars on his brown skin. So much pain... Every man's hand was raised against him. His father and mother were gone. His only future was grim, that of running and hiding and pirating until he was caught or killed. Either way, Richard Neville was doomed.

He pulled on his trousers and buttoned them. "What on earth are you staring at, boy?" He grumbled. "You want a bath? Then climb in the tub."

"I'll, uh, get one later."

"Then empty the damn water. It smells of perfume. I swear, Billy," he said, "it's like having a wife at hand when you're about."

"Um," Tess said. "But you don't really mind it so much anymore, do you?"

"Ha!" he snorted. "It was a foul bargain I struck with you. I suffer every day."

"Sure you do."

Growling, he tugged on his shirt and buttoned it. A moment passed as Tess watched him, in one of her weaker moments when she thought she was going to blurt out the truth, but it passed. What good would it do him to know she was a woman? At this point it would only complicate matters. But, oh, just to see the expression on his face, to have him look at her the way he did those barmaids of his, to feel his arm around her waist and taste his lips on hers. . . .

"Empty the tub, Billy! Are you deaf, too?"

They walked to the Laughing Parrot that night, Richard declaring he needed an ale or two, that he was sick of being cooped up awaiting news of Thomas's whereabouts. He spoke of that special floozy of his, Matilda, and threatened that Billy might have to pull the curtain in their quarters tonight.

Tess tugged the collar of the jacket he'd given her up around her neck. "She's just a whore, Richard."

"So?"

"How can you be fond of a whore?"

"Fond? I am not fond of any woman. Don't you know yet what a woman is for?" he asked, disgusted.

"Sure I do. But I wonder if you've ever, you know, been in love."

"Love? Who would love a bastard? What decent woman?" He laughed bitterly, the rain dripping down his face.

"Oh," Tess said, hurrying to keep up despite his limp, "I know a few thousand or so who'd be swooning at your feet, Captain."

"Ha!" But he shot her one of those curious looks.

The Laughing Parrot was packed, but then many ships were in port because of the stormy weather. Even pirates and privateers had their limits as to what seas they'd sail for possible sight of a fat Spanish galleon laden with treasures.

"Why don't you go on home?" Richard suggested as he glanced around. "You know you dislike this place, Billy."

"Um," Tess said, "I think I'll hang around awhile."

"No doubt to interfere with my wenching," he said under his breath.

"Maybe," Tess replied just as quietly. It was true, though. She'd been keeping him engaged in conversation, diverting him, when he would have sought out one of his trollops. What good it was going to do her, Tess never decided. She knew only that she couldn't abide another night listening to him make love to some other woman.

"Are you coming then?"

"Yes. Yes, I'm right behind you."

She regretted her decision to play mother almost immediately. The place truly was a nightmare, every whoremonger, pirate, scalawag, thief and cutthroat in attendance. It struck Tess that Hollywood had portrayed pirate hideaways much too kindly. This place was a hellhole. Even the swill buckets hadn't been emptied.

Matilda, Richard's doxie, spotted him right away and sashayed over. She gave Tess an assessing look then smiled at Richard, asking if he'd buy her an ale. It sounded like: "Aye, matey, 'ave ye got a place in yer lap for a woman ooze got a dretfil thirst?"

Tess made a face.

"Sit you down, Matilda," Richard said. "I've always got room for you, love."

This was not a part of his life that Tess could tolerate. Like all seamen when they entered the taverns, Richard took on an air of belligerent carelessness. She'd come to know him as a gentle man, a bold and dashing sea captain whose wounds ran deep. He was a man of great potential, but had been stymied at every turn by the rules of his own time. His education had been wasted. The free spirit that was essentially his had been squelched by a world that spawned men such as Thomas Moore. That was the Richard that Tess was coming to care about, not this buccaneer who was forced to live behind a facade. And if he took Matilda home with him tonight, Tess decided, feeling a gloom settle over her, well, if he took her home, Tess was going to spend the night at Ruby's. The Salvadors would take her in. Maybe she'd never go back to Richard.

"Ales all around!" Richard was calling to a barmaid.

The evening proceeded on that note, though Richard actually drank very little. Instead, he would leave the table every few minutes, spotting a comrade, and go to ask if anyone had word of the *Mermaid*'s whereabouts. He offered rewards, threatened Tess and the whole table that he was going to sail out despite the inclement weather and keep on sailing until he found his murderous half brother. "He won't escape me long," Richard said, banging the table with a hard fist.

The question was, though, how was it that Thomas had not found *him?*

Where was he? It had been nearly two weeks. Thomas Moore could sail into Red Turtle's harbor just like any other man. On this island, there were never any questions asked. Surely, she thought, Richard knew that, too.

But Tess didn't get the chance to wonder about Thomas anymore that night.

The fight wasn't her fault. Later, Tess would swear she'd done nothing to encourage the attention that the captain of the privateer *Dark Wind* lavished on her. But at the time it sure must have looked as if she'd asked for it.

She'd gone outside to use the facilities out back, as unseemly as they were. After coming back in from the slanting cold rain and heading to their table, she had quite unwittingly bumped into Roger Duncan, a young pirate who was known to have a huge appetite for women, ale and defending his male prowess.

He was drunk. And in his inebriated state, he was the first and so far only person who recognized Tess for what she was—a woman.

"What a jaunty lass!" he beamed, snatching her to him when Tess tried to keep going. "By God, I like the look of this wench!" And then he tried to kiss her, one hand on her short dark hair, the other encircling her waist. Tess tried to knee him in the groin, but they were too close and he was too strong. Panic surged through her. Not at his kiss, but because she was about to be discovered.

She swore at him viciously, twisting her mouth away from his, crying, "I'm a boy! Stop it! I'm a boy!" Around her, laughter arose, toasts were made, and she had no idea what they were thinking. Had she been discovered? Or did they all think Duncan was assaulting Neville's cabin boy?

Tess never found out. As abruptly as she'd been pulled into his arms, she was suddenly free, falling backward, landing on the filthy, ale-slick floor with a thump.

Shocked, Tess looked up to see Duncan in Richard's grasp, Richard's fist, as if in slow motion, going back, back, then coming forward, slowly, to land firmly on the man's jaw.

Duncan might have been drunk, but his jaw was a rock. The next thing Tess knew, the men were at each other's throats, their bare hands flying. The crowd moved in around them, taunting, cheering. Wagers were made. Tess scrambled to her feet and, on tiptoe, tried to see what was happening. Finally she climbed up on a bench.

They were on the floor, rolling, panting, still swinging fists. Then they were up. Fists slammed into hard bodies. It was Duncan who picked up a tankard and heaved it at Richard. It was Richard who picked up a heavy bench and, using it like a battering ram, forced Duncan clear through the back door into the muddy yard.

Along with the throng Tess tried to make her way outside, too, but she was a calf among bulls. And then, the next thing she knew, it was over. Richard reappeared at the door, his lip swollen and cut, but he was alone.

"What happened?" came a few calls.

And then, "'Twas the bench that got young Duncan! He's out there retching like a pig!"

Tess barely had time to sigh in relief, however, because it was her turn to catch Richard's fury. Without ceremony he caught her around the waist, and like a sack of flour against his thigh, he hauled her out of the front door into the street. Still furious, he flung her aside.

"You despicable twit!" he yelled, wiping the blood from his lip with a forearm. "I knew you leaned in that direction! By God, I knew it all along! You couldn't even keep your unholy ways private! By God!"

Amazingly, once she caught her breath, Tess felt a wave of relief. He still thought she was a boy! It never even crossed his mind that he might have been mistaken all along!

"I didn't start that," Tess said, righting herself. "And if you weren't so bent on insulting me, you'd know that."

"You scoundrel!" he roared. "Haven't I enough on my mind! Haven't I?"

Tess studied him through the rain. She pushed her bangs out of her face. "Tell me something," she said, challenging him. "If you think so damn little of me, then why come to my rescue?"

It was as if she'd slapped him. His jaw slackened and then grew rigid. His fists balled at his sides.

"Come on," Tess said again, "tell me *that*. Why not let me get what's coming to me if I'm asking for it?" She didn't wait for an answer. "I'll tell you why," she rushed on. "It's because you can't stand to see another man's hands on me, can you?"

It was a long, long moment before Richard Neville, the black pirate, found his voice. "That...that's a lie," he finally said weakly.

HE DIDN'T SPEAK A WORD to her that night. Nor did he say anything the next day. Tess was coming to believe that the game was up; she had to tell him now or he'd throw her out, his very manhood at stake.

But it never came to that. On the second day of silence, on the evening tide, a ship sailed into the harbor at Red Turtle Cay. Within the hour Ruby was in Richard's quarters. He looked like a man who'd just seen the devil.

"The Spanish have him," Ruby said, his gaze averted from Richard's. "They took him and his ship when it sailed out of Saint Christopher. They towed them to Havana and turned the whole crew, Thomas along with them, over to the Spanish governor."

"The Spanish?" Richard repeated, barely comprehending.

"Aye, Captain. He's lost to us. They'll hang him sure or at least put him in prison."

"No," Richard whispered, "no. I'll never have my revenge!" And then suddenly, in a rage that boiled up from his soul, he picked up the table, the dinner still on it, and smashed it into the wall. "God's miserable teeth!" he roared.

The ensuing days were hell. Richard ranted and brooded. He rationalized. "Good," he'd say. "Let the Spaniards have his bloody hide. As long as he suffers. As long as he dies."

Then, "Why? Why can I not have my revenge? Thomas's accursed soul is mine! *Why!*"

Tess cringed. She tried to cheer him. She even yelled at him. Nothing brought Richard out of his black mood.

Another day passed. She was ready to give up, to beg him for money and talk one of the other captains into sailing her to Key West, pay him handsomely, anything. But to leave Richard like this...? He was a man in torment. There was also the puzzle still eating at her—his mother's necklace, and the necklace she'd been holding when she'd been torn through time. If they were one and the same, then there had to be a reason she'd been brought here. A purpose. But what?

No. She couldn't leave Richard just yet.

And then more word of Thomas Moore's fate arrived on the island, and Tess never had to make a decision.

Ruby and a captain of a Dutch privateer arrived at Richard's quarters at dinner time. Ruby was grinning. "Fate has intervened," he told Richard. "It seems your half brother has struck a bargain that runs in your favor, my Captain."

The Dutchman explained, but not before exacting a reward from Richard for his trouble. "Here's your gold," Richard snapped impatiently. "Now tell me this news, man."

"I have it on good authority that Thomas Moore has bought his freedom with a promise."

"Aye, go on."

"He has offered your head on a silver platter, and he's on his way here to collect it."

"Bah!" Richard declared. "Why should the governor of Cuba trust him?"

"Because it is agreed that when your head arrives in Havana, the governor will also pay Thomas Moore a handsome reward."

"I see," Richard said thoughtfully. And slowly, a merciless smile twisting his lips, his fingers touching his eye patch, he turned to Ruby. "If this is true," he said, "if Thomas is coming to me, then this is indeed the happiest day of my life, old friend. At last, after a lifetime, one of us will live. One will most certainly die."

Richard's change of mood was almost worse than his brooding. He went about Red Turtle Cay with a cold, calculating smile, his being still consumed with this need for revenge, but now he was calm, deliberate in everything he did.

Tess was afraid. She watched Richard stand by the window in his quarters, looking out to sea, and she knew that whether Richard lived or died, he was doomed. If he killed his half brother, the English would assuredly not rest until he was hanged. Already the Spanish were out for his blood, but if he slew Thomas Moore, there was going to be hell to pay.

And it didn't seem as if Richard knew or cared.

"We should just leave," Tess said as she brought him a bowl of stew.

"Leave?"

"Yes. Don't you realize how bad this is going to be?"

"If I die?"

"No. If you *live*."

He laughed. "And would you miss me, boy?"

Tess eyed him for a moment. "Yes," she said, "I would."

She lay on her pallet that night and realized she no longer cared so much about getting to Key West. She was now utterly, intricately, tied to Richard in this mess, damn it. Night after night she lay so close to him, her throat tight, her insides yearning. Day after day she dwelled on every nuance of his movements, the pitch of his head as he stood at the window, his long hair stirring in the hot summer wind, the whorl of whiskers on his chin...

Oh, yes, Key West and her former life were growing less and less important because Tess was truly, for the first time, falling head over heels in love.

But there were problems. So very many obstacles to her love. First, she was Billy to him. And then, of course, she could never, *would* never, be content in this world. And Richard. *His* troubles were insurmountable.

An image of Thomas Moore came to her—wealthy, dressed in his finery, throwing Elizabeth Neville out of her home and into the squalid streets of London. And stealing her only means of survival, left her by her lover of thirty years... the necklace. It was no wonder Richard hated him so desperately.

The next day Tess had a moment of unbearable fright. She tried to conjure up the faces of her loved ones—Paul, her parents—but nothing came to her whatsoever. Maybe they never existed, would never exist. Maybe it was all a dream.

"Gad, Billy," Richard said, seeing her, "you are pale. We need to be asea. We will be as soon as I dispatch my beloved brother."

"Yes," she mumbled, "that's it. We need to set sail."

It wasn't a dream, though, Tess kept telling herself. She'd come through time. She almost felt as if she'd somehow been sent through that portal to meet Richard, perhaps to help him escape his terrible fate. But how? He couldn't exist in her world and she had to escape his. What could she do then? Again she conjured up the necklace. Could it really have belonged to Elizabeth? Was the treasure the link?

Her head ached with questions.

"What is the trouble?" Richard asked gruffly, annoyed.

"I need to lie down," Tess told him.

"Then go! What a lazy soul you are, Billy." But still he gave her that curious glance, as if there was something he was trying to get straight in his mind. Tess pulled the curtain closed and thought she'd seen something else there, too. Had she detected a flicker of regret in that flinty blue eye? Could the captain be harboring feelings for his cabin boy? *Wishful thinking,* she told herself.

With her heart pounding sickly, Tess awaited the arrival of Thomas Moore those awful days and nights, panting in the heat that followed the stormy week. To make matters worse, she got her monthly flow and had to hide that fact carefully from Richard and the innkeeper. It was hard. But then nothing was easy in this time and place.

The necklace stayed in her thoughts. There had to be a connection. But the necklace was in London. And even if Thomas Moore had carried the jewel with him, how could it end up on a Spanish galleon?

"Is there a ship called the *Isabela?*" she asked Richard.

"Not that I've ever heard of," he told her.

She racked her brain. Had the *Isabela* been built in the shipyards of Havana? Or in Cadiz, Spain? And when? She'd sunk in 1622, Tess knew. This was 1622. She'd sunk in a hurricane, yes, on September sixth, which was coming up soon.

"Now you've spilled my ale!" Richard yelled at her, the tension growing in him each day. "What has come over you, Billy?"

Tess fought tears. "Nothing!" she yelled back. "I'm just sick of watching you sit here and wait to die with that damned cold smirk on your face!"

"If I die," he said, "Ruby will protect you. Does that suit you?"

"Sure, sure," she said, "anything."

But he was watching her intently now, his head cocked. "What is it about you, boy, that perplexes me?"

"I wouldn't know."

That whole afternoon he watched her, though, and it was as if comprehension was about to dawn in him at any moment. She'd just about made up her mind that tonight she was going to spill the beans. If he were to die and never know... He wouldn't throw her out. He wouldn't even hate her for the deceit. No. And she imagined him taking her to his breast and searching her eyes, his feelings for her at last set free. He had to feel something. He had to! She'd seen it in his face, his disgust for himself.

Tonight she'd tell him. Yes.

But that night was not at all what Tess envisioned.

CHAPTER NINE

THOMAS MOORE ARRIVED on the evening tide, boldly sailing into the harbor at Red Turtle Cay on the *Mermaid,* the English ensign flying from the mainmast and his own London Trading Company pennant flying from the mizzen. He knew, everyone knew, he was as safe there as anyone, criminal to royal heir.

Word of his arrival flew, swifter than the west wind blew, and ship's mate Jamie Talbot came pounding up the narrow stairs of the Crow's Nest to bring Richard the news just as Tess was setting his supper down on his table.

"He's here!" Jamie said breathlessly. "Thomas Moore on the *Mermaid!* Just heaving to in the harbor, Captain!"

Richard froze, his face hard as stone, his mug of ale halfway to his mouth.

Tess stopped dead in her tracks, too, staring anxiously from one man to the other, knowing something was going to happen now but not knowing what.

"You're sure," Richard said then, his voice so quiet, so deadly still, that Tess shuddered inwardly.

"Aye, Captain, I saw the *Mermaid* with me own eyes," Jamie said.

Richard set the mug down carefully, not spilling a drop, his movements deliberate and slow. "Does Ruby know?"

"I sent Colin to fetch him, Captain."

"Good. I thank you, Jamie. You may go now," Richard said.

But Jamie stood there, undecided, and asked the question Tess was dying to ask. "Uh, Captain, sir, will you be needin' us, that is, I mean, what are you going to do now?"

Richard turned to Jamie and flashed him a wide smile, a completely humorless smile, one that Tess supposed was meant to disarm. What it did was to chill her all the way down to her bare feet.

"Jamie, my lad, thanks, but I'll not be needing you. I appreciate your offer, though."

"Aye, aye, Captain," Jamie said uneasily.

When Jamie was gone, Richard rose and went to where his cutlass and scabbard hung from a peg on the wall and took them down.

"What . . . what are you going to do?" Tess choked out.

Richard gave her a glance and commenced buckling on his sword. "I'm simply going to meet my dear brother, who's so kindly come to visit me," he said.

"Richard . . ."

"This is none of your affair, Billy."

"You're trying to get yourself killed."

He leveled a cool gaze on her. "Not at all."

"What do you think you're going to accomplish?" she asked, putting a hand on his arm.

He stood stock-still and looked down at her hand. She drew it back as if burned, and she knew then there was nothing on earth she could do to stop Richard.

Deliberately he finished buckling on his belt, stuck his two knives in his sash, took a long drink of ale, then headed for the door.

"Where are you going?" Tess whispered.

"To the dock, of course."

"I'm coming." Her heart pounded with an awful apprehension.

"You stay here, lad," Richard said offhandedly. "It won't take long."

She didn't argue, but as soon as he was gone, Tess raced down the stairs after him and headed toward the harbor. There would be a fight, a terrible fight. Richard had sworn to kill Thomas. She was terrified. What if Richard died, cut down by his half brother? What if she had to watch him die, his blood pumping out on the ground, his heart pierced? How good was Thomas? Better with a sword than Richard?

It seemed that the entire population of Red Turtle Cay had heard the news and was on its way to watch the fight. Men and women, even children, trod the muddy paths that led down to the sea. Excitement was in the damp air as if a circus had come to town..., a spectacle.

Her pulse pounded in her veins as she shouldered her way through the festive throng. When she could see the masts of the *Mermaid* in the harbor, her sails furled, Tess broke into a run, pushing people aside, panting in the heavy air. The crowd grew thicker, and she knew she was close. Pushing, worming her way through, she felt herself growing slick with sweat, short of breath, her heart drumming too fast. *Richard,* she cried inwardly, *Richard.*

A space had been cleared on one of the wooden quays. Tess burst through the mob crowded tightly there, panic knifing through her insides. Rough voices swore at her, hands snatched at her ragged shirt, but she shoved through, and then she was out in the open, gasping, sweat running into her eyes, and she saw them.

Thomas Moore. A slim man, dressed impeccably in a blue doublet and pale breeches and hose. A long English face, a high-bridged, aristocratic nose, dark blond hair like Richard's in a pageboy to his shoulders. A smile on his face, a hand on the pommel of his sword, he'd just stepped out of the longboat that had rowed him ashore.

And Richard. Facing Thomas, his expression set, his legs apart in their soft high boots, his rage banked but ready to flare.

Tess stood still in the suddenly hushed crowd, and she heard each word uttered by Richard and his brother as clearly as if they'd been hammered into her heart.

"You're looking fit, Richard," Thomas said with heavy irony. He was cool, unmoved by the crowd, the place, the cold intent he must have read on Richard's face, and Tess began to see what kind of man he was, this half brother of Richard's.

"You, too, Thomas, although I heard you had an unfortunate run-in with the Spanish," Richard replied.

"Not at all unfortunate. The governor and I got on famously. Why, his hospitality was such that I had to present him with a gift, one whose value you will appreciate, my dear *frère*."

"I assure you I have no interest in what you gave the man," Richard said. "I'd rather discuss the bargain you made with him."

Thomas's mouth stretched out into a thin smile. "Ah, I beg to differ. You should be interested, for I gave the governor that lovely gold and emerald necklace that belonged to—"

Richard lunged toward Thomas so suddenly the crowd gasped in unison, but he stopped himself, and Tess could see him fighting for control. Thomas had merely stepped back a pace, keeping that chilly smile on his lips. "Ah," he said softly, "I thought you'd be interested."

"You gave my mother's necklace to that Spanish pig?" Richard asked in a deadly voice.

"It was the least I could do. He's about to set sail for Spain in the new galleon, the *Isabela,* and he was quite thrilled with it. Said he might even present it to the queen," Thomas said, and then he laughed. "As for the bargain, well, I simply had to promise him something, didn't I?"

Tess felt dizzy. The necklace. On the *Isabela.* That's how it got there. But she had no time to pursue the thought because Richard was drawing his sword, his face stark and set, his body going naturally into the fencing stance, and Thomas, laughing, was drawing his, too, mockingly saluting his brother.

"Shall we see who comes out best this time?" Thomas asked, taunting.

"I'm grown now, Thomas. I'm no whelp for you to take advantage of," Richard said between his teeth. "I've had my share of practice."

Thomas flicked the end of his sword in the air with insouciant grace. "You always had too much to say for yourself, bastard."

Tess saw the blood leave Richard's face, but he smiled without humor. "And you, brother, are a murderer. As such I take it upon my honor to do away with you."

"You have no honor," Thomas sneered.

"Shall we begin then, and may the better man win," Richard said levelly, slashing at the air with his blade.

The crowd was muttering now, making wagers, excited with spectators' blood lust. Tess wanted to cry out to someone to stop the fight, but no one would. She saw some of Richard's crew, Colin and Joseph and Jamie and old Benjamin. And there, across the way, was Ruby, but his face was unreadable, and even he, Tess knew, would not interfere.

Oh, God. She wanted to sob, to beg, to throw herself between the men but she couldn't. Someone would only drag her off, and they'd be at each other again.

It was a vicious fight. The brothers were well matched, Thomas a bit taller, slim as a whippet but strong and quick. Richard broader, powerful, practiced. Both were out to kill.

Richard feinted, feeling Thomas out, the tip of his sword slashing, his feet moving lightly. Thomas waited, that cold smile always on his lips, holding off that dancing tip with ease.

A fine rain began, first as a fog turning to mist then to droplets that hung in the hot air, wetting everyone, shining on the swordsmen's skin, soaking the rough boards underfoot. Tess stood there, not even feeling it, her heart in her throat, her belly clenched into a knot.

The men lunged fiercely at each other then; metal grated, clanged and shrieked apart. A slice opened in Thomas's doublet but no blood. The crowd breathed as one, and more wagers were offered. Richard backed up and tripped over a crate, avoided a sword edge, regained his balance, pushed Thomas back until one more step would have him in the water. They battled mightily back and forth, the crowd surging with them, then slowed finally, their arms growing tired, their clothes sticking to them with sweat and rain. Thomas had cuts on his arm and cheek, Richard one on his side. Their garments pink where rain diluted their blood, still they fought, breathing harder now, hacking at each other two-handed.

Thomas went down on a knee, holding off Richard's attack. Richard flung himself at his brother, but he could not reach him. Thomas rolled away, regained his feet like a cat, came in again, straight, sighting along his blade, running, so quick.

Tess cried out as Thomas's sword ran through Richard's left shoulder, up under his collarbone, then was yanked away, blood spurting after it. The crowd sighed in unison, eager now for the kill, waiting. It would come soon.

For a moment, Richard stood as still as a statue, and Tess was afraid he was going to collapse. Blood soaked his white shirt so quickly that she had to stuff her hands into her mouth to keep from screaming. The crowd waited, hushed.

Thomas lowered the point of his sword and grinned with pleasure. "Shall we call it quits, then, Richard? If you yield now, I will take you back to England to stand trial for mutiny. You'll have your miserable life for a few more months, at least."

"I'll see you in hell first," Richard said through gritted teeth.

"You may at that, *frère,*" Thomas said. "So? It's not over yet? Splendid!" And he raised his blade again.

Richard said nothing more. He seemed unaffected by his wound, although that could not be, Tess knew. It was as if he'd turned to something deep inside, some well of strength, and he went at Thomas, pressing him fiercely, crashing away at him, one-handed now. Thomas slipped on the wet wood underfoot, lurched sideways for a split second, and in that heartbeat of time Richard raised his blade high and brought it down toward Thomas's unprotected side, and it bit into his neck, halfway through skin and bone and gristle and arteries, and it was over.

Thomas's body fell like a tree, straight and hard, and his blood mingled with the rainwater. The sun was setting, fuzzy behind the rain and fog, the light growing dimmer. Richard stood, head hanging, cutlass still in his right hand, blood flowing down his left arm, his side, dripping onto the glistening dock, the last copper rays on him, so that he seemed dyed crimson. He stood for a few moments. The crowd was utterly silent. Then his body turned to rubber and he slowly slipped to his knees there on the wet dock, putting out a hand to support himself.

The people roared then, in appreciation, in satisfaction, in fulfillment, and Tess ran to Richard in the mad confusion. She reached him at the same moment Ruby did.

"Oh, God, Ruby," she cried, kneeling by Richard, "help him!"

Ruby had Richard on his back, the rain on his face, and he was pulling off his own shirt and pressing it to Richard's shoulder. Tess leaned over, her hand behind Richard's head. "I'm here," she said to him. "Richard, we're here. We'll take care of you, Richard."

He opened his eye and saw her and a faint smile pulled at his mouth. "I killed him," he said.

"Yes, you did. Oh, Richard," she said, biting her lip, horror welling up in her. "You're going to be all right, you hear?"

He closed his eye, his face waxen and shiny wet and peaceful. "It does not matter anymore," he breathed, and then his head lolled lifelessly against her.

"Richard!" she cried brokenly, despairing, holding him against her chest, his blood mingling with her tears and the rain, washing away in pink rivulets on the deck.

"Billy, Billy, lad, he's only passed out. Come away, boy, we've got to get him home," Ruby said, pulling at her, trying to pry her hands off him.

His crew carried him along the mud-clogged streets, Tess running alongside, holding the shirt pressed to his shoulder. But it turned pink, then red, then even darker blood welled up under her fingers, and she was so terribly afraid. Up the stairs of the Crow's Nest, through the plank door. It was growing dark now, and someone lit a few candles. They laid him on his bed, and Ruby cut the soaked, bloody shirt away and looked at the wound.

Tess was afraid to say a word and crouched, soaked, shivering, by the bed.

"Well?" Joseph Bellows asked.

"It's hit nothing vital," Ruby said, "praise God, but it must have nicked a vein to bleed like this."

Tess looked up. "Ruby, will he live? Ruby, tell me."

"It's in God's hands, Billy. If he hasn't lost too much blood . . . It's a clean wound, at least."

"Pressure," Tess mumbled to herself, remembering snatches of a first-aid course. "Elevation and pressure." She stood up and looked at Richard, lying there so still, so pale, so like a corpse. "We have to prop him up," she said. "Elevate him so that the blood can't run out as easily. And keep pressure on the wound. Direct pressure," she said, remembering. "And he has to be warm so he doesn't go into shock."

They looked at her oddly, those rough buccaneers crowded into Richard's room. "Shock?" Ruby asked.

"When the blood leaves the internal organs. It's due to trauma like this. He could die of shock," she said.

They stared at her, eyes narrowed, doubtful frowns on their faces.

But Tess was oblivious. She got some pillows and arranged them behind Richard's back so that he was propped against the wall. She found clean shirts, ones she'd washed for him, ripped them into rags and pressed them, hard, right on the wound.

The men watched Billy the cabin boy as he leaned over Richard, his heavy lower lip caught between his teeth, intent, working over their captain. They looked at one another then back to Billy and shook their heads, bemused.

"Please, someone, help me get his clothes off. Here, hold this, hard now. Press on it with your hand," Tess said.

While old Benjamin held the wadded-up shirt over the wound, she and Ruby peeled Richard's soaked clothes off. Joseph pulled his boots off, and Tess didn't even notice the length of his nude body as she covered him with a blanket and pushed his tangled, wet hair back off his forehead.

And then there was nothing to do but sit by him and wait to see when . . . if . . . the blood stopped flowing.

Ruby had grog and food sent up from the kitchen, but Tess couldn't eat. She sat there tirelessly, changing cloths when one became saturated with blood. *So much blood,* she thought, *he must be drained dry by now.* He'd fall into shock, his blood vessels would collapse, his heart would simply stop.

The men left after a time, when it got late, but Ruby sat there with Tess, and finally, finally, they could see that the bleeding slowed, and they looked at each other, the grizzled pirate and the girl he thought was a cabin boy, and they smiled wearily.

Tess sat up all night, watching Richard. He breathed shallowly, lying there as if dead. His pallor was frightening. "What do you think, Ruby?" she asked once, her voice a wisp of sound.

"I don't know, I just don't know. I've seen men lose blood before," Ruby said tiredly, "and it can go either way."

A transfusion, Tess thought. A simple transfusion was all Richard needed. An ambulance, an emergency room, doctors, an IV in his arm. Oh, God damn this primitive time!

At dawn Ruby left, worried about his family missing him. Richard was still alive, holding on, still unconscious. Tess nodded, dozing, jerked awake, dozed again. The candles had burned down, guttered out, and half-eaten food on the table was attracting flies. She fell asleep in the chair and woke, panicked, hours later, drained, sticky with Richard's blood, needing desperately to relieve her bladder.

He was alive, his chest rising and falling. *Oh, thank God,* Tess thought. She left him for a moment to visit the privy, then ordered the cook to send up buckets of warm water and some red wine.

"You promise payment?" the cook whined.

"Just do it, lady," Tess said in a hard voice. "Richard Neville is good for it and you know it!"

She washed Richard with the warm water and a rag, cleaned the blood and grime from him, patting carefully around the wound. She wiped his face, going under the strap of his eye patch, over his cheeks and forehead and lips, down his jaw to his neck. She touched him with reverence, breathing life into him with her hands.

At midday Ruby returned.

"He's still alive," Tess said.

"Aye, that he is."

She ate a few bites that day. People knocked at the door, but Ruby spoke quietly to them and sent them away. The crew of the *Marauder* kept a vigil under their captain's window, but Tess was unaware of them. She sat and cooled Richard's forehead with a wet cloth and willed him to live.

It was late afternoon, and it had begun raining again. Ruby had fallen asleep. Tess dozed, weary and aching in mind and body, her head hanging, her hands resting in her lap. The air in the room was thick and close, hot. Droplets of moisture clung to every surface. Tess stirred, half-awake, aware of her shirt and pants clinging to her, her hair plastered to her forehead. So hot, so humid. If only there was an air conditioner...

"Billy," she heard in her daze, and she struggled to answer, but no sound came from her throat. "Billy."

She jerked up with a start, and her gaze fell on Richard. He was looking at her with one blue eye. He was awake. "Richard," she breathed.

"Billy," he said again, trying to smile. "You were damned hard to awaken."

"Oh, Richard."

"Aye, it's me, all right. Gad, I feel weak as a kitten. What did you do to me?"

"You lost a lot of blood."

"Tell me I didn't dream it, lad. Tell me I bested Thomas."

"You did."

He closed his eye and smiled a little, weakly running a hand across his sweat-slick chest as if to see if he was truly still alive.

"Now, Richard, I want you to drink a lot of fluids. You'll be weak until we get your blood built back up. And sleep. Rest a lot. You'll be fine," Tess said.

"Aye, you've got me where you want me now, lad, under your thumb. How bad is my wound?"

"Clean. Ruby says it didn't hit anything vital. You bled a lot." Tess rose and put a hand on his forehead. "Can you drink something now?"

He drank some wine mixed with water, Tess helping him, spilling some down his chin. When he finished he fell asleep again, and that's when Tess put her face in her hands and wept with relief.

Ruby woke up, heard the news and leaned out of the window to relay the news of the captain's improvement to his men.

When it was dark, Ruby's wife, Edith, came to relieve Tess. Tess argued, irrationally afraid that if she slept he'd die, but tiredness overcame her, and she fell asleep on her pallet even as the words came out of her mouth.

Another night went by. The sun woke Tess and she sat bolt upright. "He's well," Edith said calmly. "He drank, had some soup, and he's peacefully asleep."

Matilda arrived at the plank door that morning, her red hair frizzed up on top of her head, her cleavage indecent, her skirt above her ankles. "'Ow is he?'' she asked Tess.

"Get out of here," Tess muttered.

"Mind yer tongue, boy. I've come to offer me services to the captain," Matilda said haughtily.

It was Ruby who held Tess back. "Go on, Matilda, it's best you leave. He's well taken care of," he said, one big hand restraining Tess.

Richard sat up that afternoon. Tess fed him soup from a big tin spoon, held the tin cup for him to drink from.

"Ah, Billy, that's good. I just feel so bloody weak," Richard said.

"You're lucky you aren't dead."

"That I am. But, God's teeth, no poxy knave like Thomas Moore can kill me," he said lightly.

"He almost did."

"Not to worry, lad. Give me some more of that good wine, will you?"

The next morning he tried to stand with Ruby's help, shaky, his pallor worse, and go sit in a chair at the table. He swore at his own helplessness.

"Take it easy. What's your hurry?" Tess asked. "You should be in bed."

But Richard cursed richly and turned his splintered-sapphire gaze on Tess. "I have something to do, Billy. God's sweet mercy, boy, can't you ever leave me be?"

"What do you have to do? For goodness' sake, Richard, you almost died and now—"

"I need to get to Havana, if you must know. I need to find that sodding governor and get my mother's necklace back before he sails to Spain," Richard said tightly, "and I'll be damned if I know why I'm telling you my mind."

"Havana?" Tess repeated, then stood up and bent over him, her face red and splotched with emotion. "You're half-dead and you want to go to Havana?"

"Aye, Billy, Havana. It's something I have to do," Richard said soberly.

She spent the rest of the day agonizing. She, and she alone, knew that his mother's necklace was not within Richard's grasp, certainly not in Havana. It was going to end up on the ocean floor with the wreckage of the *Isabela*. September sixth. That was the day the galleon would sink off Key West. But she couldn't tell Richard, not without telling him everything.

The next day he walked a little farther, and Tess knew she couldn't keep him there much longer. He was mending quickly; already he'd given orders to prepare the *Marauder* for sailing.

Tess had thought about it a lot, and she'd come to the same conclusion time after time. When Richard set sail she'd go with him; despite the danger, despite his stubbornness, despite everything, she would accompany him. She knew somehow that she must be with him on this quixotic quest of his, that the necklace belonging to Elizabeth Neville bound Tess to Richard in some bizarre way, and had beckoned Tess through time, as though . . . as though Elizabeth were protecting her son by bringing Tess together with him.

She could no more deny her destiny than Richard could his. She'd go with him and she'd stay by him and try very, very hard to keep him safe.

Richard was healing and he was brooding. He was restless and impatient now, his mind taken up with plans. His arm was in a sling, and he moved more confidently, even going downstairs to the taproom. Tess watched him, growing more and more afraid, but trying to repress it. The future held nothing for Richard but violence and misery, and she couldn't save him from any of it.

"What if the governor has already set sail for Spain?" Tess ventured once.

"I'll follow him to hell then. The necklace will be mine. It's the last and only thing of my mother's."

Tess could say nothing.

That evening, as the fiery tropical sun set over Red Turtle Cay, Richard leaned on the windowsill and stared out over the town, and beyond that to the silvery blue sea. He stayed there for a long time, so long that Tess was about to say something, but then she heard him mutter to himself. She listened, holding her breath, and she caught his words. "What life have I here?" he said. "I am a man who should never have been born."

What loneliness, Tess thought. What hell.

Her feet moved as if of their own accord. She came up behind him, and saw the scars on his back, faint white lines, as if he'd been lashed long ago. Tenderly she touched the scarred skin, wanting so badly to comfort him.

He flinched from her, and without even turning around, he snarled, "You only make matters worse, Billy."

Tess bit her lip. She was desperate to tell him she was a woman, unable to bear the way he shrank from her now that he was better. She'd decided all those days ago that she would confess, but now she was afraid again. Would he sail off to Havana and leave her alone on Red Turtle Cay if he knew?

And yet if Richard were to die on this quest for the necklace . . .

"Get away from me, Billy," he was saying, still flinching from her, and in a split second Tess made up her mind. The consequences be damned, she thought.

She touched his back again, gently, whispered up a silent prayer and spoke the words. "Richard," she whispered, "I'm not Billy, your cabin boy. Richard, do you hear me? I'm not a boy. I'm a woman. My name is Tess Bonney. Richard . . ."

His back grew rigid, stiffened. Tess couldn't move, couldn't say a word. Her heart beat against her ribs like a bird trying to escape, and she went cold all over. Cold and weak.

CHAPTER TEN

RICHARD WAS NUMB. Not Billy Bonney. But *Tess* Bonney. A woman. A bloody woman!

His first reaction was shock. His next was a sudden spurt of knowledge. He'd been battling his feelings all these weeks, cringing inside with shame whenever by chance they touched. He'd thought himself the most corrupt of men!

A bloody woman!

For an endless time Richard could only stand there and gaze at him...*her,* his heart hammering. He drank her in—Tess, her shape, those delicate hands and feet, those dimples, the curve of her mouth and those long, long dark lashes framing big sable eyes.

"Richard," Tess started to say, the high-pitched voice now a dead giveaway, "I—"

"You—you lied to me! You deceived me in the most vile manner!"

"You're angry."

"God in heaven, I am! How could you...put me through this...this torment!"

"I didn't mean to. I—"

"Enough!" he shouted, his emotions gone berserk. "Get out of my sight!"

She stood there for a moment longer and then finally turned from him, walking slowly toward the door, her shoulders shaking.

Rage and disbelief coursed through Richard. He stared, furious, at the gentle sway of hip, the slimness of Billy... no, *her,* the bow of this Tess's head. He recalled in a sane corner of his mind his cabin boy donned in the mauve silk, the swanlike white column of neck, that heady, cloying female scent. Gad! The torture she'd put him through! The unholy, ugly thoughts he'd been suppressing all these long weeks!

Something inside Richard burst then, a thing so wild and primitive and pent up he was taken by utter surprise himself when he strode after her in two long steps and grabbed her arm. "Where in hell do you think you're going?" he demanded, his brain reeling.

"You told me to—"

Before he could think, Richard crushed her to him, muttering, "Damn you," as his head descended to hers.

Tasting Billy's... Tess's lips, the feel of small, firm breasts pressed to him, rocked Richard. And her response... It was as unleashed and violent as his. She clutched at him, those slim fingers grabbing at his back, her mouth twisting against his, and he felt her warmth beneath her rags.

They stumbled backward, clutching, clinging, until they fell together on his bed. Richard let out a cry of pain.

"Your wound," she groaned, her mouth to his.

"My wound be damned," he breathed, panting, his hands tearing at her shirt.

And then she was his to see at last, lying there next to him, pulling her clothes off while he managed his own. He could feel his wound, but now it was only a distant ache, and soon it was forgotten.

He couldn't stop staring at her, the slender limbs, the curve of her hips, those small, firm breasts. He never asked, nor thought to ask, if she'd have him. He knew down deep in his soul that this was Providence. Truly there was a benevolent God who'd sent this woman to him in his loneliness.

He kissed her tenderly, drinking her in, his hands on either side of her face. Then he kissed her with abandon, his senses going mad when she pressed her warmth to his in response. His mouth found her breasts, her navel, her hip. He could not get enough of his Tess.

"How could you have denied us this?" he whispered hoarsely.

But she only moaned, her breasts rising and falling with the rapid beat of her heart.

He entered Tess with care, a passion he'd never before known welling inside him, a wave building, building, ready to crash on a new and wondrous shore.

Tess met his thrusting as he eased his hands beneath her buttocks and brought her up to meet him, again and again, heat clutching heat, releasing, clutching. It was she who cried out first, her dark eyes moist and surprised, locked onto his. And then Richard felt the pounding of his own blood in his loins and his wave crashed, too, on the shore, until he was spent, collapsing onto her. He pressed his mouth to her neck, tasting her still, a warmth so wonderful suffusing his body he could find no words to tell her his joy.

Richard looked up at the ceiling and felt her lean warmth snuggled close to his side. He still could not get over his shock. Tess. Not Billy. How could he have been so blind? He recalled her again in that mauve gown. And he recalled his frustration. He should beat her for putting him through such hell. And yet the very notion of any harm coming to Tess, even inflicted by himself, was so foreign, so remote, he could not imagine it. He realized then that he'd been protecting her all along. Perhaps a part of him had known, then. Perhaps he'd not been as despicable as he'd thought.

Later, while they still lay in his bed naked together, he finally had the presence of mind to question her. "It was perplexing enough that the Spaniards had you, you, Billy, the boy. But Tess? You must tell the truth now, the whole of it."

She sighed, and he thought it was much like the purring of a cat at his side. "You'll think I'm lying, Richard."

"Not if you tell me it is the truth."

"Easy to say now."

"Come," he said, "no more games between us, Tess Bonney. That time is done."

She kissed him lightly then and met his gaze. "You have to promise to hear me out, Richard. I don't want you to move or speak until I'm done."

"Why would I?"

"Just promise."

"On my honor, then, I swear it. But tell me, Tess, for this has been too long in coming."

She took a deep breath, took his hand in hers and held it tightly. "My story begins three hundred and seventy-odd years from *now*, Richard," she said. "I'm from the future."

Richard lay there next to her in silent and unimaginable shock. At first he thought she was making a jest, but when she went on and on, her tale so astounding it was either truth or the greatest lie he'd ever heard, Richard began to ask himself: Could such a thing have happened?

She told him of a world so wonderful that, despite his enormous doubt, his heart began to sing. "It's called the United States," Tess said. "You remember I told you that once before."

"Aye, you did," he managed to say.

"Well, it's not perfect," she said, "but we have the Constitution that's our law, and there's the Bill of Rights that guarantees freedom of speech and establishes that all men are created equal."

"No slaves, then?"

She shook her head. "Not for a long time."

"Incredible."

"But medicine, Richard, you'd never believe it. We've cured the pox and dozens of other diseases on a worldwide scale. We have machines that take pictures of your insides. Doctors can replace your organs if you're sick. There're drugs to cure infections and almost everything that ails you. And now the scientists are experimenting with cloning."

"Cloning?"

She did her best to explain. Richard took it all in with disbelief, yet no woman could invent such tales, could she? "Men have walked on the moon," she told him, and he declared this impossible. "And cars, Richard, they can go a couple hundred miles . . . knots per hour."

"No. There is nothing to propel such a thing."

"Engines propel them. I'm no expert, but they're called internal combustion engines. It's like this fuel, called gas, can make little explosions, creating energy." She thought a moment. "There are lots of inventions I can't explain. Like TV. And telephones and satellites." But she tried, and all he could do was lie there and listen and wish, from the bottom of his heart, that he could see such things if, by some miracle, they existed. Or *would* exist, he corrected himself.

"Ships," Richard said. "Tell me about ships."

"Wow. That's tough. First, sails were mostly replaced by engines, steam engines. And now it's all so advanced you can cross the oceans under nuclear power. There are even submarines that go under water."

He listened and listened, mute, at one time thinking her daft, at another time deeming her sane. What was he to think?

"But it's funny," she told him, "a lot of men and women prefer to sail just like you do."

"Is this so?"

"Absolutely. There're plenty of people who think we've taken technology too far. Our lives can be complicated. Yours is so simple."

"Simple? Where hundreds die of the pox and men hate men because of their parentage?"

"Like I said, we don't have a perfect world. We have new diseases, hunger, riots. There's still hatred among men."

"But not everyone."

"No. Far from it."

"Wars? Are there wars?"

She told him about the two great wars that had plagued her twentieth century, but said that people and nations were coming to believe in world peace.

"This is good."

"If we achieve it."

He listened to more of her tales and said, "I do hope the Spaniards do not get hold of you, Tess. It's sure you'd be burned by the Inquisition as a witch."

"Do *you* believe me, though?"

"I . . . I do not know," was the only reply he could give.

What he did know, however, was that a huge burden had been lifted from him. He'd been stricken with a fever for this strange, marvelous woman all along, reproaching himself cruelly for his vileness. But now he could allow himself to feel this passion for her. Such a fey creature, Richard thought, pushing her short dark hair from her brow with a gentle finger. He could almost believe she truly was from some future where men and women were free and equal and magic machines were making life wonderful. And medicine. That man should no longer have to suffer the torture of diseases, the pox, the plague, malaria. And children could grow up where their parentage did not brand them. Such happiness! Such justice!

He looked at her demure face. And this small female with her sweetness and sharp mind, her astonishing *freeness,* with her smoothly tanned skin and short hair and supple body said she was from such a time. "By all the stars in heaven," he avowed, "I'd like to leave this misbegotten world behind and go to yours."

"Oh, Richard," Tess said fervently, "I wish you could, too."

He asked her a dozen questions at a time, testing her, loving these marvelous tales she related to him. A battle waged within him; he wanted all this to be true but knew it could not be. Still he listened, rapt.

"There's so much that's happened in almost four hundred years," she said, "though most advances have really come in the last hundred and fifty." She went on about economics and politics and history. "I'm a history major myself. I teach as an assistant at a university in Florida."

"A *woman?*"

"Women are into most everything, Richard."

"I suppose men bear the children in your time, Tess." And he laughed.

"Not quite. But they do stay home and raise them sometimes while the woman works."

"That I should not like."

"I didn't think you would."

They talked, well, mostly Tess did the talking while Richard listened on into the night. He began to form clear pictures of her world in his mind and suffered the knowledge that he'd never see these wonders. "Perhaps you should not tell me so much," he said, frowning. "I'll never see these miracles."

"Oh, Richard," she replied, "I know it's unfair, but you have to hear these things to know who I am."

"No," he said. "I think that at any time or in any place I would be...fond of you, Tess."

"Really?"

"Aye. But don't press the matter, woman. I have not forgotten Billy."

"I had to do it. At first it was an accident. And then when everyone took me for a boy, well, can't you see it was safer?"

He made an annoyed sound. "You should have known I'd never harm a woman."

"I did know, after a while," she admitted softly. "But I was...attracted to you, and I guess I was afraid you wouldn't be interested in me."

"Um." He thought a moment. "So, what you have not told me is how you came to this time. One of your machines?"

"Good God, no!" Tess said.

"Then how?"

"This is the weirdest story of all," she began. "I'm just afraid you'll never believe a word of what I'm going to tell you."

"I shall be the judge of that."

She started at the beginning, telling of research she'd been doing at archives in Seville, Spain. She told him all about Paul and Mack Solomon and his twenty-year quest for the *Isabela*.

"The very galleon of which Thomas spoke?" he asked, bemused.

She nodded. "One and the same. And now here comes the really strange part. I think I was somehow sent back in time because of this ship and because of a treasure that's on it." And then she told him about the necklace, a series of gold links that held an emerald pendant.

"But—but," he stammered, "that's my own mother's!"

Tess nodded slowly.

"This cannot be."

"Think," Tess said, holding his hands in hers. "I'm diving for treasure. I pick up this necklace. Next thing you know I drop it and I'm whisked back to the very time the necklace existed in the past."

"Ridiculous!"

She shook her head. "No, it isn't. The necklace is the connection. It's on the *Isabela*. It's got to be the same one—your mother's. It's part of the lost treasure of the *Isabela*."

"Ha!" he said sharply. "You are wrong there. The *Isabela* is afloat and soon to be on her way to Spain, if my brother was correct."

Tess took a deep breath. "She's afloat and sailing now, Richard," she said. "But she won't be for long. She'll sink a week from today, on the sixth of September. She'll go down in a hurricane off the coast of Key West."

CHAPTER ELEVEN

"THIS IS UTTER tomfoolery," Richard declared, leaning over Tess's shoulder. The oil lantern in his captain's cabin swung with the ship's movement over the chart they were examining, casting long shadows across the table. Above deck the square black sails cracked in the wind as the *Marauder* skimmed across the sea, her wake a silver hissing in the moonlight.

Tess tapped the chart with a finger. "Look at it from my point of view," she said. "History dictates that the *Isabela* will be here on the morning of the sixth."

"In a hurricane." He snorted.

"Yes. And she *will* go down."

He straightened, his hands on his hips. "You are mad, woman. But then to be sailing my ship toward your Key West is just as mad. What has gotten into me? Are you a witch, Tess Bonney?"

"I'm not a witch and I'm quite sane, and when the *Isabela* goes down I want you to say how sorry you are for questioning me. Is it a deal?"

"Ha!" he said. "I'll go you one better. If we run into your hurricane I'll... Let's see. I know, I'll bring you a meal in your bed. Is that not what a twentieth-century man would do?"

"You're catching on."

She knew he didn't believe her, not really, not about her traveling through time and not about the *Isabela* and his mother's treasured necklace. What he was doing was covering all bases. As soon as he proved her wrong, he'd head straight to Havana, hell-bent for leather to get his mother's pendant, his only worldly link to her. Sadly, Tess thought, he would never recover the necklace, for it was destined to rest in a watery grave along with the *Isabela*, not to be seen again for almost four centuries. She could tell him that, but her heart broke to even think about it.

Tess kept thinking about another thing as the *Marauder* sped toward Key West. It was driving her crazy, too. The *Isabela* was going to sink. Okay, fine, she knew that despite Richard's skepticism. And she knew that in the latter half of the twentieth century she was going to be born. That much she could comprehend. But what of the moment her hand first touched the necklace in that distant future? Was she going to somehow touch the necklace again when they caught up to the *Isabela?* Could touching it again set off a chain of events that would transport her back? Or was she stuck in this time and everything had been random happenings?

Play it as it comes, she told herself. *Wait and see. But there are no real coincidences.*

Tess turned in the cabin's chair and caught Richard studying her. She'd just spent the whole stinking hot summer trying desperately to get back to Key West, risking life and limb with this black pirate. And yet . . . as the time neared and the hours closed on the

sixth of September, Tess was not at all sure she truly
wanted to go home. It would mean leaving Richard.

A scene filled her mind. She was back home, sitting in a library, researching Richard Neville, Black
Pirate, who'd sailed the Spanish Main in his dark ship.
She'd find out that he survived a terrible hurricane and
went on to plunder more Spanish ships. But she'd
know he did it with a sad heart, his mother and the
necklace lost to him forever. And then she'd read he
was caught. Tortured. Hung from a yardarm.

But to stay here, in this time with him . . . it was in-
conceivable. She couldn't, she *wouldn't*. She'd found
that whirlpool once—or it had found *her*—and she
could find it again. Still, Richard . . .

"What are these tears in your eyes?" he asked,
watching her closely.

"It's nothing," she said. "Just the smoke from the
lantern. No big deal."

She was afraid for him. She knew that hurricane
was out in the mid-Atlantic even now, amassing
strength. The *Isabela* and twenty-eight other Spanish
vessels in the convoy were going to be lost. How then
was the *Marauder* to survive? And Richard? Was she
going to lose her life alongside him? If so, Tess
thought, she'd accept her fate, knowing that she'd at
least loved and, she prayed, been loved. Her parents,
Paul . . . they wouldn't mourn her loss for another three
hundred and seventy-some years. Crazy.

Then again, she pondered, perhaps the whirlpool
awaited her.

She wished, oh, how she wished, that she knew
more about the fate of the Spanish convoy and espe-

cially the *Marauder*. Had Richard's ship survived?
Would it? Would *he?* Oh, God, she thought, if only
she knew more, had read up on the storm, the fate of
the ships. And here she was, living history itself and
still needing a crystal ball!

She dried her eyes surreptitiously, but Richard noticed. "What is it, Tess?"

"Nothing," she breathed.

"You lie badly," he drawled, and he sat down on
the edge of the table and tilted her face up with one
hand. "Tell me, my love. Are you afraid?"

"I'm afraid for you, Richard," she said softly.

He smiled. "Silly twit." Then he leaned over and
kissed her on the lips, a sweet, soft joining.

She reached up and put her arms around his neck.
"Love me, Richard," she whispered ardently.

They came together in his narrow bunk with slow
tenderness. Tess showed no shyness or coyness and
Richard had no doubt of his male ability. He took the
lead and kept it, treating Tess as he would a precious
object.

She liked it. History had taught her mistakenly that
men in previous centuries had had their way with
women and, with no concern for a woman's pleasure,
had rolled away when they were done.

But history, at least in Richard's case, was wrong.

Richard was a practiced and careful lover. He kissed
her forever it seemed, unhurried, as if they had all the
time in the world to love each other. And then he
slipped her out of her clothes, button by button, his
mouth warm on her exposed flesh. He set her on fire,

slowly, deliberately, until she breathed that he was tormenting her, teasing her, trying to drive her wild.

"Ah," he whispered, his lips against her neck, "what would you do in your own time, Mistress Bonney?"

"This," she said, her body so ready to receive him it was a physical pain. Her eyes liquid and dark, Tess positioned herself above him, her slender legs straddling his hips. She put her hands on his chest and felt the tip of his hardness between her legs. "Am I too bold?" she whispered. "Am I hurting your leg?"

He groaned. "Never mind my damned leg!"

Tess rode him that way, her neck arched, her hips moving with his. He put his strong hands on her waist and guided her, and when she was about to cry out, her blood pounding, he flipped them both over so that he was on top of her and he thrust himself into her hard, once, and then she did cry out, grasping him to her, feeling his body as it shuddered against hers, inside her.

They made love again that night. Tess had awakened to the feel of him moving languidly against her until later, much later their loins again burned and ached for release.

It was Ruby who bestirred them. "Captain," he called through the door, rapping loudly, "we've made the Florida Straits!"

Tess raked a hand through her tousled hair and sat up, orienting herself.

"I'll be on deck shortly," Richard called and he pulled her down to him, kissing her soundly on the lips.

"What if Ruby...?" she began, grabbing the cover.

"Ruby knows your secret. He won't come in."

"Still..."

"But you best put on your breeches for the other lads, *Billy*. I won't be having them know I've brought a wench aboard."

"Billy I stay then," Tess said, and she extricated herself from his hold, playfully and teasingly looking over her shoulder as she dressed. "We *do* have a few minutes," Tess said, turning to him, her shirt unbuttoned provocatively.

But Richard was frowning. "Shh," he said, and that was when she first noticed it, too, the slapping of large waves on the ship's hull. "The sea's astir," he said, holding her gaze.

"The storm?" Tess held her breath.

"A storm for sure. A hurricane? That, my woman, only time will tell." Richard dressed in less than a minute's time, was out the cabin door, up the companionway and onto the quarterdeck before Tess even finished buttoning her shirt. It was then, as she stood there, that she realized it was the morning of September the fifth. In twenty-four hours...

THE STORM STRENGTHENED that afternoon, the *Marauder* running before a strong wind with only her storm topsails raised. The ropes groaned under the strain as the black-hulled ship dipped down into the trenches of the sea and came up shuddering, spilling froth across the deck and through the scuppers.

Tess stayed on deck, holding on to the rail, watching Richard brace himself at the helm. Every so often a tremor would course through the ship as the storm took on a life of its own, its breath fierce and growing worse.

Wiping the sea spray from her eyes, Tess glanced up at the bow lookout. It was a job for only the strongest at heart, for every pitch and roll on deck was multiplied tenfold at his position aloft.

"He's having a time of it," Ruby said at her ear, pointing upward.

"It's awful. Has he spotted the Spanish fleet yet?"

"Not yet. And in these seas . . . ?" Ruby shrugged. "Would you not be more comfortable below?" he asked.

Tess shook her head. "You wouldn't ask Billy that, I bet."

"Most assuredly not," Ruby agreed. "And I'll keep your secret if you'll tell me one more." He was practically shouting now over the howling of the wind in the rigging.

"What?"

"How is it you think the Spanish will be in these straits?"

"I can't tell you that, Ruby," she said. "But I will tell you something that you must swear to listen to no matter how crazy it sounds. Okay?"

"I'll listen," he said, but he looked puzzled.

"If anything happens to us, anything at all, I want you to promise you'll buy up a whole bunch of Red Turtle Cay and keep it for your sons."

"The land?"

"Yes. And you have to tell them to keep it for their sons, too. Okay?"

"Well . . . why?"

"I can only tell you that someday it's going to be worth a bundle. Now promise you'll try to do that."

"I . . ."

"Promise, Ruby."

"All right then, lass, I promise. But naught will happen. It's just a squall. She'll blow past by the evening bell. You'll see."

"Uh-huh," Tess said, "sure."

"And," Ruby said before he went to join Richard, "I want you to know that I pegged you for a lass the first minute I laid me eyes on you, Tess Bonney."

"Uh-huh."

Ruby's storm did not blow past them. By evening the sea was a furious mass of foam and towering waves, and the wheel was lashed in place as the ship rode the roiling waters, a black devil on the angry sea.

Every inch of the *Marauder* protested. The halyards and spars and rigging creaked and groaned, and the rudder strained to keep them on course. Richard remained at the helm, the ocean spume in his eyes, his legs braced to the pitch and roll of his ship. And still the Spanish had not been sighted.

Tess stayed on the deck until the water cascading through the scuppers threatened to carry her along and then, reluctantly, she made her unsteady way below.

The hours ticked away. Eight o'clock, nine, ten. No one could sleep, though there was little they could do except batten down as the ship was on her own, riding the violent sea, on course through the straits, a course that Tess could no longer guess. They were at the mercy of the oncoming hurricane.

Just before dawn, Richard, dripping, his face waxen, crashed through the door. Tess lifted her head from the table and blinked.

"We've sighted them!" he cried. "The bloody Spanish!" And just then the *Marauder* nosed into a trough. It seemed to take forever before she rose, nearly foundering before she shook and shuddered and Tess was thrown across the cabin, still on her chair.

"The storm?" she breathed, suddenly afraid as she tried to right herself.

"A full-fledged hurricane," Richard said as he made his way to her.

"You owe me breakfast in bed," Tess said with false cheer. "Remember, you promised."

"Tomorrow," he told her, helping her up, "tomorrow I'll string my mother's necklace about your white throat and serve you a fine meal. I swear it!"

"Oh, Richard," she said, "oh, God, I wish you could! But the necklace—"

"We will change your history," he said fervently. "Who's to say we can't?"

Despite the storm, the *Marauder* dogged the Spanish fleet as a gray, raging dawn took hold of the endless night. The *Marauder*, a black speck on the darkened sea, was nearly invisible. Richard gave orders for his men to prepare for battle, shouting against the wind, his eye never leaving the sight of the Spanish convoy as it scattered before the storm, a handful of gray vessels coming into his view when the *Marauder* rose upon the waves.

"Topsail ho!" he yelled from the quarterdeck, and his men scurried across the heaving deck to man the ropes. Untying the wheel, Richard put the ship on a new heading. Then, with all his strength, the waves now racing in to broadside them, he slipped the lashing back through the spokes of the wheel and tied her off. Still below deck, Tess felt the ship head on her new tack. No longer was she being slammed from fore to aft; now Tess was fighting the pitch from port to starboard. She could only assume Richard had a plan, perhaps to intercept the fleet at an angle. But in this storm... and with so many of them...

He wouldn't.

After struggling up from below, she made her way on deck, holding on for dear life, grasping at ropes, slipping, clinging to a crate, sliding, the sea a looming monster at one moment, a fallen beast the next. Somewhere a halyard gave and a block and tackle swung wildly until the crew untangled it from the rigging and secured it. And then she saw Richard at his post, shouting orders against the hurricane's fury. Everywhere the men prepared for a fight, lugging grapeshot to the cannons, fixing ropes, their strong, seaworthy legs braced against the pitch of the heaving deck.

Tess tried to keep her balance, watching the sea, gauging the next violent roll. And then she was beneath the helm, spray stinging her eyes, her clothes sodden. "Richard!" she yelled. "Richard!" But he couldn't hear her. Panic began to roil within her. They were all going to die! Right along with the crew of the *Isabela!*

The ship rose, riding a swell, the timbers shuddering and groaning in the wind, and Tess suddenly saw it to their port side—the towering *Isabela*.

"Ready fore cannons!" someone yelled above the unearthly howling of the wind.

"Ho! Load the grapeshot!"

They seemed to be heading directly at the galleon now, as if to broadside her, but Tess knew Richard would never risk it. No. He planned on putting a hole in her side and somehow, in this wild, hellish storm, boarding the vessel.

They'd all die, Tess knew suddenly, and Richard was never going to possess the necklace. Panic shot through her. She looked up, trying to see him through the slashing rain and spume. She cried out, "Richard! Let it go! Richard, no!"

Tess never finished her pleas. Driven on a hundred-mile-per-hour wind, a wave stopped her words cold in her throat. All she knew at the time was that one moment she was intent on getting Richard's attention, and the next instant she felt a crash against the hull of the ship. The giant swell heeled the *Marauder* over and washed Tess clear across the pitched deck.

She grabbed at anything and nothing, coming up with splinters in her hands. She screamed, seeing the rail ahead of her and the sea coming up to grab her. Then she was clutching at the rail, still being swept away, and insanely she thought she could hear his voice. "Tess! My God, Tess!" But the sea was coming up to take her, reaching for her, beckoning, and she was gone, sucked under, the gray and violent beast consuming her.

THE FOAM ROSE around her, oddly warm but choking, and once again she was falling into a trench as the sea surged and the wind drove the waves mercilessly.

I'm going to die, screamed through her mind as a wave crashed over her head. *This time I won't survive!*

And then she thought she heard her name carried on the slashing wind. "Tess! Tess, hold on!" She didn't have time to think or even to allow herself regret that in moments she was going to die; she could only fight to keep her head above water, to spit out the sea and gasp in air. And that was when she saw him, desperately making his way toward her, hanging on to a piece of planking. Richard. Thank God!

"Hold on!" came his cry again, and he disappeared for a moment as Tess was carried over the crest of a breaker. Then he was back in sight, swimming toward her. She fought furiously now, her arms exhausted from keeping her afloat. But he was so close now, only a few more seconds and . . .

He had her, grabbing her shirt and hauling her up and across the wood plank, yelling against the wind for her to hold on.

She couldn't speak. She coughed and choked and let her limbs go weak as she clung to the board with him. It didn't occur to her then that he'd given up his ship, his quest, his own life for hers. At the time all they could do was fight the mountainous ocean, and Tess thanked God that Richard was there to save her.

At some point she was aware of the *Marauder* nearby and hope sprang in her breast. But as they rode the crest of another wave she could see his ship being carried on the fierce wind, carried away from them.

"The ship!" she choked out as she felt his arm tighten across her back, holding her against the plank.

"She can't fight the wind!" he yelled against the howl in their ears.

It must have been only seconds before they saw another ship, though, bearing down on them, not the sleek black *Marauder,* but the fat-sided galleon, the *Isabela.* And just before it seemed that it would sail directly over them, a colossus looming so tall that Tess let out a scream, suddenly there was a rope in Richard's hand, the knots ripping through his fingers as the great ship swept past.

"I've got it!" Richard shouted. "Tess, hold on to me!"

She was aware of Richard's arm around her waist, the rope burning through his fingers, and suddenly they were being swept along, crashing through the huge waves as Richard got a firmer grip. They were hauled up then, up along the side of the galleon, slamming into it, twisting and turning as they rose from the water, two half-drowned souls that were being spared the gullet of the enraged sea.

After that everything happened quickly. Tess was aware of being dragged up and over the rail, Richard next to her. And then they were on the deck, lying facedown, panting and spitting up seawater. It raced through her dazed mind that she'd been in this exact spot before—at the mercy of the Spaniards on a great galleon.

Tess, however, was of little interest to them as the ship was flung across the sea. It was Richard they'd wanted all along. It was no miracle or humane attempt on the part of the Spaniards that had saved them. It was their hatred, their rage against Richard, because clearly they knew exactly whom they'd pulled from the ocean. One of the sailors dragged her to her feet, his big arm encircling her, and Richard came up from the deck growling, only to receive a boot in his ribs.

They treated him cruelly. Shoving Tess aside as if she was of no consequence, they vented all their fury on their deadliest enemy, *Ricardo Negro,* Black Richard Neville, the pirate.

Despite the storm and the imminent danger to the *Isabela,* the vice admiral and the governor of Cuba both appeared on the pitching deck, clinging to rails and lifelines, trying to brace themselves for the confrontation. Tess huddled against the rail and watched, horrified, as the governor made his unsteady way to Richard, who was lashing out, struggling against three sailors who were trying to hold him down.

"Richard Neville," the governor said, spreading his legs to keep from falling to the heaving deck, "you will hang this day!"

English, he spoke English, Tess registered, but then the governor and the vice admiral began to speak in Spanish and she couldn't understand a word.

A noose was being prepared, though; that much Tess could see. A scream began to well up inside her but something unfathomable kept her still. No one

was guarding her now. If she could just remain un-
noticed. . . .

"Go to hell!" Richard was shouting, lunging toward the governor. "You recall my brother, Thomas
Moore, you poxy swine? He's dead. *Muerto!* You understand! Your hellish bargain failed!"

The governor hurled back some insults in Richard's face, a babbling of Spanish and English. Tess
caught the word "hang" and the noose was brought.

It all was happening too fast, and her brain kept
screaming at her to do something, anything, and
Richard wasn't making it any easier, struggling, kicking out, cursing their souls to perdition. She was still
aware of the storm, with the waves crashing against the
hull and the wind tearing through the tall timbers of
the masts. And on the horizon, scattering before the
storm, she sighted the Spanish treasure fleet, fighting
for survival, each ship on its own. Even if the *Marauder* was out there among them she'd be battling the
storm, too, trying to flee to deeper waters. There'd be
no help coming from that quarter.

Through the veil of rain she looked back toward
Richard and saw that the governor was not there.
Where . . . ? Then she saw him coming down the steps
from the forecastle, just barely holding on with one
hand, his feet slipping out from under him when he hit
the main deck. Sailors, whose legs were more seaworthy, swarmed to him, righted him and helped him back
toward Richard and the vice admiral.

Tess looked up. Someone was fixing the rope to a
yardarm above Richard's head, the noose catching in
the wind, whipping from side to side until the vice ad-

miral shouted an order and one of the sailors caught it and dragged it toward Richard's neck.

The *Isabela* fell into a trench then, listing badly, and the vice admiral shouted orders, and the great ship creaked and groaned, righting herself until the next wave smashed into her.

Tess began to cast about frantically, aware that the two sailors who'd been watching her had raced off to their posts, far more afraid of the storm than the puny cabin boy who cowered on the slippery deck. She switched her gaze back to Richard, and that was the moment she saw it—the necklace, his mother's necklace dangling from the governor's hand. The man had gone to get it, gone to fetch the one thing he knew could further torment Richard before he was hanged!

Richard cursed, his words torn away on the screaming wind. Even as the noose was put around his neck, he fought furiously, lunging at the governor, damning the man to hell, the veins in his neck swelling.

A cry shuddered through Tess, a primitive, agonized shriek at the terrible injustice. Richard should not die at their hands! Not like this! *No!*

Her leg muscles tensed, her brain worked. As she was ready to claw her way to Richard's side, it came to her with sudden insight, an explosion of knowledge, and her rage seemed swept away in the howling wind, to be replaced by a strange calm.

This was all supposed to happen! The whole thing! From the moment she'd found that letter in the archives at Seville, this was the inevitable outcome.

Richard here. His mother's necklace. The ship. The storm . . .

And the whirlpool.

Her calm took hold. Even as Richard's fate at the hands of the Spanish was nearing, Tess knew that history was about to intervene. The question was: before or after Richard was hanged?

She waited, panting, the sea spray stinging her eyes. The vice admiral was giving orders, the governor grinning, his fear forgotten. The noose was tightened around Richard's neck and the wind keened eerily through the ropes.

The vice admiral took a halting step as the *Isabela*'s deck rolled. He started to nod at the three sailors who would haul the other end of the rope, and Tess felt her heart go dead. Richard . . .

"And now you die!" the governor roared as he held onto a crate for support, the necklace clasped in his free hand. "Die, Ricardo Negro!" he raged when the shout came abruptly from the poor, damned soul in the crow's nest. Suddenly Richard, Tess, everything was forgotten as sailors scrambled up the rigging and desperately tried to raise a foresail. Fascinated, horrified, Tess watched history unfold, knowing they were about to strike the reef, knowing that their attempt to claw their way back to deeper water was futile.

Shouts came from the vice admiral as he raced to the side of the ship, slipping, catching himself, slashed by rain and wind. Anchors were lowered, thrown into the sea in a last-ditch effort to keep the great galleon from being swept aground. But, again, Tess knew nothing would matter.

She looked back at Richard, her calm replaced by cold purpose. The instant they struck the reef she'd make her move. The whirlpool, she thought. Somewhere in that furious, foaming sea below them had to be their salvation.

She began to come to her feet, her eyes on Richard and the governor who still guarded him where he was bound to the mast. And that was when the impact came, rending her guts.

The sound was awful, a grinding and tearing, the death cry of the great sailing ship as she struck the reef, her hull opening in a mortal wound.

And then she listed terribly.

Tess scrambled across the heaving deck as bedlam reigned throughout the galleon. Men were slithering, thrown right past her against the rail. The governor crashed to the decking, his body utterly still, the necklace gripped in his beringed fingers.

She crawled toward him and heard Richard shouting her name, crying for her to save herself. But Tess shut out his words, saying to herself over and over, "We'll make it, we'll both make it. Please, God, please..."

She reached the governor and pried the necklace from his fingers. Clutching it, she clawed her way, hand over hand, across the crazily tilted deck toward Richard.

"No!" he yelled. "Save yourself!"

Men were rushing everywhere, terrified, fighting for balance as the ship continued to list, over, over, onto her side. Screams and frenzied cries tore through the rain-slashed air. A mast cracked like a musket shot, splintered, fell, crushing passengers who were crawling out of a door. Tess kept moving, clutching at ropes, crates, tackle, pulling herself along toward Richard, closing her mind to the terrible death around her.

She reached him and dragged herself up by the ropes binding him to the mast. "You fool!" he yelled, "go over the side! I beg you, Tess!"

"Shut up!" she screamed back at him as she ripped at the ropes holding him, the knots soaked, swollen, impossible.... She got one loose.

"No!" he shouted again. "Save yourself!"

She freed one of his arms. He pulled the noose over his head and it caught in the wind again, a chilling sight as it stood out against the black, raging sky while the galleon wailed and groaned her pain.

"Your feet!" Tess screamed, "I can't get the ropes—"

But Richard got them, struggling desperately against his bonds, trying to keep Tess upright while freeing himself with his other hand.

The *Isabela* was spinning helplessly now, masts cracking, cannons falling into the churning sea one by one. The wind was ferocious, watching the ship's torn topsails and dragging her across the reef. Sailors and passengers alike leaped into the hungry sea, screaming, grabbing on to anything that might float.

"So what now?" Richard yelled into Tess's ear as they clung to the mast and a huge wave slammed across the deck. "What is your plan?" He grinned into the face of death.

"We go overboard!" she shouted back.

"And die in the sea?"

"No! We live! You have to trust me!" She looked into his face, her body buffeted by the wind and rain. "We have to go! But hold my hand tight! Don't let go of me!"

"You are a fool! A brave fool! But I'll die by your side, lass, and to heaven we'll ride together!"

A body swept by them and Tess, the necklace clutched in her hand, took a long, deep breath. "Now!" she cried. "We'll go together now!"

Richard put an arm tightly around her waist and she saw him loosening his grip on the mast, hesitating.

"Now, Richard! We're going to a new life!"

He gave her one last searching look as the *Isabela* shuddered beneath their feet and then he let go. The last thing Tess felt was the strength of his hold on her and then they were in the sea, sinking, sinking, swallowed by its furious, hungry maw. Somewhere, somehow, as if she were in the last dredges of a dream, Tess was aware of the necklace being ripped out of her hand, torn away, and there was only blackness and Richard by her side.

CHAPTER TWELVE

TESS FOUGHT THE CURRENT, her lungs bursting. In a second she'd have to take a breath, but there was only water around her, racing, murky water that tossed her like a scrap of buoyant trash. Above her was brightness, and she fought toward it, knowing that she'd done this before, that she could do it this time, once again, before she was swallowed and drowned. But Richard was with her, a shadowy figure grasping her in an iron grip, and he was also battling his way up to the sunlight.

The whirlpool was weakening, the light was stronger, and just as Tess began to suck in that deadly liquid breath, she was spit out, her head breaking the surface.

She drew in a lifesaving lungful of air, gasping and sputtering, her legs scissoring automatically, trying to keep her head above the glassy, sunlit surface of the sea. And then she turned to Richard, who was gulping in air next to her, and cried out in wonder, "Richard, I think we—"

She heard it then and so did he—an engine, the roar of a motorboat nearing. Her mind registered for a split second that this would be incredibly strange to Richard, but she heard a voice calling, "There she is!" and it was Paul's voice. My Lord, it was her brother Paul!

THE MAIN CABIN of the *Seahunt* was a shabby affair, except for the bank of controls, the radio, the wires and antenna and ship-to-shore apparatus. Four people sat in the cabin: Paul Bonney, Mack Solomon, Tess and Richard. The atmosphere was supercharged with disbelief and tension and heart-stopping relief.

"You were under too long," Paul said. "When I surfaced I realized it pretty quickly. You should have been up by then because I knew you'd be out of air. God, I panicked. So I jumped into the motor boat and gunned it, and when I got to the reef you popped up with—" Paul gestured toward Richard "—with this guy."

"I've told you a dozen times already," Tess said, her head bowed in weariness, "his name is Richard Neville."

"Right. And he's from the seventeenth century. Right."

"Believe what you—" Tess began again but Richard put up a hand.

"It's no use badgering the woman, Paul Bonney," he said. "Believe what you will." He smiled thinly and from his seat glanced around at the bare metal walls and cabin controls on the *Seahunt*. "I'll say one thing. I am damned glad to be here, no matter the circumstances."

Paul and Mack studied him. "So you're English," Mack said, his weathered hand rubbing his chin.

"And you say you were chasing the *Isabela* in a hurricane."

Richard turned to him. "Aye, that we were."

"Look," Paul insisted. "You both must have passed out or something. Dreamed the whole thing."

"Our clothes, too?" Tess asked. Paul fell silent. "And how about Richard himself," she went on. "How'd he get here?"

Richard rose, still in his wet clothes, his high boots and breeches and torn white linen shirt, his gold earring and his patch, and even before he spoke, his presence commanded the men's attention. He stood in that aluminum and plastic cabin, in a place and a time that he couldn't even conceive of, and he looked calmly from Mack to Paul. "Gentlemen," he said, "I suggest we refrain from trying to answer these riddles. I fear it'll get us nowhere. The problem here, as Paul pointed out earlier, will be to explain my presence."

Paul hadn't pointed it out, Tess thought. He'd just not believed her story, but Richard wasn't giving anyone time to consider that.

"I feel that I know you good men already," Richard continued. "It is truly a great pleasure to meet brethren who search for the treasure that I once lost. Men after my own heart," he said in his strong, ringing voice, and then he flashed them both his arrogant, charming smile. "And, by God, I repeat, I'm glad to be here in your time and not at the bottom of the sea with the poxy *Isabela!*"

"Well spoken, young man," Mack Solomon said, breaking out in a genuine smile. "You're welcome here, wherever you're from, but I have one question."

Richard regarded him levelly. "Ask away."

"Are you going to be satisfied here? What I mean is, are you going to try to find that whirlpool again?"

Richard threw back his head and laughed, striking the exact same pose as the first time Tess had seen him. "Not bloody likely," he said.

"I still don't get it," Paul said. "I mean, there is no such thing as time travel."

"I'm not so sure," came hesitantly from Mack. And then he looked up and swallowed, holding Paul's gaze. "What I'm saying is that I thought I saw something out on the open water."

"Oh, come on," Paul began but again Richard put up a hand.

"Let the man have his say."

"I don't know," Mack started once more. "There was a bank of fog on the reef. You saw it, Paul. I pointed it out just before you took the launch to find Tess."

Paul thought back a moment. "I suppose there was."

"It was odd," Mack went on. "A perfectly clear day. Odd."

"What did you see, Mack?" Tess urged.

He gave a nervous laugh. "I, uh, thought I saw a ship in the fog…a galleon," he barely managed to say. "Just before the fog dissipated. A goldarn Spanish galleon riding the sea."

There was a long, hushed moment in the cabin. Mack looked from one to the other for help.

"It was the *Isabela*," Tess whispered finally. "You saw her!"

Mack gave another short laugh. "Yes," he said, nodding now. Mack, the visionary, the romantic, the man who'd spent over half a lifetime searching for the elusive mother of all treasure ships, the *Isabela*, said, "Yes, by God, I really did see her!"

Richard had a twinkle in his eye as silence once more held them in its embrace, each with his own thoughts. Paul sank onto a bench, Mack kept rubbing his jaw and Tess breathed a sigh of utter relief.

After a time, Richard moved toward the window and gazed out on the sea, his hands clasped at his back, his legs astride to the roll of the boat. Quietly he said, "The sea holds many secrets. She is a fickle woman, but a lady nonetheless. This day she has given us a miracle—she has given me a new life. And the *Isabela*? Aye, I suppose she is a lady, also," he said, giving a short laugh. "Even I felt a sadness when the fat-sided beauty began to founder."

"You saw her sink?" Mack asked.

"I daresay the ship went down shortly, though Tess and I were rather busy." He turned to Tess. "Weren't we?"

She nodded, remembering. "And then I dropped the necklace. I'm so sorry, Richard."

"Hey," Mack said, "if your story's true, then you had to drop it, Tess, for the necklace to show up in the future. Well, *now,* that is."

"My head hurts," Paul said.

"No, wait," Tess persisted. "Mack's right. It's still down there. Of course it is!"

Richard's face was resolute. "If that's true, God willing, I lay claim to that one piece. I set out to get it back from the Spanish, and it seems my search is not yet over."

"We'll find it, Richard," Mack said, "just like I'll find the *Isabela* herself, the mother lode. Sooner or later we'll find it."

"We *will* find it," Tess said, "but first, Richard, what are we going to do about you?"

"Me?"

"You've got to have come from somewhere. People will wonder."

"Let them."

"No," Mack said, "Tess is right." He thought a moment. "Why not just say he's from one of the remote British islands, a recluse, whatever. Tell people he lost his boat on the reef, and he's staying in Key West doing some work for me until he can afford a new boat. No one will question that. It's not even much of a risk for him."

"A risk?" Richard said. "I don't mind a bit of a risk now and again, you know."

"Oh, God," Tess whispered, and Paul gave her a curious glance.

It was Paul, though, who offered his apartment to them for the night. "There's this all-nighter out on the Trenville boat," he said. "Someone's birthday party. I was going, anyway." Then he looked at his sister. "Or maybe I should stay home, Tess? You gonna be okay?"

"I'll be fine, Paul. You go ahead. Sounds like something you shouldn't miss. We'll be okay."

Paul narrowed his gaze and gave a sharp look at Richard. "You sure?"

"Oh, for goodness' sake, Paul, I'm a big girl," Tess answered, flushing.

The *Seahunt* docked that afternoon, and Paul drove them to his apartment. Richard wore some dry clothes Mack had provided, and Tess had put on the shorts and T-shirt that she'd left on the *Seahunt* that morning, even though it still seemed to her she'd been gone for months. Her rags and Richard's shirt and breeches and boots had been weighted down and tossed into the water.

She watched Richard, wondering how he was taking all this newness bombarding him. She remembered her own bewilderment, the alien strangeness of everything. Richard seemed to be taking it in stride, though, curious about everything, asking questions, marveling. His exuberance was infectious, and even Paul had allowed a grin when Richard first saw the pickup truck and said, "Gad, where are the bloody horses?"

"Under the hood," Paul had replied.

But Tess remained very quiet, squeezed next to Richard on the pickup's narrow seat, thinking uneasy thoughts. Shouldn't Richard be horrified, paralyzed, as she had been when she'd found herself in a different time? At least a little nervous?

But, no, Richard seemed to be untouched by what had happened to him, to them. Heck, this was all an exciting new adventure for him. He was a thrill junky. She'd been right all along.

"Does everyone here drive a carriage like this?" Richard asked Paul.

"A truck, or a different kind called a car. Almost everyone. You have to be sixteen years old and take a test. Then you get your license," Paul explained.

"Would you show me how?" Richard asked. "Is that an acceptable thing to do here?"

"Sure, man, I'll teach you to drive. It's a cinch."

"A cinch," Richard said to himself.

Richard turned his face up, and Tess wondered for a moment, but then she heard the drone of a plane. She leaned forward and said, "That's an airplane. I told you. They have engines that pull them through the air."

"I recall that, yes," Richard said. "And all these moving things of yours, they all use the same source of power?"

"Gas," Paul answered. "Gasoline, which comes from oil, which is in the ground in certain places."

Richard turned in his seat and continued to watch the commuter plane as it banked on approach to the Key West airport. "I vow," he said, "only a madman would leave the safety of this solid earth to fly through the air."

"There's a lot of folks who agree with you whole-heartedly on that one," Paul concurred.

It was only a few blocks more before Paul pulled up to his apartment, unlocked the door and showed them in, flicking on the ceiling fans.

"Listen, you guys, I'm going to take a quick shower and change and then I'm outta here. There's some food in the fridge, I think," Paul said, shrugging apologetically.

"Don't worry about us, really, Paul."

Her brother put his arm around her shoulders and gave her a squeeze. "I'm sure glad you're okay, Tess. You had me scared there for a minute."

"You don't really believe what happened, do you?" she asked quietly.

"Not really, but then I don't *not* believe it, either. I guess I'll just have to take it on faith," Paul said thoughtfully.

"That's fair."

"Besides," he said, "Richard here seems like an all right guy."

"I am grateful," Richard said facetiously, bowing like a courtier.

"Nice move," Paul said admiringly.

While Paul showered, Tess sat on the sturdy wicker chair in the one big, partitioned room that was his apartment. Richard paced, going from the kitchen to the big windows and back, touching the humming refrigerator, gazing at the passing cars outside, feeling the paint on the walls. She tried to see the place through his eyes: blue-striped carpet, tiled floor, three ceiling fans turning lazily, the entire place decorated in shades of pastel blue with a full wall of shelves covered with old bottles found on the ocean floor, seashells and turtle shells. There was a ship's wheel in the corner, and through glass doors could be seen a patio with a grill and a hammock and Paul's gray cat crying to be let in.

"Uh, I'll let the cat in," Tess said, suddenly uncomfortable. She got up and slid the door open, and the cat darted in and went to his food dish. Then she sat down again and stared at the floor, at her lap, at the wall of shells and bottles, and couldn't think of a single word to say.

"This is Paul's house?" Richard asked, breaking the awkward silence.

"He rents it."

"Do you, too, have a house like this, Tess?"

She shrugged. "I have a small apartment in Miami, where I work."

"Who is turning the fans?" Richard asked. "I vow, I am curious about that." He stared at the ceiling.

"Electricity runs them. Lights, too. I'm sorry, but I'm not really sure about how electricity is produced, or I'd explain it to you. It's a kind of power that comes through wires to our houses."

The uneasy silence fell again. All that had been between them—the love, the passion, the closeness and caring—seemed to have evaporated in this mundane present-day reality. For a moment, Tess wished she could be back on board the *Marauder* as Billy the cabin boy. She sighed. Richard, of course, wasn't in the least unsettled. He was bursting with that energy of his, excited, seeing her world with unjaded eyes.

He noticed her finally, sitting there stiffly. "You are sad, Tess," he said. "Why? We have come to your time. Is that not what you wanted? You held me to our bargain, lass, and here you are."

"Yes," she said, "it's just that... I don't know. Everything's different. I didn't think you'd be here, too."

"You're not comfortable with me here, Tess. I intrude," Richard said, uncharacteristically serious.

She looked up quickly. "Oh, don't say that! I wished... I wanted... Oh, God, Richard, you had nowhere else to go." She stopped short and looked at him. "Is this what you would have wanted, Richard? If you'd been given the choice?"

He gave a low laugh, completely at his ease, an elegant, proud figure even in Mack's faded old clothes. "Is this—" he gestured around him with a hand "—is this what I would have chosen? Aye, Tess, that it is. It's as if I had died and gone to heaven, my girl. You know it, you said it yourself. I had no life left in that time past. Nothing save Ruby, and he was a good friend, the best, but he has—*had*—a family of his own, a life. I had none. I was alone. No one will miss me." And then he cocked his head. "I do wonder what became of Ruby and my ship, though. Ruby was a skilled sailor. Perhaps the *Marauder* survived the storm."

"It could have," Tess said. "Other ships did that day."

"Mmm," Richard murmured.

Tess had to smile a little. "And what about Matilda?"

"She'll find another man, the wench." Richard looked at Tess abruptly, a dawning knowledge in his eye. "It comes to me that you were there, Tess, that first night we got back to the Crow's Nest.... Gad, and I thought you were—"

"Don't remind me," she said, blushing.

"I owe you an apology for that one," Richard said, and Tess saw that he really was discomfited.

"Never mind," she said. "It was an honest mistake."

"She meant nothing to me," Richard said hastily.

Paul came out of his room then, his dark hair damp and combed neatly, wearing white slacks, Top-Sider shoes and a patterned madras shirt. "So, I'm off. You need anything before I go?"

"No, Paul, we're okay."

Then Paul offered, "Richard, you're welcome to use my electric razor. Just clean it out when you're done, okay?"

That uncomfortable silence filled the room again as soon as the door closed behind Paul. Tess got up and wandered around, touching the old encrusted bottles, spinning the ship's wheel. "I'm going to take a shower," she said. She laughed self-consciously. "I've been waiting months to take a real shower."

"This shower, can you show me what it is?" Richard asked.

"Sure, it's in the bathroom. Well, some people have bathtubs, too, but Paul only has a shower stall." She led him into the bathroom. "See, that's the toilet, the sink, the shower there. Water comes in pipes from storage reservoirs into our houses, and it's pumped to faucets like these."

"This is a privy, too? Right inside the house?" he asked.

"It sure is."

"Well, I'll be damned!" He put his head back and laughed. "And how does this contraption operate?" He nodded at the shower stall.

"It's easy. One knob controls hot water, the other the cold. You mix them and get the temperature that's comfortable for you."

"Show me this."

Tess leaned into the stall and turned both knobs, feeling the water with her hand.

"Hmm, I see. It looks to be a simple task."

"It is," she said, straightening, turning.

Richard was there, close behind her, so close she drew in her breath. "Does one take a shower while dressed?" he asked softly.

"Uh, no," she said, "your clothes would get wet."

"I thought not. See, already I am becoming a modern man. So, I must disrobe, Tess?"

"Well, sure, if you want to take one first, I'll just—"

"Not at all. You've waited months, you said. But I think you should show me how to do this new thing." A small smile tugged at Richard's lips. "What say you, Tess?" He began to unbutton his shirt in the close, steamy room as the water rattled against the walls of the shower stall.

"Richard..." she breathed.

He took off the shirt and started on the pants. "Does one always take a shower alone? Is there some rule I am not privy to?"

"Usually, uh, well, there's no rule, but..."

He stepped out of the pants and stood before her as she remembered him, hard-muscled and beautiful, the scars of his new wounds still livid, the old ones white lines and ridges on his smooth skin. "Well, Tess? Are you afraid of me now? You were never afraid before," he said gently.

"I'm not afraid."

"Shall I help you take those garments off?" he asked. "We wouldn't want them to become wet, although, I confess, they don't seem to be very sturdy. They barely cover you, lass. Do all women wear such scanty things?"

"Yes. No," she said, feeling heat curl in her belly.

"Why, men must be at them like billy goats if they wear such clothes in public," he said, reaching out to gather the bottom of her T-shirt.

"They get used to it."

"Aye, I believe that." He pulled the shirt over her head and dropped it. "And this—" he touched the fly front of her cutoffs "—what do you call it?"

"A zipper."

"Mmm, a zipper. Clever invention, and is this how it works?" He pulled it down and the shorts fell to the floor. "Ah, I believe I've mastered it."

"Richard," she said again, "you don't have to...are you sure?"

He looked at her, searching her face, levity gone. "Aye, Tess Bonney, I'm as sure as ever a man could be."

"But...it's different, Richard. Everything's different," she said breathlessly.

"Is this different?" He touched her lips with his, softly, then harder, and her mouth opened under his. "Is it, Tess?"

"No," she whispered, her arms going around him.

"Or this?" He ran his hands down her back with long, smooth strokes and bent his head to kiss her neck, her shoulder, the white swell of her breast. "Tell me, lass," he asked, his lips against the tender skin of her throat, "do men and women make love differently in this time of yours? Must I learn a whole new technique?"

She moaned a little, deep in her throat, and held him close. "No, Richard."

"Do we go under this shower now?" he asked. "I'm curious."

For a long moment, Tess studied his bronzed face, the blue surety of his eye. Richard knew what he wanted. He was a man whose life followed straight and unbroken lines despite anything and everything fate threw in his path. It was so easy for him.

"Come," he whispered, "join me."

Still, she hesitated, even as he stepped into the stall and reached a hand toward her. She wanted him, every fiber of her being craving this man, but suddenly her desire was tinged by anxiety, some unknown obstacle crouching deep within her.

"Come, lass," he coaxed, "it is only me." And slowly, uncertainty eating at her, Tess took his hand and went to him.

CHAPTER THIRTEEN

TESS MADE THE BED the next morning, then headed for the shower, forcing herself not to look out the window another time. Richard had insisted he could walk the two blocks to the Cuban grocery store and purchase espresso coffee for them, a Key West morning ritual. She'd given him a few dollars, gone over and over the procedure. He'd laughed at her worry.

"I could stand on your street corner and announce I was from the past and do you think anyone would believe me?"

"They'd lock you up."

"There," he'd said, "you see? And besides, my Tess, I'm going to relish handing money to a Spaniard who will not seek to see me hanged!"

"Oh, God," was all she'd said.

Dripping wet, towel wrapped around her, Tess hurried to the window. Where was he? But then she saw him, standing on the corner, holding two plastic coffee cups and shaking his head at the morning Conch Train that ran through Old Town filled with tourists.

She heard the driver saying over the intercom, "And this is the Haitian Art Gallery on your left. Just ahead is the cemetery."

Someone even leaned out the side of the open train and snapped a picture of Richard standing under a palm tree with his coffees and distinctive eye patch. He must have thought Richard a true conch—a local, and a funky one at that. Richard bowed facetiously, enjoying himself.

"Oh, boy," Tess whispered. He was having himself a swell old time, seemingly unconcerned about the many problems he was going to face adjusting to this new world and new time. Anyone else would be gaping and cowering, at least a little intimidated. But not him. Oh, no. It was Tess who was doing all the worrying.

They took a walk later that morning, Richard as curious as a cat at everything he saw, full of a thousand questions, Tess just plain concerned about his future. "You'll need a social security card and a driver's license. Oh, God, how are we going to get you that? And a bank account. A credit card, too."

"Stop fretting," he said, marching alongside her, tucking her arm into his, "we've all the time in the world."

"Someone's got to worry," Tess complained.

"What in God's name is *that?*" he asked, steering her across the street.

"The local eyesore—the power plant." She had to explain how it worked and provided the island with the energy it required.

Cameras really fascinated him. Tess finally took him inside a camera shop and paid a salesman five dollars to snap their picture with one of his Polaroid cameras. Richard stood there holding it as their shapes took form and color. "'Tis a miracle," he kept saying, "a treasure."

"He's from Mars," Tess quipped to the salesman.

When they left the shop, Richard still staring at the picture, he said, "I shall keep this forever."

"It's a real work of art," she said and led him on.

He was drinking in every new sight and sound and experience like a man long denied water. And he was thoroughly enjoying himself, not a bit out of place, confidently striding alongside Tess, laughing and making jests, already deciding which model car he preferred.

"Aren't you the least bit taken aback by any of this?" Tess asked.

"Certainly not," he said cheerfully. "I'm a man reborn into the most wonderful of times."

"It's not *that* wonderful," Tess snapped and then asked herself why. Why were his good mood and self-assurance annoying her? She should be happy for him.

They headed toward the waterfront, Richard wanting to see what ships and boats there were, declaring he'd need to decide what kind of vessel he would prefer.

"And how will you pay for this vessel?" Tess asked pertly.

"I daresay I'll manage," he told her. "I always have."

A cruise ship was in port, and the narrow streets and shops were packed with Swedes. Richard listened to their speech, marveling. "Vikings," he remarked, "but somewhat tamed."

Tess explained that the ship would be gone by five, but that tomorrow another one would dock from some other foreign port.

"Railroad trains, great ships and your airplanes," Richard said. "Man is free to go where he will, when he will. It truly is a grand world I've come to."

"Money's the key," Tess said, shrugging.

"And so it was in my time."

He couldn't fathom the number of shops on Duval Street, all crowded with tourists. "Does everyone in this new world wear T-shirts?"

"Just about."

And then they stopped by a coin shop where Tess pointed out pieces of eight and silver coins from a treasure ship salvaged ten years ago. "Of course this ship went down at the end of your century," she said, and Richard vowed he was having a hard time getting history straight. She laughed. "Nothing new there," she said. "You should hear my students on the subject."

They walked on and Tess thought about her students and her job. She'd only been gone from this time for a few minutes, and yet it did seem like centuries.

At lunch in an oyster bar where Richard wanted to watch the boats coming and going inside the harbor, Tess couldn't help notice the attention he drew. She realized he'd been getting this attention all along, everywhere they went. From women.

She sipped on her conch chowder and stared at him, the spoon poised midway to her mouth.

He *was* one handsome man. Four hundred years ago. Today. Four hundred years in the future. Richard Neville was always going to turn female heads. It was his charisma, she decided. It oozed from every cell in his body.

An unaccountable gloom began to settle over her. She tried to identify it. She began to wonder if she was upset because he was taking everything so easily, as carefree as a bird. He didn't need her. Maybe that was it. In his time she'd needed Richard to survive. In her time he was adjusting quickly and almost carelessly. She ate her lunch lethargically, her mind working. What *did* he really need her for? She'd expected him to lean on her, but apparently it wasn't going to happen like that.

Richard held an oyster shell to his lips and let the raw flesh slide down his throat. "You do not like your soup?" he asked.

"It's fine."

"But something is amiss."

"Nothing's *wrong*. We don't say amiss anymore."

"It seems a small thing to be upset over, Tess."

"You're right. It doesn't matter. People will just think you're an eccentric Englishman, that's all."

"Well," he said, laughing, "and so I am." He went back to his oysters and stared out the window at a lovely, white-sailed schooner that was navigating the harbor buoys.

"Pretty, isn't she?" Tess asked.

"A real beauty in any time. Perhaps I'll have one like that."

"You should have brought your treasure with you. You could afford one then."

"Ah, there are always treasures to be made and lost, Tess. Half the pleasure is in making them."

"But surely it bothers you to be broke...penniless."

He shrugged. "With all this new world surrounding me, how can I be penniless?"

They finished eating and Tess suddenly announced, "Listen. You seem to be doing okay on your own. I've got an errand I want to run and—"

"I'll be fine," he said. "You go about your business."

"Are you sure?"

He only shook his head at her indulgently.

"Then I'll see you back at my brother's," Tess said. "I guess you remember the way."

"That I do."

She had no errand; she only wanted to get away from Richard for a time to think. He was so overpoweringly optimistic that he confused Tess. She knew there would be more problems for Richard than he expected, and she was worried.

She felt glum, worse than at lunch. A knowledge was settling in her, and Tess did not like it at all. She'd believed Richard needed her, imagined he might even cling to her for a while, but just the opposite was happening. She walked, head bowed, and thought that he'd loved her in his time, loved Billy and later a courageous Tess, but women like her were commonplace in the 1990s, and soon, real soon, Richard was going to make that discovery.

When she got to Paul's apartment she flopped down into one of his wicker chairs and tried to think. She didn't try for long, though, because the phone rang.

It was Mack Solomon. "Is Richard there, Tess?"

"No, he's still downtown. Can I take a message?"

"No, actually I wanted to talk to you. Can you come over for a bit this afternoon?"

So Tess walked over to Mack's lovely old conch house and settled herself on a lawn chair across from him with a glass of wine in her hand.

"Well," he said, leaning forward, elbows on his knees. "I have an idea, but I wanted to try it out on you first. It's about Richard."

"Go on," she said.

"I think I'm in a particularly good position to help Richard."

"Richard is sure going to need help," Tess said. "Although he doesn't even know it yet."

"I know. He's going to need identification, a place to live, some money."

"Yes," Tess said. "I just can't figure out what to do. But Richard doesn't seem to worry about anything."

"And you're worried sick. I can see that," Mack said kindly. "But I believe I've got it all figured out."

"What are you thinking?"

He drank from a beer bottle. "It's going to take time for Richard to adjust," Mack said. "I know he's enthusiastic...."

"Very."

"But there'll still be problems. Bound to be a few, anyway. I think he should come and live here in my son's old room. Live with us. I've spoken to Kitty. She agrees. It would be good to have a young man around again."

Tess felt tears brim in her eyes. "I'm sorry," she said, wiping them away. "But you're so nice to do that."

"It will be our pleasure. And yesterday, when we spoke about a cover story for him, working as one of my crew, I was serious. The pay's terrible, but he'll get along, especially if he lives with us until he's situated. Heck, Tess, he'll be one big asset to my crew."

"I guess he will be at that," she said. "What better crew member to have around than the man who sank the ships in the first place?"

"Exactly."

"And identification? All that? It's going to cost."

"I'll see to it. I'm sure Richard will repay my investment a thousand times over."

"You...you're a very good man, Mack Solomon."

"I try to be." And then he looked at her solemnly. "What about you, Tess? I thought you fitted into this scheme somehow. If I'm off base, tell me and I'll shut up."

She told him, her eyes averted, a finger rubbing the rim of her wineglass, around and around. "I think it's for the best," she finished. "He needs his space now. And I guess I do, too. I've got my job and my life up in Miami."

Mack eyed her soberly. "Does Richard know you're planning on going back to Miami, Tess?"

She couldn't meet his questioning gaze. "No," she said, knowing in her heart at that moment that she'd really have to give Richard up. For his sake and for hers. "But I'll tell him."

"And how's he going to take it?"

She looked up then and tried to smile. "Oh, I suppose he'll take it in stride, just like he's taken everything else."

Mack nodded. "So, you'll suggest it to Richard? I thought it might be better coming from you."

"Sure, I'll do it."

After she left Mack, she wondered what was the best way to handle the situation. It needed planning and Tess planned to do it just the right way. She walked back toward Francis Street in the close September heat, the flowering vines and shrubs drooping lifelessly, and played the upcoming scene out in her mind. Watch the sunset. Have dinner. Walk the nighttime streets and tell him gently. He'd object, being the gentleman that he was, but he'd also know she was right.

What a martyr you are, Tess thought, but she knew in her heart this was the only way. She put a smile on her face and trudged on through the thick heat.

RICHARD WAS WAITING for her in Paul's apartment when she returned. She listened as he talked a little about the afternoon's adventures, but her heart was heavy and she found it hard to concentrate. A little later, Tess, proceeding with her plan, invited Richard to go for an evening stroll with her. Together they watched the sunset out on Mallory Square with hoards of tourists. Another island ritual. And it was a perfect close to the day, the sun sliding into the silvery water, the sky glowing orange and pink and lavender through the ever-present humidity haze over the Gulf of Mexico, music drifting on the heavy air, sweating glasses clinking in salute.

"I never watched the sun setting before. Well," Richard said, "I did, to take a directional reading, of course. But I never saw the beauty of it, the finality of the day."

"Nice, huh?" Tess said.

"Another thing I'll come to enjoy about this world."

"So," she said, propping her feet on the rail of the pier, "what else did you do all afternoon?"

He looked at her and seemed to make up his mind. "I observed your women."

"You... Oh, of course you did. Their clothes, or lack of them?"

"Precisely. I vow, Tess, you should have warned me. I damned near got run over by a car once when this pair of six-foot-long legs caught my attention."

Tess laughed. Inside she died. Her predictions were coming true. "So, do you like *my* shorts?" she asked, showing him a trim leg.

"I do. But then so does every man on this dock."

"Jealous?"

"No. Just making an observation."

"Mmm," Tess murmured, disappointed despite his honesty.

They finished their drinks and left the pier, milling along with the crowds. Street people hawked their wares on Duval Street. Young college types stood on corners handing out leaflets for restaurants, island tours, deep-sea fishing trips, seaplane excursions.

"It's the tourist business," Tess explained.

"Is the whole world in this business?" he asked, taking a leaflet from someone.

"No. But it sometimes seems that way." She went on to tell him about the Florida coasts, the many resorts. She explained about skiing in the north then had to explain how every corner of the earth was populated now. Mexico City alone had a population of about ten million people. "In your time England and Wales had only about three million, so you can see how people have multiplied. We'll buy you an atlas," she said, "and you can study it, get a feel for the world."

He announced that he was hungry, but he was uncomfortable using Tess's plastic card for his needs. "I intend to speak to Mack Solomon," he said, "and seek employment. I think the man will have me. After all, I do possess a fair amount of knowledge I'll wager he'd find of use."

Tess stopped and stared at him. "You make that sound like... Don't you think you're being pushy?"

Richard frowned. "Not at all. A business arrangement is all I will ask. You must understand, I have not forgotten, nor will I ever forget that my mother's necklace lies at the bottom of the sea. I still want it back."

"What about the rest of the *Isabela?*"

"Oh, I can locate her for Mack Solomon and—"

"*Richard.* You're sounding awfully egotistical. It's been almost four hundred years and Mack's been searching for twenty years and..."

"Ah," Richard said, steering her toward a tiki-style, open restaurant, "you forget. We were on board when the galleon began to break up. We knew the wind direction, the ocean current—"

"Maybe *you* did. I was kind of busy."

"It's in my blood, Tess. I recall those details without real thought. You understand?"

"And I suppose you know where other treasure ships are located?"

He grinned wickedly. "A few, lass. I do have that knowledge."

She wanted to ask him just how much he'd extract from Mack to divulge this knowledge, but thought better of it. Mack was a romantic, true, but he was also a darn good businessman. He'd handle Richard just fine. Still, as they were seated at a table in the lush gardens, Tess couldn't help seeing Richard as the pirate he was. In the past he'd had an excuse, the world against him at every turn. But here . . . ?

The night was hot. Windless. And a fine mist covered everything. Above their heads the palm fronds were utterly still, a canopy keeping in the heat. But then, it *was* summer.

"Tomorrow," Richard said, taking her hand across the table, "I will speak to him first thing."

And then, of course, she had to tell him about the arrangements Mack had already made. "Mack really wants you to live at his place until you're situated," Tess went on, her eyes on her folded hands. "I think you should take him up on the offer. A job, a place to stay. It's not that easy to get settled here," she finished lamely.

He was silent for a minute, studying her. "I believe you feel a responsibility toward me," he said at last. "But I assure you, Tess, I will do well on my own."

"I guess we should have asked you first."

"Aye, that you should have. But I understand. In truth you've been ill at ease for the last day."

"You're right. And I don't see why you aren't. How can everything be so simple for you?"

"I came from a hard time to a far better one. I feel nothing but enthusiasm. Is this so wrong?"

"No," Tess whispered. "I'm the one who's confused."

He squeezed her hand. "Don't be, my lass. I'll see to our needs."

She told him the rest of her plans while they walked the waterfront after dinner. She didn't know how he was going to take the news that she was leaving; she knew only that Richard was going to be starting a new life—he already had begun it—and that she owed him his freedom. Besides, Tess wasn't sure how she felt anymore. She loved him whether or not he loved her. But she needed her space, as well. *Time will tell,* she thought.

"I'm going home tomorrow," she announced and forced a smile.

"Home?"

"To Miami."

"But..."

"Richard, I've got to finish my thesis. I have a job." She shrugged matter-of-factly.

He stopped striding then and stood, legs braced, arms folded stiffly across his chest as he stared out across the darkened water. He was too still, as still as the night, a part of the setting, the harbor, the sea, the heavy hot air. They could have been on Red Turtle Cay, and instead of that sleek fiberglass yacht moored a hundred yards offshore, she could have been looking at the *Marauder*.

Richard fit. In any time or place he'd fit right in, a man so full of self-assurance she felt insignificant in comparison. What on earth did a man like that need her for?

Tess felt her skin begin to crawl and a nerve jumped in her neck. What a coward she was, running away because everything was changed and she had no idea how to deal with it. If he would tell her he needed her, he loved her, she'd stay with him forever. But Richard was never going to say those words because they were untrue.

"So," he said at last, the hot, sticky tropical air moist on his smooth face, "you've made a decision. But, I think, you are telling me you have obligations when there is another reason for this decision."

He was not stupid. Tess took a ragged breath. "You're right. I . . . I feel like I'm extra baggage right now."

"Can you put that in English?" His tone was hard.

"What I mean is, I feel as if I was somehow sent to the past to show you the way to a new life."

"My guardian angel?"

"I guess. But I don't think I figure in your scheme any longer."

"You know this as fact?"

"No. It's a gut feeling."

"Hmm."

"Listen," she said, "give yourself a week, a month. You'll see that I'd only be holding you back."

"From what?"

"Your new life. All the adventures you're about to begin."

"That is absurd."

"It's the way I see it."

Tess saw the angry set to his jaw. "You're wrong about me," he said. "You're mistaken about my intentions."

"Maybe. I don't know anymore." Then, "What *are* your intentions?"

"To learn about this new world, to learn how to live in it. To explore. To sail the seas again, but this time as a free man. To start over."

"And to salvage treasure ships," Tess added. "Don't forget that."

"Yes. Why wouldn't I? It's what I can do."

"I don't know." She felt frustration gnaw at her. "I don't understand you. In your time, okay, you were forced to be an outlaw, a pirate. But now... I don't know. I just remember you freeing those slaves from the Spanish. It was so... so noble, so honorable."

"And to become another hunter for treasure is not. Is that what you are saying?"

"It must be."

"I would still be a pirate in your eyes?"

"No... Yes. Oh, how in hell do I know!"

They walked back toward Paul's apartment, Richard bursting out with an argument every few blocks. He just didn't want to see, Tess decided, that in her time there were no extraordinary situations to bond them together. If she thought for one moment he really loved her, then . . .

"I'm not going to hold you back," Tess told him in front of Paul's door. "You'll see I'm right."

"What I see," he stormed, "is a frightened little woman! I know what I want. It is you, Tess Bonney, who is confused."

"Give it time," she whispered. "You'll see."

They found Paul asleep on his couch, cat in lap, a six-pack of sodas on the glass table. He stirred when they came in. "Heck of a party you missed last night," he said, putting a hand to his forehead. "I bet it would have been right up your alley, Richard."

"No doubt," Tess said under her breath.

It was Paul's idea that they could use the bedroom, but Tess wasn't about to, for many reasons, not the least of which was if Richard so much as touched her she'd burst into tears and not be able to stop. So Paul and Richard shared the queen-size bed and Tess made up the couch. A digital clock sat on a counter, blinking at her all night, and she counted the minutes till morning when Paul would drive her to the airport and she could run, run as fast as possible from the pain in her heart.

CHAPTER FOURTEEN

"IMPERIAL SPAIN in the New World, 1563–1638", Tess typed on her keyboard, then she sat and looked at the words for a long time.

She tried again. "In the sixteenth century Spain controlled the axis of a far-flung imperial system that claimed exclusive rights to most of the New World."

That was it. She couldn't think of another thing to say—her mind was empty. Worse, it simply was not functioning. She looked at the piles of notes that she'd been organizing for two weeks. She checked her detailed outline again, then she sighed and pushed herself away from her word processor. It just wasn't any good.

It seemed so long since she'd left Key West, ages and ages. She hadn't heard a word from Paul or Mack or Richard. Especially Richard. He could have called her. He was a smart guy. Surely someone had shown him how to use a telephone by now. He could have phoned—if he'd wanted to.

She'd made up her mind when she'd left Key West that under no circumstances would she call Richard. He had to be left alone. She'd begun teaching her sections again, only a few a week, and she found herself distracted and restless. She'd also set herself to work on her research, trying to drown her misery in routine, but every note card she looked at only sharply reminded her of something that she'd done in the past. With Richard.

She'd sit for long minutes, note cards spilling from her hand, and remember the feel of the *Marauder* flying across the silver-tipped waves, or Ruby and Edith hugging each other, or the raucous voice of the cook at the Crow's Nest, or the smell of the harsh lye soap she'd used to wash Richard's shirts. She could see Thomas Moore in her mind's eye, his elegant clothes, his sword, the blood... She remembered old Benjamin, Joseph the pilot, Stretch Tilden, Jamie the second mate, and all the rest of the crew. Gone, all gone. Dead and buried four hundred years ago.

What was history? she asked herself. Was it trends and dates and politics and religion? Or was it the men and women who lived those trends? It was both, she guessed. You had to know both to be a historian. Well, she should consider herself lucky. She'd analyzed history objectively, and she'd lived it, too. She should write a book, the definitive history of the Caribbean. Unfortunately, all she could do was feel sorry for herself.

She knew she'd been right to leave Richard. She had no hold on him; they'd promised nothing to each other. It had merely been coincidence that Tess had picked up the necklace. Why, any of the divers might have come across it that day, and then...

Except that you don't believe in coincidences, Tess reminded herself. So, did that mean *she* had been fated to rescue Black Richard Neville? That no one else could have done it? Ludicrous. She rubbed her temples with her fingers, and tried to put Richard out of her mind. He wouldn't go easily.

He'd have new clothes now, she supposed. Shorts and jeans and T-shirts and Top-Sider shoes like the other guys. She could see him so clearly in her head: laughing, rakish, proud. He'd have style in his new clothes, just as he'd had in his old ones. She wondered whether he'd gotten his hair cut and tried to picture him with short hair, but she couldn't. And his earring. But so many of the divers had long hair and earrings; Key West was full of rugged individualists and Richard would fit right in.

No, he didn't need her.

Tess stared out of her apartment window, out over Miami and its waterways and high-rise hotels, and listened to the hum of the air conditioner.

Where was Richard right now? Out on the *Seahunt?* Had Mack taught him how to use scuba gear? Maybe he was wandering around Key West, inquisitive, quick, learning about things, absorbing everything, four hundred years' worth of living. Maybe Paul was teaching him to drive—or maybe someone else was. She pictured a gorgeous young shapely blonde in a sporty convertible, her hand on Richard's as he shifted gears. He would laugh and kiss her and fondle her bare, tanned skin as he had Matilda's. Oh, God.

Enough, Tess told herself. *Forget him.*

Tess met a friend, Gene, another teaching assistant, at a cheap Cuban restaurant for dinner. He was a nice man, very smart, tall and skinny, with freckles and fair hair and glasses. He liked her, she knew, maybe a little too much.

"So, Tess," he asked, "how was Spain?"

"Tedious but worthwhile. I found a reference to the *Isabela* that may help Mack Solomon locate it," she replied.

"Your brother still involved with the salvage operation?"

"Yes."

Gene shook his head. "They're all crazy, those guys."

"A little."

"Dreamers," Gene stated.

"They'll find her, though," Tess said. "They're getting close."

"I won't hold my breath." Then he reached across the table and covered her hand with his. "You're much more sensible, Tess. You'd never go running off on a wild-goose chase like that."

Tess stared at his freckled hand where it touched hers and felt prickles rise up her arm. She wanted to pull away, but that would be unforgivably rude. She raised her eyes to Gene's. "Don't be too sure," she said, trying to smile. "I'm beginning to find out that I don't know myself as well as I thought."

"Is your thesis getting to you?" he asked sympathetically.

"I guess so."

"Don't let it. We all have to get through it, Tess. It's worth it when it's over."

"Is it?" she asked.

Gene dropped her off at her apartment building, and she walked past the pool and up the stairs to her door. She threw her purse on a chair, kicked off her shoes and sank down onto the couch. Why didn't she like Gene enough? *Why?* she asked herself angrily, and then the phone rang.

"I've been trying to get you! Where have you been?" came a voice.

"Paul?"

"Yeah, it's me. Guess what?"

"What?" Tess switched the phone to her other hand, wiping her suddenly damp hand on her skirt.

"We found the necklace!" His voice was excited, thrilled. "The emerald one!"

Tess felt her heart give a leap. "You did?"

"Today, right where Richard told us to look."

"And it's the same one?"

"Richard identified it positively as his mother's. I mean, can you believe it? His *mother's!* Too weird, Sis."

"Yes, isn't it," Tess said drily.

"Aren't you excited?"

"I think it's wonderful," she said.

"You don't sound excited. Anyway, what it means is that we're close, real close to the *Isabela,*" Paul said. "Richard thinks we're wrong about the true site. He thinks the *Isabela* got carried on a ways, didn't sink right away. She was still afloat, and there was a northwest wind, so he figures she's southeast of the place we were looking. He really knows his stuff, Sis."

"That's nice," she said noncommittally.

"Well, it's really *great*," Paul said, "not just nice. I mean, we'd have searched the wrong place for months, maybe years. God, Tess, he's a gold mine!"

"I think it's terrific. I'm glad for you all. I knew Richard would be a help. After all, he sank Spanish ships. What better man to locate them now?"

"You sound funny. Aren't you excited? You should see the necklace! Thick gold links, all twisted strips, and three huge square-cut Colombian emeralds. It's worth a fortune!"

"I did see it," she said quietly.

"Oh, yeah, that's right."

"Uh...does he...I mean, how is Richard doing?" Tess fumbled.

"Great. He's quite a guy. He's been working real hard, even diving some. He caught on quick."

"I'll bet."

"Mack knew this fellow who makes up false IDs for the Cubans and South Americans and all, so we got him a Social Security card, a birth certificate, all that stuff. He even took his driver's test and got a license. At least that's not fake," Paul said, chuckling.

"So he's all set."

"Sure is. It cost Mack plenty, but when we find the *Isabela* it'll be worth it. We'll all be rich! And it's going to be soon. I know it. Oh boy, this time I can taste it!"

"Well, I hope you're right," Tess said, then she couldn't stop herself from asking, "does Richard ever, uh, ask about me?" And she could have died of shame.

There was silence on the line for a time until Paul cleared his throat. "Well, he did tell us a story about this redhead and how he thought you were a boy and..."

Matilda. Oh, God, he'd told them about Matilda and about this dumb little cabin boy cowering in the alcove with his hands over his ears, only it wasn't *him,* it was *her,* Tess. "I see," she said, swallowing the lump in her throat.

"Hey, Sis, it was a funny story. We didn't know you pretended to be a boy. Richard just—"

"Oh, sure, I know. It *was* funny," she said, forcing a laugh.

"None of us could figure out how he could have thought you were a boy, though. We gave him some crap about that, I'll tell you," Paul said.

"And what did he say to that?"

"He was suitably embarrassed."

"I'm glad to hear it," Tess said. Then, before she could stop herself, she asked, "Is Richard, uh, is he...well, dating anyone?"

"I don't know," Paul said. "He's a grown man and he lives at Mack's. I can't keep track of him, Sis. Hey, if you're so interested you should have stuck around."

"I couldn't. I had work to do," she protested.

"Right. Well, I don't know what was between you two, but you sure put the kibosh on it."

"There was nothing between us."

"Whatever you say, Tess. Anyway, I gotta go now. Richard wants to try pizza tonight, and there's this place I know...."

"Okay, sure. Say hi to Mack for me and good luck, Paul," Tess said.

"You want me to say hi to Richard, too?"

"Why not?" she replied lightly.

She hung up and instantly felt melancholy. They were all down there in Key West, on the verge of an exciting discovery. All of them, Mack and Paul and all those divers, men and women, and Richard. She felt left out, unloved, unappreciated, miserable. Why *had* she left? It seemed now that it had been a stupid thing to do, and Tess really couldn't recall why she'd thought it so necessary at the time.

Richard, that was it. She'd had to leave him to find his own way. She hadn't wanted him to stay with her out of some misguided sense of obligation. He'd be living a lie. Well he wasn't living a lie now, that was for sure. He was having a wonderful time, a fantastic time.

Still, for the life of her, Tess couldn't imagine that she'd gone through all that, traveled through time and almost starved and drowned and been killed, just to meet Richard and bring him to the present so that he could eat pizza and carouse and get rich!

A WEEK PASSED. Tess tried to work and got a few more pages on disk. She even went out with Gene again, trying desperately to forget, to put things behind her. She wasn't very successful.

On Saturday morning she woke up, and it was as if her mind had made itself up in her sleep. All she knew was that she couldn't sit in front of her word processor in her sterile apartment another day when everything she wanted and needed and loved was in Key West.

She called the airlines and got a reservation on a ten o'clock flight that morning. She packed; she drove to the airport and parked her car on the hot, tacky asphalt. She was calm the whole time, as if a crucial obstacle had been overcome. She was calm when the plane landed and when she got a cab to Mack's house. She felt as if she weren't in her body, as if she were a spectator. She was calm when she rang the doorbell of the Solomons' white conch house.

Of course, no one was home. They were all out on the water searching for the *Isabela*. Weekends didn't matter to Mack Solomon; everyone worked until they found what they were looking for. They were out on the *Seahunt* and they wouldn't be back till late.

Tess began to get nervous. Maybe it was the anticlimax of finding no one home; maybe it was the fact that she was so close to Richard. For a few minutes she stood in front of Mack's house feeling lost and despondent. Then she shook herself mentally and started to walk. She strolled up and down the streets of Key West, along the harbor where she thought she might see the divers coming in on the *Seahunt,* even though she knew it was far too early.

She ate something from a bakery and remembered when she'd been right across the street at The Quay Restaurant with Richard, watching him eat oysters. It was hot, a stagnant heat that was wearying, but Tess still wandered around the waterfront. Once she called Paul's number from a public phone, but it only rang over and over on the other end until she hung up.

What a terrible mistake she'd made coming here. No one wanted her or needed her. She was intruding self-ishly.

In the late afternoon, when the heat was a palpable burden, she made her way back to the Solomon house and rang the doorbell again. Mack's wife, Kitty, opened the door, then looked surprised.

"Oh, you're home," Tess said stupidly. "I was here before—"

"I was at the office and Mack's out on the site. My goodness, you should have called, and we would have picked you up at the airport," Kitty said. "Come in, come in. You look hot and bothered."

"Thanks. I really came down here on a moment's notice. I hope I'm not intruding. I can always—"

"No, no. Here, will you have some iced tea, lemon? Sit down, Tess. Did you come to see Mack?"

"Well, in a way. Uh, Paul called last week and told me they were real close to finding the *Isabela*."

"Oh, they are." Kitty beamed. "This morning Mack said, 'Today's the day,' and maybe I believe him this time."

"Do you expect him back soon?" Tess asked.

"Oh, probably. Now you just take your drink out to the patio. It's so much cooler out there. You sit and relax, and I'll start dinner."

Tess sat in a wrought-iron chair at a glass table on the shaded, lush patio that was overhung with a tan-gled jungle of huge leaves and writhing creepers and bright flowers. She leaned back, closing her eyes, and tried to relax. In the house Kitty turned the radio on and rattled around the kitchen. It should have been restful, but Tess sat there growing more tense by the minute. Questions bombarded her: What would Richard's reaction be when he saw her? Why on earth had she come? What would she say?

She should leave. Yes, she'd just get a plane back to Miami, get a motel room, anything. The tropical growth around the patio seemed to hem her in frighteningly. She almost did, she almost got up and gave Kitty some excuse and walked out, but she was too embarrassed to do it, too hot and tired and, finally, just too damn stubborn. No, she'd see this farce through. Richard had always called her brave, and she'd let him believe that at least to the end. She'd never let him see the sad, shattered wreck she was inside. If Black Richard Neville had his pride, so did Tess Bonney.

She sat and waited, her white linen shift growing damp under her arms and where it folded across her hips. She bit her lip and ran her hand through her short hair.

"You need a refill?" Kitty asked, standing in the doorway.

Tess looked up. "Oh, no, I'm fine. Thanks."

"Just let me know. I'll be out in a minute, soon as I get the fish in the oven."

Tess smiled, but her face felt stiff. What was she doing here? She glanced at her watch. Six-oh-five. What if they never came, and she sat here forever, waiting and waiting? She sipped her iced tea and her hand shook. *Stupid,* she thought angrily.

Kitty finally joined her outside, and it couldn't have been ten minutes later when she heard the crunch of gravel from the front of the house. A car. Her heart lurched in her chest, and she set her glass down quickly. Then a horn honked, loud and long, then another. Car doors slammed, lots of them.

"Well, for goodness' sake," Kitty said, "I guess they're all here. I don't know *what's* going on."

Tess rose and stood there, not sure what to do, her pulse throbbing in her temples, her breath short. *All here.* What did that mean?

"Come on, Tess," Kitty said, "let's go see what those guys are carrying on about."

But before she took a step, they poured up the side walk and into the patio—the divers, the dredgers, the mechanics and boat captains, all the handsome, tanned, fit dreamers who worked for Mack. They were loud, yelling, laughing, exuberant, carrying bottles of liquor and six-packs of beer, their arms draped around one another. Singing, shouting, dancing with excitement, they jammed the patio.

Paul was among them, his expression hectic, two spots of red on his cheeks. He was so excited it never occurred to him to wonder at her presence. "We found her," he yelled to Tess. "We found the goddamn *Isabela!*"

Tess had time to feel a stab of elation—they'd found it!—when she saw Richard walking up the path, and her heart fell to her feet like lead, and her knees went all watery.

He didn't see her for a second. His head was back in laughter, his strong neck arched. He wore a pair of beige shorts and an olive green shirt, unbuttoned, open on his smooth, brown chest. He was tanned, muscular, a man among men. Her pirate. Even his eye patch added to his allure, his mystery. *A man for all seasons,* Tess thought.

A girl, one of the divers, threw her arm around him just then, draped herself on him and laughed and nuzzled her face into his neck, and Richard's arm went around her waist as naturally as if he'd known her for years.

Tess switched her eyes away. Mack Solomon kissed his wife, then popped the cork on a champagne bottle. Everyone was dancing, shrieking, chattering, opening beer bottles. Tess felt as if she were on an island, wrapped in a cocoon of stifling, choking misery. She couldn't escape, bumped and shoved by the happy throng, in a crowd but so very alone.

And then she felt his gaze on her, knew he'd seen her, and his presence dragged at her senses just as the moon tugged at the tides. She turned her head and looked where he stood with the girl's arms around him and met his eye. She was frozen there, not breathing, not feeling, not hearing.

Richard stopped laughing. Slowly he untangled the girl's arms and said something to her, leaning close, and the girl glanced in Tess's direction, nodded, then faded into the growing crowd. Richard stood there by himself regarding Tess soberly, not surprised, not anything, she thought dismally, and suddenly she wanted the earth to crack beneath her feet and simply swallow her up.

Slowly he began to move toward her.

CHAPTER FIFTEEN

"WELL, TESS," he said.

"Hi, Richard," she murmured shakily.

"I had no idea you were coming to Key West," he said, holding her gaze.

"Oh, well, it was a spur-of-the-moment decision.... Uh, Paul called me last week..." Her voice trailed off, and she realized she'd been unconsciously wadding up a damp cocktail napkin.

"I see."

"Quite a party."

"Yes." He said nothing more, but stood there watching her, waiting. The moment stretched out, fragile as spun glass, and Tess was acutely aware of him. She'd almost forgotten his good looks, the aura of power surrounding him. Her heart began to beat furiously and the late-day heat bludgeoned her.

She shifted her weight awkwardly. "Well," she finally said and had to clear her throat, "eat, drink and be merry, right?" Tess held up her glass. Her fingers were quivering.

He cocked his head. "Are you quite all right, Tess?"

"Fine, perfectly fine. Well," she said brightly, "I guess we're here to party, right, Richard? I think I'll just get something more to drink. Uh, see you around.'' And she escaped.

She stood in a dark corner under a palm tree and closed her eyes tightly, willing her heart to slow down and the burning behind her eyelids to go away. She'd thought he was going to follow her, talk to her, say *something* . . . but he hadn't. Damn him.

Within the hour the yard and back porch were spilling over with people, not just the crew now, but their friends and relatives and reporters from the two local newspapers and a couple of radio personalities. Tess had heard that it would be only a matter of hours before CNN arrived. The *Isabela,* the mother lode of all treasures, had been found at last.

She allowed herself to be pushed up against a stone wall that ran along the alley. Only a few feet away was a gate.... But no, she decided, her head pounding, she wasn't going to run. Tess watched as a well-guarded portion of the day's find was carried in and set carefully on a backyard table. A hush fell over the assemblage while the scattering of artifacts was laid out to be photographed.

''Wait till the media gets a load of this,'' she heard someone say.

The treasure, though only a tiny portion of the mother lode, was exquisite. There were dozens of silver ingots, a small encrusted chest containing as yet uncleaned jewels, two gold dinner plates, intricately designed, even a poison cup—Tess thought it must have been the governor's—with the bezoar stone, that supposedly neutralized arsenic, still intact.

There was a showing of silver ware, a few silver buckles and a six-foot-long gold chain. Even a bosun's whistle had been uncovered. And all this, Tess thought, in a matter of hours. What would the weeks and months ahead produce? The *Isabela*'s manifest told of the entire lower hull having been crammed with chests of silver coins, enough treasure to sustain the monarchy of Spain for years to come.

In a dramatic conclusion the find of the day was laid down. The crowd stilled and the hush deepened as a lovely gold inlaid cross with an engraved image of the Madonna and Child on its reverse side was revealed. "My God," voices whispered.

Several of the divers watched over the table as the throng moved in closer, awed, every single person speculating on the enormous wealth still lying buried in the sandy ocean floor. Tess couldn't help remembering when she stood on the tilting deck of the great galleon, moments before the sea swept her away. Despite the oppressive heat and heavy air, goose bumps rose on her arms.

"God," Tess heard one woman say to another, "it's like every one of these divers just won the lottery."

"Yeah," the other one replied, "and what did they do to deserve it? Just have some sun and fun out on the water. Some people have all the luck."

Jealous, Tess thought, but of course a lot of folks would be. However, who other than Mack would have risked half a lifetime on the search? He'd lost a child, lost his own personal fortune twice over, but never wavered in his resolve. She had to ask herself if she was jealous—but no, she wasn't, at least not over the wealth. Richard, on the other hand, had so quickly been absorbed into the hunt that she could honestly say she envied his quest for adventure, which left her out in the cold.

She glanced around, hoping to see him, but it was so crowded.... She realized then how heavy her heart was and how very, very much she loved Richard Neville. When she'd first seen him coming up the walk tonight she'd been rocked to the core with that love. And she'd run off. Afraid. Hurting. She just didn't know how to deal with him, Tess realized. He was, perhaps, too much man for her. And yet the thought of someone else meeting the challenge of his love infuriated her, wounded her so deeply it was like a knife in her belly. What was she going to do?

"Yo, Tess," she heard at her side and she had to shake herself. It was Paul, pressing a glass of champagne on her. He looked about to burst with joy. So many years of searching, hoping. And now, the mother lode. "There's no feeling in the world like it, Tess," he said over the din. "I can't even describe it."

"Is it just the money?" she had to ask.

"The money's gonna be great," he told her. "I can buy a house, my own boat and put something in the bank. Sure, that's a dream come true. But it's more, Sis. It's a thrill I can't describe. You touch history, hold it in your hand. And it's taken years. Every day you wake up and pray this is the day."

"I guess it's like a sickness," she said before thinking, eyeing the treasure-laden table.

"A sickness? Hell, it's more like a miracle drug that cures everything in the world. You were *there*, on the

Isabela. You can't tell me it wasn't the biggest thrill of your life.''

"It was . . . exciting, yes, but scary. Real scary."

He laughed and shook his head at her. "Where's Richard? I thought you two would be celebrating."

"Oh, he's around." She shrugged.

"What a guy. This morning, when we found the mainmast, he was over the side of the *Seahunt* in a flash. He stayed in the water all afternoon, even when the rest of us were ready to call it a day."

"*Richard* found the hull? The treasure?"

"Sure as hell did. He was the first to spot the buried timbers sticking up in the sand. It wasn't thirty feet away that we found the first silver bars."

"I suppose he'll be on TV and all that."

"You bet! Mack pulled him aside not more than five minutes ago and told him CNN was on the way in on a chopper from Miami. Mack wants him to do an interview."

She wanted to scream. Three weeks into his new life, four hundred years removed from his birth, and already he'd located the *Isabela* and was ready for TV interviews! The arrogant, self-serving—

"Come on, Tess," Paul said, sensing her mood, "give the guy a break."

She saw Richard shortly after that, surrounded by well-wishers and the curious, even posing for pictures. He seemed to be doing just fine, no one questioning his accent or his rather strange use of English. But why would they? As he'd said on his very first morning here, no one would believe him even if he shouted the truth to the world.

She watched him and fought the urge to run off again. She stood there feeling the sweat on her neck and the dampness of her waistband and stared at him until he twisted his head and saw her. His expression sobered. He disengaged himself from his fans and shouldered his way to her.

"I thought you'd gone," he said.

"Oh, no, I just got lost in the crowd. It's quite a mob, isn't it?" she replied breezily.

"There're a few souls about. Well, Tess, have you seen the treasure?"

"Uh-huh. I hear you were the first to spot the hull."

"Aye. Sticking up in the sand like the rib cage of some beast. It was not difficult to find."

"Paul said it was mostly buried." She shrugged and took a drink from her plastic cup, noticing the tremor was still in her fingers. "So I guess you're the hero."

"One with a definite advantage," he said, and then he laughed. "But tell me, Tess, how have you been? When I realized the number of days that have passed since you left, I was—"

"I've been busy. Real busy."

"Too busy to use a telephone to call me?"

She looked up sharply. "Yes," she lied, "my associate and I have been working long hours. I hardly get any sleep as it is."

But he wouldn't take the bait. "Well," he only said, "I did much thinking on you, Tess."

"I bet."

His face grew sober, and he put a hand out to touch her cheek. "Have I ever been dishonest or—" He never finished his sentence, however, because they were interrupted by the CNN crew, who had just arrived and were setting up their lights and cameras next to the table.

"Over here!" Mack called to Richard. "I want you next to me for this! Come on!"

"We will talk later," Richard said, and he took hold of her chin firmly, tipping her head up. "We *will* talk." And with that he let her go and strode away with the confidence of a man fully in charge of his life.

The interview was interesting, Tess had to admit. Mack described the triumphs and trials of the last twenty years and his own tragic loss for the exquisitely groomed female reporter, whose face was familiar to everyone. He spoke of the treasure being worth a hundred million dollars after taxes, and even the seasoned woman holding the microphone had to collect herself before saying, "Then this could be called the richest find in history, Mr. Solomon?"

"Absolutely," Mack said.

"And how do you know this treasure is really from the *Isabela* and not another ship?" She indicated to the cameraman to pan the objects on the table.

Mack smiled. "The silver bars and coins were printed in the New World," he explained easily. "Each bar has a number stamped on it that's listed on the ship's manifest. The coins come from several mints in Mexico and South America. They bear the individual stamp from that mint along with the date."

"I see. And you have the manifest?"

"We've had *that* for almost four hundred years."

"So what now? You haul up the treasure and divide it among the workers, your financial backers and the government?"

"Not quite." Mack grew serious. "The salvage will go on for years. We have a piece of history here that must be preserved as best we can. Our archaeologist will excavate the site with the same care as you would any ancient ruin."

"Some of your critics say you'll destroy the find. That you've done it before. Can you reply to that?"

"In the past, when we salvaged a ship, there was not as much regard for the historical significance of the site."

After another five minutes of questions, he finally put a hand on Richard's shoulder and urged him over. "This is the man who actually spotted the hull today."

Richard handled the interview quite well. The best, Tess thought, was his fielding of the inevitable question. "Mr. Neville, I'm unfamiliar with your accent. Are you British?"

"Actually," Richard replied, smiling, "I have had citizenship in America for some time now. But, yes, I hail from the shores of England, though I have spent much time sailing the remote corners of the Caribbean."

"Fishing? Treasure hunting?"

"No, to be truthful, I was a pirate." He gave the woman a merciless smile.

"Cut! Oh, that's good, Mr. Neville! Did you get that on camera, Fred?" Then, "Can I ask you how you lost your eye?"

"You may ask."

"I'm asking then."

"In a most vicious duel with the deadliest of enemies, mistress."

"Cut!" she said. Then, "Great! This stuff is really great! You're going to have a fan club nationwide, Mr. Neville. They'll love you!"

They'll love him, all right, Tess thought.

The woman wouldn't stop asking questions. "And now what, Mr. Neville? A big house and boat? How will you spend your fortune?"

He gave her a charming, flashing grin. "I will spend my treasure on my love."

"And she is...?"

"The sea, lass. What else?"

"That was cute," Tess said to him after the interview. "Why didn't you just tell her you're in it for the money?"

"I merely told the woman what she wished to hear."

"Uh-huh," Tess grunted.

They threaded their way through the crowd, Richard saying, "I vow, the atmosphere reminds me of times in the Laughing Parrot when the ships were all in port. Let us go to my room and talk, Tess."

"Your room?"

He nodded to the second floor and a balcony that was overgrown with lush greenery. "You have spent some time in my quarters before, have you not?"

"Yes, I have, but..."

"But now you are afraid," he said, putting both hands on her arms, his eye searching hers. "And I would know more of this fear."

"I'm not afraid," she said, lying. "I just don't think it would be such a good idea."

"Have I made some terrible mistake in this time that I know naught of? Tell me, Tess. For everything that was between us has vanished," Richard said quietly, seriously.

His words, his tone, struck Tess like a blow to the solar plexus. Her knees went weak and there was a tightness in her throat that ached, holding in all those words that craved release. She looked down, anywhere but at his somber expression, and swallowed hard. "I . . . just can't," she said miserably.

"Why not?"

"Oh, God, Richard, please . . ."

He snatched his hands away. "So there, I do not touch you, I do not force you. I request an explanation, that is all."

"It won't work, Richard." The words were wrenched out of her.

"What won't work?"

"Please . . ."

"Is this a riddle?" His tone was angry now. "A game? There were never these games between us before. What has happened?"

Tess felt a pressing against the bottom of her heart. She couldn't tell him the truth that more than anything in the world she wanted him to fall to his knees and declare his undying love and devotion. He'd throw back his head and laugh. Richard loved, all right. He loved his ships and his sea and his treasures! Someday he'd find a woman like Matilda, who'd traipse after him, sharing his bed, waiting on him, but Tess couldn't, *wouldn't* be that woman.

"I'm going home," she announced, raising her eyes to his, fighting back tears. "Where's the phone? I need to call a cab." She felt a sob welling in her chest and it hurt. God, how it hurt. She had to get out of there. She cast around desperately.

"I shall drive you," Richard said, his voice suddenly soft. "If you must go, I shall get the keys to the car and at least see you safely onto your airplane."

"I don't—"

"I insist."

"Richard," she asked, breathless, "can you really drive a car?"

"Aye."

"I guess if you could sail the *Marauder*, you can drive a car."

"Shall I get the keys?"

Richard *could* drive. He borrowed Mack's old Ford station wagon and headed up the narrow, clogged streets toward the far side of the island. He'd picked up all the usual traits males exhibit when driving: legs splayed, an elbow propped on the open window of the door, the other hand draped casually over the steering wheel.

"At least you keep your eye on the road," Tess said, unaccountably irritated, glad for the stab of anger that protected her from the abject misery she was still battling. She breathed deeply, closing her eyes, fighting for control.

"I would strike something if I did not." He gave her a glance.

"How'd you pass the written test?"

"I nearly didn't. But Paul was my coach, and I managed somehow."

"Good of Paul."

"He's a fine man." They were quiet for a moment, then he said, "I would like it if you remained here, Tess."

"Why would you like it?" she dared to ask, looking straight ahead, her heart beating too quickly.

"I enjoy your company."

"Oh? You mean our *conversations?*"

Richard said nothing. Not one single word. But he did pull over to the side of the road and stopped. To the right were the waterfront, the public beaches, deserted at this late hour. Tess stared out at the water and felt tears burn behind her eyes again.

He leaned close. "In the past," he said, "we shared something, Tess. But you have changed. I fail to understand this change in you. Can you enlighten me?"

She bit her lower lip and wished to God she could hate him. "It's you who's changed. Not me."

"I am the same."

She was silent.

"Is it because I hunt for treasure now? Is that it?"

"Partly."

"And the rest?"

She turned to him abruptly. "Once you freed slaves...you shared your wealth with those who needed it. Are you going to take your share of the treasure and give it to the poor here? I don't think so," she said and pressed herself against the door, away from him.

"Ah, I see," he said after a moment. "You think me a buccaneer still."

"Yes."

"It was all right in my time, but in yours it is wrong. Is this the trouble?"

"In your time you were forced into it. Here...I don't know. I really don't."

"I think," Richard said slowly, "that this is only an excuse, some notion you've taken to keep your distance from me. Is that true, Tess?"

"Maybe," she whispered.

"So what would you have me do, Tess Bonney?" He was so close, too close. "I...I don't know."

"You do not seem to know very much at all of late," he said, then put the car in gear and drove on.

The airport was quiet at that hour. Only two more commuter flights were due to arrive, reload, and head up to Miami that night. Tess bought a ticket and turned to Richard.

"You could have just dropped me off," she said, looking at her sandals. "The party's still going on, and I'm sure everyone is wondering where you are."

"I'll await your airplane."

She looked at him. "Richard," she said, "I don't want you to. I wish you'd go back to Mack's."

"Is this what you truly want?"

"Yes, I do."

He walked toward the double doors, his shoulders stiff. Suddenly he stopped, stood there with his back to her for a moment then spun on his heel. He strode back to her, his steps loud on the tile floor. "Something has indeed changed," he said angrily. "It is you.

Once you braved a world that was both terrifying and exciting to you. That Tess I came to know well. But here you are a sniveling coward. I fail to comprehend this."

"Richard," she began.

"No!" He put up a hand. "It is curious, Tess, but in this new and wonderful world it is you who are out of kilter, not me." And with that he turned and left her there, alone.

TESS LOOKED UP FROM her computer and rubbed her eyes, realizing the time. It was almost noon. She was still in her robe, a cold morning cup of coffee beside the stack of notes and books and file cards at her side. She was supposed to meet Gene at twelve-thirty. Damn. She reached for the phone and dialed.

"Gene?"

"Yes. Is that you, Tess?"

"It's me. And I'm so sorry, but I can't meet you for lunch. I got up at six and started to work and I just this minute noticed the time."

"We can meet later."

"Uh, no, I mean, I'm behind on everything. I've got a bejillion errands, a class I have to sit in on at three. My folks want me up for dinner...."

"I see. Well, I was just hoping to read over some of your paper. Maybe another time."

"You bet. A rain check. And thanks, Gene, you're a pal."

"I was afraid of that," he said before hanging up.

By six Tess was frazzled. She called her mom. "I can't make it. I'm up to my ears in this thesis and I can't get a word typed."

"Well, we'll miss you, honey. But are you sure you're okay?"

"I'm fine."

"You haven't been fine, dear, since that first trip to Key West a month ago."

"Oh, Mom..."

"Your father and I have been worried. Oh, and by the way, dear, pick up a copy of this evening's *Sun*. There's a lead story on the *Isabela*."

"I will."

"And tell Paul not to spend a cent until he talks to your father's stockbroker."

"I will."

"Take your vitamins, Tess, you really do sound strange."

"Yes, Mom."

Tess got dinner in a cardboard container at the neighborhood Chinese take-out. She hadn't meant to buy a copy of the newspaper, but it seemed to reach out at her, saying, *you can't resist.* Maybe there would be a word or two on Richard....

She hated the headline: Richest Treasure In History. She ate the greasy egg rolls, dipping them in hot mustard, and hated them. She tossed the paper on the carpet and turned on the evening news. It wasn't going to do her any good at all to read about the treasure or Mack or Richard. None whatsoever.

Fifteen minutes later her hand reached down of its own volition and picked up the front page again. What she read stunned her.

Estimates of the value of the *Isabela* treasure are far greater than first expected. Salvor Mack Solomon at a press conference today in Key West stated that appraisers have now quoted the treasure to be worth $150,000,000. Much of the anticipated increase in value is due to a discovery by Richard Neville, a thirty-year-old English salvor working with Solomon, who yesterday brought to the surface a sackful of pieces of eight. Neville stated that these were just a sample of many more to be found.

The discovery of the Spanish gold, minted in Mexico in 1621, is of great significance to the salvors, as passengers on the Spanish galleons often carried with them secret contraband from the New World in the form of gold coins, so that the king's taxes would not have to be paid. Of course there was no way for Solomon to know how much contraband gold was on this particular ship as it was not listed on the manifest. Neville is quoted as saying, "All the Spaniards cheated. We'll find many treasures in contraband, on that I'll wager."

Tess let the paper float back to the floor. She stared straight ahead. Her brain was spinning. So much money. And what would Richard's share be—five million, ten . . . more?

CHAPTER SIXTEEN

RICHARD STOOD in the florist shop that was just off the cavernous art deco lobby of the Fontainebleau Hotel in Miami Beach. He looked around in carefully disguised wonder at the profusion of colors and blossoms and greenery. He inhaled the aroma of cut flowers and damp soil, that unique hothouse smell.

God's teeth, this world was stupendous, he thought again. Miami was the farthest from Key West he'd been so far, although Mack had shown him his collection of *National Geographic* magazines, which Richard had studied religiously, seeing every corner of this fantastic world, right there on the colorful, glossy pages.

He'd driven to Miami, a long, tiring drive in a rented car, but he'd wanted to see the countryside and he'd wanted to do it alone. But Gad, the speed! Fifty-five, sixty miles an hour! In his day, it had taken weeks in execrable conditions to do what he'd just done in three hours.

He walked over to a refrigerated glass case of roses and gladiolas and stared at the wealth of color. Unbelievable.

"May I help you, sir?" the well-dressed shopkeeper asked.

"Perhaps in a short time. I am deciding," he said, and that seemed to satisfy her.

Sometimes Richard wearied of the constant barrage on his senses. The crowding and noise and rushing, the intensity of this world. Too many people, cars, shops, things for sale. Too much communication: TV, radios, movies, print everywhere, so cheap, so easily obtainable. Too much of everything. Sometimes he wanted to retreat, to rest, to sit by a smoky fire and eat simple food and hear men speak as he was used to, but those nostalgic moments were few and far between, and Richard considered them objectionable and weak. He'd never been one to shirk or go backward or be afraid of what fate offered.

Oh, he knew he put on a good front, impregnable, that of the carefree buccaneer, ready for any adventure, but ofttimes, deep inside... The worst, he supposed, was when he'd had to take that test to get his driver's license. Lord in heaven, but he'd been near undone! Paul had coached him carefully. The mechanical part, the driving, was not taxing, but oh the rules. Gad, these people had to know so bloody much. Red lights, green lights, yield signs, double yellow lines, stopping distances. He hadn't let on to Paul or Mack or Kitty, but he hadn't slept a wink the night before.

The roses, yes. Red, yellow, white, pink. Where had all these colors come from? And the prices. He peered closer, astonished. For something that grew in tumbling confusion, free, in front of every cottage in England, he must pay eight dollars for a single rose! One of the oddities of this century was the cheapness of some things and the dearness of others. He'd just have to accept it and not go into shock every time he read a price tag. Besides, he could afford all the flowers in this shop, if need be.

What would Tess prefer? Ah, that was the rub. Paul had told him Tess loved flowers, every woman did—that at least had not changed—but he was well aware that this choice was very important.

Tess. He missed her shamefully, the damn stubborn woman. But he should have expected that; even as Billy he, she, had been intransigent. She was making herself miserable for no reason. Did she think he would fall out of love with her just because the times were different? People were the same. He'd tried to tell her, but she'd closed her ears, her mind, her heart. Silly twit.

So, he'd come to Miami to storm her castle of obstinacy. He'd decided it couldn't be done by telephone. No, this delicate task must be accomplished in person.

Red. He decided on red roses, a color he was used to, a proper color for roses. A dozen. "Excuse me," he said finally, "I have decided. A dozen of those, if you please, to be delivered to this address." And he laid down on the counter Tess's address, copied from Paul's small black book. He'd learned already to be carefully prepared in this world. Information, that was the key. Names and numbers, phone numbers, street numbers, social security numbers. But with so very many people, he supposed it was the only way to keep order.

The woman began choosing the flowers, conscientiously picking out the freshest ones. "I may write a note to accompany the flowers, is that not correct?" Richard asked.

"Of course." She handed him a folded card, with the hotel's crest in gold on the front. Quite tasteful.

He chose his words selectively, writing in his old-fashioned, curling script. "My dearest Billy, I am here in Miami and I am causing a car to be sent for you at eight this evening. I implore you to join me for dinner. Please. Richard."

There. She could not refuse. Not even sweet, stubborn Tess. Or perhaps she could. He frowned. Then he'd just bloody well go and find her and . . .

"That will be a total of $102.72, sir, including delivery and tax," the clerk said. "Cash or credit card?"

"Cash," he said. Those plastic cards still made him a bit nervous. They were so very improbable. He understood the idea; Mack had told him about credit and checks and so on, but Richard felt more comfortable with hard currency, although that, too, was a misstatement. The money was paper. Ah, this world!

Carefully, deliberately, he counted out the bills and coins, and when he walked out of the florist shop, he felt as if he'd surmounted another hurdle, passed another test. His days seemed filled with them, one after another, endlessly.

It was a long afternoon. He walked on the beach, still quite unused to the sight of people lying in the sun, their bodies glistening with oil. They sprawled there for hours and every so often they put lotion on so that they wouldn't get too much sun, the one canceling the other out. The logic of it escaped Richard. So much skin exposed. So many old people, so very many. They retired to Florida, he'd been told. In his day a man retired when he was either dead or in his dotage. Yet these people were here, being neither, their fat bodies or skinny bodies exposed to the naked eye. Indecent. Well, mayhap he'd get used to it.

And many of the women, although advanced in years, looked marvelously attractive. Plastic surgery, Kitty had told him. "A tuck here, a tuck there," she'd said. "I might do it myself soon."

"They...*cut and sew?*" Richard had asked, aghast.

Then he thought of the contrasts. In his time, a woman was bent and wrinkled and toothless by forty—a crone. Even his mother, bless her soul, had lost a few teeth, and she'd been well taken care of most of her life. One lived in filth, with fleas and rats ofttimes, and a full bath rarely. Clothes grew stiff with dirt. Ignorance and superstition were rife. My God, he could never go back to that.

He walked on, noting everything he saw, the highrise hotels, the traffic, the tiki bars on the beach, and he thought again about Tess, his lady love. Did she have the flowers yet? What was she thinking? Was she with another man? Oh, he hadn't missed her mention of an "associate." He'd not let on, but he'd heard. What, precisely, did Tess do with this associate? Read history?

He accepted that Tess was a teacher, well, a university teaching assistant. Paul had corrected him on that score. Women did all kinds of things these days, from driving trucks to working as doctors. But would Tess want to stay at her university? How important was it to her? Because Richard knew, without a doubt, that he must live near the sea and he must sail a ship.

He'd thought about Tess endlessly after she'd left Key West. He'd asked Paul and Mack many questions about modern females, although they'd been largely unable to answer his queries. It seemed womankind, although equal now, by God, was still an absolute mystery to mankind. So he'd had to use his own experience, plus some hints from a fascinating thing he'd discovered on television, much to the merriment of the salvage crew. Soap operas.

It had been Kitty's idea. She'd implored him to take a day off and relax. Mack had insisted. So Richard had given in, sleeping till past eight, breakfasting on the patio. And then Kitty had called him inside, asking him if he'd ever heard of a soap opera, and they'd sat down in front of her television, a whole, new, amazing world revealing itself to him over the next few hours.

Aye. Every facet of modern male-female relationships was on those programs. He watched, he listened, he bore Kitty's teasing and, bloody hell, he *learned*. The flowers had been on one soap, the limo on another, the room-service dinner he'd ordered for that evening on still another. And his clothes—he'd chosen them carefully to look like one of the more admirable characters. By all that was holy, there was even a character on a soap who wore an eye patch! And the women loved him, too.

He also got from soaps the germ of an idea about what ailed Tess: she was afraid she was presuming too much and backing Richard into a corner. There was one problem, however, that he couldn't solve by watching "A Guiding Light" or "The Young and the Restless." It was the fortune Richard would soon have.

Tess was put off by what she saw as his greed; to Richard it meant nothing beyond freedom. The money itself was an encumbrance, what with all Mack's talk of dividends and accountants and tax shelters. What Richard wanted was precisely what he'd wanted for four hundred years: freedom and a ship and the woman he loved.

He'd considered what Tess might think of him, treating her with the roses and the limo and the expensive hotel. But it was just this one time, and he owed Tess and he owed himself. He wanted very much to prove to this intractable woman that he was quite comfortable in her world. He knew instinctively that he could not command Tess's love and respect from a weak position. He would not embarrass her, acting like an oaf, an ignoramus. He would court her, as he'd never done in the past, and he'd win her over.

He glanced at his watch—marvelous invention. Mack had given him one for diving. Black plastic with numerals and dials. And it ran on a battery with no winding. Someone had tried to explain to Richard how a battery worked, but the diver hadn't understood it either, it seemed.

He had hours yet. He bought a drink at a stand. Orange soda. Too sweet, but he loved the exotic taste of orange. And a hot dog. Odd name for a cheap sausage. Odd taste, too. What a world. Richard looked in store windows for a time. Boutiques, especially men's clothing shops, fascinated him. He wandered into a bookstore. There were, as usual, too many items to make sense of. He picked up a tome here, a tome there. Every subject in the world.

On one "paperback," as he'd been taught to call them, he saw a picture of a pirate like him, cutlass in hand, patch and all, in an intimate embrace with a fiery-haired wench. Unfortunately he could only laugh at the wrongness of the ship's rigging in the artist's depiction. The book was called *Love's Desperate Enemy*. Marvelous.

He went back to the hotel and rode the elevator up to his room. Such luxury, such privacy. He opened the sliding glass door to his balcony and let the hot, moist Atlantic air flood in, spoiling the air-conditioned coolness. Miami was an anthill, its tiny figures swarming between tall buildings. But he could look out over the ocean and breathe in its familiar scent.

He turned the big-screen TV on. He flicked the remote control, channel after channel a delight: news, travel, sports, movies. He'd learned all the terms. There were Spanish language stations on television, he'd discovered quickly enough. The English, although taking over most of North America, had never succeeded in dislodging all of the Spanish. Oh, yes, he'd been instructed to call them Cubans or Mexican-Americans or what have you, but to Richard they were all poxy Spaniards.

On the news a smooth-faced reporter was speaking from London, England. Richard sat up straight. The reporter was in front of an ornate palace, the queen's palace called Buckingham, but what interested Richard were his countrymen in the background. Ah, he decided in a few moments, disgusted, they had degenerated into shorthaired imitations of Americans, and were ruled by a rather homely queen who wore spectacles and tasteless bonnets.

Idly, Richard kept an eye on the TV and perused the newspaper delivered to his room that morning. He had time to kill, and he spent every spare moment soaking up information. Sometimes he felt like the computers he heard everyone talk so much about, taking in facts ceaselessly, analyzing, computing, coming up with new calculations. It was tiring. He still had some trouble deciphering the small, square, unfamiliar newspaper print, but he was growing used to it, although it was not so artful as print in his day.

How fortunate Edmund had insisted on a tutor for him. If he had not been taught to read, as most sailors were not, he'd have been lost in this world. *Thank you, father,* he thought, and it was the first time he'd ever thanked Edmund Moore for anything.

The hour grew later: six then seven. Neither the newspaper nor the antics of a nubile athlete on television kept Richard's attention. Where was Tess? he kept thinking. Had she been home to receive the flowers and the note? Would she come?

He showered, he dressed in shot-silver raw silk trousers and glove-leather loafers with no socks and a white silk shirt that he left half unbuttoned as he'd seen in one of Kitty's soaps. He plaited his hair neatly into a single braid and tied it with a strip of cloth, as he was used to, and then he put a small gold stud in his ear, replacing the gold hoop. He did want to look respectable for Tess.

The champagne and the dinner were delivered on the dot of eight, and Richard saw that it was fitting and elegant, all heavy silver and white damask cloths and an ice bucket that sweated drops of moisture. Everything was ready, perfect, for his Tess. By the grace of God, she'd come—any minute now—the long black limousine dropping her off at the door just downstairs. He'd woo her ardently and she'd be his.

Maybe.

Richard went out onto his balcony, stood with his legs braced, hands behind his back, and looked out over the water, smelling the sea, but only able to see the lights of passing ships on its blackness. He felt suddenly lonely, so alone in this wondrous new world, and he wondered what he'd do should Tess not come. Gad, it was unthinkable.

He stood there for a long time, leaning on the railing now, his fingers clenching it tightly, and a new, totally unexpected feeling ate its way into his heart. *What if Tess did not come?*

The knock at his door made him straighten quickly. He strode across the patterned carpet and black-and-white tile of the foyer, past the pale wood tables, the shell-patterned paper on the walls, the footed couches and floral bouquets and Erté posters on the walls and threw open the door.

They stood there, staring at each other. "By God, Tess," Richard finally said, "but it's good to see you."

"Hello, Richard," she said, a little shy, hesitating at the sight of the suite's opulence.

She was so lovely, small and pert, with her huge dark eyes and indecently long lashes and those dimples. How could he ever have thought her a boy? "Come in," he said. "Please, make yourself comfortable."

She wore a simple black dress, slim, with slender straps, high heels that made her taller than he was used to and a brightly patterned jacket thrown over her shoulders. She moved a little self-consciously, he thought, as she went to sit on the long white couch. He followed, hovering over her, wanting to do everything just right.

"You look beautiful, Tess," he said. "I'm very happy you could come."

"Thank you," she said, that one slim eyebrow arching saucily. "How could I refuse, after all the—" she made a gesture with her hand "—arrangements you made?"

"Ah, lass, you could have refused. The driver had no orders to truss you up and carry you to me."

"Hmm," she said. "You're looking well, Richard. Very—" she searched for the word "—prosperous."

He looked down at his clothes, chagrined. "Did I choose rashly? It's just that all the garments I see in your world are exceedingly dull, most especially men's. No velvet, no colors, no hose. Very commonplace."

She smiled inwardly. "Yes, I guess so. They must seem boring to you. Well, Richard, you do look very nice, very...rich."

He beamed. "Aye, don't I, though?" Then he remembered. "Would you care for some champagne? I ordered the best, the most costly. The waiter assured me..."

"That would be lovely," she said.

"And I have these things you call appetizers—fish eggs, clams and snails and such. The very best," he said, going to the silver bucket. The cork popped satisfyingly, and he poured two glasses and offered one to Tess. Her hand was damp and trembled slightly when she took the glass from him.

She looked up. "The roses were beautiful. Thank you. I was awfully surprised."

"I drove here from Key West, you know. Just to see you, my Tess," he said. "Shall we make a toast?"

She raised her glass. "To the *Isabela*."

"No," Richard said, "to someone much more important. To Tess Bonney."

"Don't be silly," she demurred.

"I *will* drink to you, who made it all possible. You can't refuse. 'Tis discourteous." They drank and then Richard sat beside her and feasted his eye on her until he could see that she flushed. "Are you hungry?" he asked.

"Starved."

"Aye, you always were. I have a fine supper for us. A beef loin with some outlandish sauce I can't pronounce, some greens and then I asked for potatoes. I do miss potatoes."

They ate, and Richard saw that she relaxed a bit. Maybe it was the wine or the food or the hot, soft, sea-damp air that flowed in through the open balcony door. "How goes your work?" he asked.

"All right." She shrugged. "More to the point, how does yours go?"

"Well, exceedingly well. Mack brings up so much, the *Seahunt* is awash at the gunwales bringing it ashore. Those grasping Spaniards."

She looked at him, her eyes shadowed, but said nothing.

Aye, he thought, *she does think me greedy.* "Paul sends his best," Richard said.

"He knew you were coming up here?"

"Aye, he told me to."

She looked flustered.

There was dessert, a tart of custard and lime and meringue. "That was wonderful, Richard," Tess said, "but, you know, you could have taken me out somewhere, anywhere. You didn't need to go to such a fuss."

He reached across the table and captured her hand. "I wanted to, lass. You're worth the whole lot and so much more. I want to make you happy."

She sighed. "Expensive flowers and dinners can't make anyone happy, Richard."

"I know that." He was feeling a touch irritated at her stubbornness. "Gad, Tess, all the gold I captured never made me happy. It was my ship and my men that did that. And you."

"Me?"

Richard made an exasperated noise. "I'm close to giving up on you, Tess Bonney. I never could abide a stupid woman."

"I'm not stupid," she said with some fire.

"Good, then listen to me. I want you. I love you. There, I've said it. And I have a gift for you."

"Oh, Richard, please..."

He stood, holding up a hand to silence her. Then he went into his bedroom and returned with it. He strode straight to Tess and pulled her upright and put it around her graceful neck.

"Oh, my God," Tess breathed.

He moved around to her back, fastening the necklace, his head bent close to her warm skin. "This is yours," he said softly, breathing in her scent.

"Oh, no, I couldn't..."

"She'd want you to have it. You saved my life." Richard felt ripples of heat in his belly being so close to her. He couldn't bear it, yet he could make no move to leave her.

She stood there silently, her head bowed, and then she turned to face him, and he saw her eyes were bright with unshed tears. "I can feel your mother's soul in this necklace. I could the first time I touched it, Richard. I felt...all her emotions."

"Aye, I believe it. She led you to this necklace so you could bring me here. It was her gift to me," Richard said slowly.

"So," Tess whispered, "it never was a coincidence, none of it." She put her small hand on the heavy pendant with its three square-cut emeralds and closed her eyes. "She's at peace now, Richard."

He thought for a second that Tess would give in then and come around into his arms. She was close, but she drew herself up and held herself stiffly and moved away, across the room to the balcony. He followed her, and in the sultry darkness she asked him a question with trepidation in her voice. "Richard..."

"Aye?"

"What will your share of the treasure be?"

He stood in front of her and put his hands on her shoulders. He was weary of her thinking him such a cad. He tipped her head up and met her gaze and said, "By all that's holy, Tess Bonney, don't you know me yet? It's not the money. I don't care a whit about the money. How can I make you see that? It's not the owning of a thing that's worth the while, it's the quest, the adventure, the challenge."

"Richard, I..."

"I shall give it all away to prove it to you. I could, in a minute."

She searched his face.

"I have spoken to Mack many hours on this. I have made plans to set up a foundation. He calls it 'nonprofit.' I can do that, he tells me."

"A foundation? For what?"

"Oh, I do not know yet. Something worthy of this beautiful world. It is a matter I will think on. I am told that there are many problems that a foundation can help to solve."

"Yes, that's true, but..."

"But what, lass? You do not believe me?"

"I believe you," she whispered.

"I will tell you this, though. I shall keep enough of my share to buy a boat, a sailing vessel. I lost one because of you, my sweet Tess, and I must have another."

"Oh, Richard..."

"So, does that satisfy you, insatiable wench? Gad, better Matilda had come to this time with me. She'd have been a sight easier to convince."

"Oh, for God's sake, Richard, don't mention that tart's name again!"

"Ah, there you go. That's better. Show me some fire, Tess. I'm tired of your quiet."

But she stood there in the warm darkness, still silent, for such a long time, that he was about to shake her. Finally she spoke, and her voice was muffled and so soft he had to strain to hear. "Richard, I owe you an apology."

"What's that, lass?" He bent his head and put a hand on her cheek tilting her face up to him.

"I owe you an apology, and I hate to apologize," she said with her old defiance.

"Aye, that you do, but as long as you see the error of your ways, all will mend itself. Come now, give me a kiss," he said lightly, not wanting to let her know how near to giving up he'd been, how bloody undone he'd felt.

"Oh, Richard," she said with a sob, and she pressed herself into his arms, her warmth and her sweet scent and slight, delectable curves tight against him, and he stroked her hair as she clung to him.

"There, there, lass," he said.

"Richard," she said into his chest, "oh, I missed you so much. I wanted to call a million times, but I thought... You needed to have a chance to choose... Oh, I don't know..."

He kissed the top of her head. "Who knows? Mayhaps there was some reason to that. But it was always you, Tess, from the first." She turned her face up and he kissed her gently, his mouth moving on hers. She reached up her arms and pulled him close and opened herself to him with all the boldness of a twentieth-century female. Ah, yes, she'd always be hard to convince, but once won over she was worth a dozen others.

"Richard," she asked against his mouth, "do you forgive me?"

"There's nothing to forgive, love."

She sighed and brushed his mouth with hers, feather light, and a small shock burst in his belly. She put a hand up between them and laid it flat against his chest where his shirt was open and nuzzled her face into the hollow between his neck and his shoulder.

"Shall we go in?" he asked. "You have not yet seen the bedchamber. The bed is so big, it could well hold half a dozen—"

"Don't tease, Richard."

"Not tonight, perhaps...."

They went in, Richard shutting the balcony door. Arm in arm, they moved across the room, dousing lights as they went, kissing, stopping to murmur and touch. It took a long time to reach the bedroom. Once there Richard stopped Tess and slipped the narrow straps of her dress off her shoulders and unzipped the back. Kissing her smooth skin, he murmured, "Zippers are lovely things. So quick, so easy. I love your world, Tess."

She gave a small satisfied laugh that turned into a gasp of indrawn breath as Richard bent to kiss one breast then the other. Then Tess unbuttoned his shirt and ran her hands over his chest, small, warm hands that caused darts of delight.

Her fingers touched the ridge of scar tissue on his shoulder where Thomas had wounded him, touched it and stopped, and she breathed, "Does it still hurt, Richard?"

"Not to speak of, Tess. Don't fret over it."

She undid his zipper and his trousers were off, their clothes together now on the floor in a sighing heap. Moonlight came through the window to touch a hip, a shoulder, a cheek, in pearly light. Carefully, Richard lifted the heavy necklace from around her neck and laid it down, where the moon glimmered on it in contented sparkles. He pulled back the satin coverlet and they slid into the huge, fragrant bed together.

Richard ran his hands over her small, smooth body and then he asked, his voice thick with desire, "Tell me, Tess, do you still make that funny little sound in your sleep?"

"What sound?" she whispered, moving against him.

"The one I listened to night after night from that damned cabin boy of mine."

"Oh, that sound."

They kissed and stroked, and she was as fine as he remembered, small and fiery and endlessly innovative. The moon had moved across the black velvet sky while they both lay together, depleted, both covered with a satin sheen of dampness, their breathing calming to a slower cadence.

"You didn't cut your hair," Tess finally said softly.

"Should I?"

"No, I like it."

Idly he ran his fingers across her silken hip. "So," he said, "I have to admit something now."

"Yes, Richard?"

"You may think I fell into your world with too much ease, Tess..."

"Yes..."

"But I want you to know that there...are...times when it is very hard. Tough, you'd say. There's so much..." He swallowed. "There are times when I crave a simpler existence, but I am a man who's had to bow to necessity...and I'll do it. But, damn it, Tess, I'd like a helpmate in this endeavor." He paused, waiting for her reaction. He prayed he hadn't spilled his guts so that she'd have no respect for him.

Tess raised herself on an elbow and looked at him in the dimness. "Has it been hard for you, Richard?" she asked softly.

"Aye, at times. I've admitted it to no one but you. A man needs to let down on occasion, Tess, to be himself with no shields up."

"I wish I'd known."

"The truth is, Tess, I need you. You know me. There's no pretense between us. I need you in this bizarre world." He swallowed. "I love you. I want you for my wife, lass. Will you have me, with all my faults and only one eye and a hide full of scars?"

"You want to marry me?" she whispered, her voice full of wonder.

He gave a low laugh, a flash of white teeth in the dark room. "Aye, Tess, *you*. I've known what I wanted for nigh on four hundred years. Of course, if you need longer..."

CHAPTER SEVENTEEN

THE TURQUOISE WATERS of the *bajamar* lapped against the wooden hull of the *Bonny Tess,* Richard's new forty-eight foot sailboat. She was a beauty, handcrafted of polished wood, not fiberglass, and without a motor. He'd insisted.

Tess sat under a blue-and-white-striped awning rigged over the ship's wheel, a notepad in her quickly disappearing lap. She was five months pregnant, she'd been Mrs. Richard Neville for six months and she was just beginning to settle down from the last year's adventures. They'd been married at Christmastime, when the school term ended and Tess could leave the university—and when winter storms kept Richard landbound.

"Now, tell me some more about your mother, where she was born and so on. How did she meet Edmund?" Tess asked.

"Enough questions, Tess. My poor head swims."

"Oh, come on, just a few." She moved in her deck chair awkwardly, licked the tip of her finger, and flipped a page in her notebook.

Richard sighed. "A tenacious woman."

"Yes, well, be thankful for that, sweetheart," she said, smiling.

"I do, every day," Richard said, grinning.

"Okay, so . . . your mother?"

Richard stepped over to the rigging and adjusted a sail to his liking, then came back to the shining mahogany wheel. "Aye, she handles nicely in this breeze."

"Richard, please . . ."

He turned to her. "You always were a better cabin boy than a sailor. I daren't let you even hold the wheel to a course, Tess. For shame."

"You knew that before we got married. Besides, I'm liberated, but I do the laundry. What more does a man want?" she asked saucily.

"And you with washing machines and driers, too," he said.

"But I'm a historian. I'm writing a book. You'll be famous, Richard."

"And you're going to kill me off."

"Well, I don't want to confuse people, do I? You're his great-great-great-grandson or something. Isn't that what we decided?"

"Aye, we did, but I hate to be drowned in that damned hurricane, nonetheless."

"Superstitious, Richard?"

He swung his eye over to her. "Maybe. What's it to you?"

Tess laughed. God, she loved it when Richard tried out the modern phrases he'd picked up! There was something so comical about her pirate mouthing things like "awesome" and "what's at the flicks tonight?"

He looked annoyed. "So what did I say wrong now?"

"Nothing. It's perfect. It's just that—" She broke into peals of laughter.

"Ah, Tess, you're not properly respectful to your husband."

"I think you're wonderful, Richard, you know that. I adore you. It's just that sometimes you're funny."

"You best raise our child to respect me better than you do," he stated.

"Of course, sweetheart," Tess said demurely. "Now can we go on? Your mother..."

"She was born around fifteen hundred and seventy outside of London," he began. "From a poor family. She was sent to the Moore house when she was fifteen, an indentured servant...."

The *Bonny Tess* skimmed the sparkling waves with Richard at the helm and Tess taking notes. She looked up from her work to admire her husband, so at home on his ship, his feet planted squarely on the oiled teak deck, his strong hands sure on the wheel. He wore white shorts and no shirt, and his ponytail blew in the breeze. His shoulders were broad and suntanned, and a sheen of sweat covered his skin. Oh, how she loved him.

True to his word, Richard had set up a foundation, funded by his share of the *Isabela*'s treasure: The Neville Foundation for Marine Research. It would target the *bajamar* and especially the fast-disappearing coral reefs that were in such deadly danger all over the world.

He had a director, a young man with a marine biology degree and a head for business, whom he'd hired on the spot. The new director's name was Gregory Salvador.

"He's from *where?*" Tess had asked when she'd heard.

"The Bahamas. It's an independent nation now, I just learned. His family, it seems, is quite large and influential there," Richard had replied smugly.

"Did you ask him . . . ? I mean, did he, is he . . . ?"

Richard had smiled. "He told me that his family has been there forever. Aye, he said 'forever,' and that some founding ancestor had been a pirate. Imagine that!"

"My God, Richard, that could be Ruby's descendant you hired," Tess had breathed.

"I am aware of that, love. And he is a most worthy young man."

"I told Ruby to hang on to Red Turtle Cay, Richard. Did you know that?" she'd asked.

"It appears he did. The Salvadors have prospered."

"Ruby would be proud."

"Aye, that he would. I miss the old lad at times. He was a good friend to me," Richard had said soberly, "and I'm glad to give this young Salvador a chance."

Greg had worked out well, and now the foundation had more employees, a research project to begin this very summer and plans for a cooperative project with Australia to save their own coral reefs. And Richard hardly ever had to go into the Key West office.

As soon as the baby came, Richard and Mack Solomon were planning a new salvage operation on the *Santa Luisa,* the slave ship that had picked up Tess. Although his crew had taken as much as they could carry from her, Richard knew there would be even more lying on the bottom of the sea with the burned, sunken hull. And he recalled with absolute clarity exactly where he'd sunk it and rescued the black slaves and gotten himself a new and practically useless cabin boy.

A hot breeze ruffled Tess's short hair as Richard changed tack. She looked up once again, studying her husband, feeling the child grow within her. Intense love filled her. He turned from his watch, caught her eye and grinned knowingly. "Is it time for a nap then, love?" he asked.

"Just a couple more questions," Tess said, teasing.

"God's teeth, lass, be done with the questions for today. Have mercy."

"Your father's company. How many shares were there? Did he own a majority? Where did his financing come from?"

"The answers are: I don't know, yes, the Dutch in Amsterdam. Satisfied?"

"For today."

"Wait, Tess. I just bethought myself of something. It is about your book. How is it that you've never asked about the women in my life? Shouldn't a buccaneer's history include his trysts and his many lady loves?" he asked slyly.

"That is not of any historical significance," Tess said primly.

"I disagree. A pirate's reputation with the ladies is of great import. Oh, I truly do think you'd best include my many and varied affairs of the heart. You could not leave out the lovely Matilda, could you?"

"Well, I don't need notes for Matilda," she said.

"Oh, but the others..." He lashed the wheel and came to stand before Tess. He was grinning, that rakish flash of white teeth, as he pulled her upright and took her hands in his. "Shall we go below and explore my history?" he asked.

"Oh, Richard," she said, laughing, "I'm sure going to have a heck of a problem listing my sources for that part of the story."

"You'll find a way, Tess. You always do," he said with utter certainty.

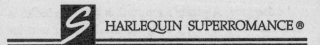

COMING NEXT MONTH

#582 MOONCALLER • Patricia Chandler
Logic told Whitney Baldridge-Barrows to hate Gabriel Blade. He
was planning to turn the Havasupai village at the bottom of the
Grand Canyon, where she worked as a doctor, into a posh tourist
resort. But logic had nothing to do with Whitney's response to the
man....

#583 IF I MUST CHOOSE • Lynda Trent
After her divorce, Lacy Kilpatrick wanted nothing to do with
romance—but she hadn't counted on sexy Austin Fraser showing
up. Nor had she counted on her family calling him "the enemy" and
forbidding her to see him.

#584 McGILLUS V. WRIGHT • Tara Taylor Quinn
Never mind that sparks flew between them—Tatum McGillus and
Jonathan Wright should never have said hello to each other. The
timing was wrong, and they couldn't agree on anything. As if that
weren't enough, they stood on opposite sides of the law. This was
one relationship that would need a miracle to survive.

#585 DIAL D FOR DESTINY • Anne Logan
The last thing Lisa LeBlanc's sister Dixie said before she disappeared was that she was going to meet a man named Gabriel
Jordan. Lisa managed to track Gabriel down, but the man denied
ever speaking with Dixie. Somehow, Lisa was sure he knew more
than he was telling. To uncover the truth, she had to stay close to
Gabe. An idea that was not altogether without appeal.

AVAILABLE NOW

#578 THE LAST BUCCANEER
Lynn Erickson

**#579 THE DOG FROM RODEO
DRIVE**
Risa Kirk

#580 SIMPLY IRRESISTIBLE
Peg Sutherland

#581 THE PARENT PLAN
Judith Arnold

MEN MADE IN AMERICA

Fifty red-blooded, white-hot, true-blue hunks
from every State in the Union!

Look for MEN MADE IN AMERICA! Written by some
of our most poplar authors, these stories feature fifty of
the strongest, sexiest men, each from a different state in
the union!

Two titles available every other month at your favorite
retail outlet.

In January, look for:

DREAM COME TRUE by Ann Major (Florida)
WAY OF THE WILLOW by Linda Shaw (Georgia)

In March, look for:

TANGLED LIES by Anne Stuart (Hawaii)
ROGUE'S VALLEY by Kathleen Creighton (Idaho)

You won't be able to resist MEN MADE IN AMERICA!

My Valentine
1994

Celebrate the most romantic day of the year with
MY VALENTINE 1994
a collection *of* original stories, written by
four of Harlequin's most popular authors...

MARGOT DALTON
MURIEL JENSEN
MARISA CARROLL
KAREN YOUNG

*Available in February, wherever
Harlequin Books are sold.*

HARLEQUIN ®

VAL94

NEW YORK TIMES **Bestselling Author**

Barbara DELINSKY

returns in January with

THE REAL THING

Stranded on an island off the coast of Maine,
Deirdre Joyce and Neil Hersey got the
solitude they so desperately craved—
but they also got each other, something they
hadn't expected. Nor had they expected
to be consumed by a desire so powerful
that the idea of living alone again was
unimaginable. A marrige of "convenience"
made sense—or did it?   BOB7

 HARLEQUIN®

HARLEQUIN SUPERROMANCE ®

Women Who Dare will continue with more exciting stories,
beginning in May 1994 with

THE PRINCESS AND THE PAUPER by Tracy Hughes.

And if you missed any titles in 1993
here's your chance to order them:

Harlequin Superromance®—Women Who Dare

#70533	DANIEL AND THE LION by Margot Dalton	$3.39	❑
#70537	WINGS OF TIME by Carol Duncan Perry	$3.39	❑
#70549	PARADOX by Lynn Erickson	$3.39	❑
#70553	LATE BLOOMER by Peg Sutherland	$3.50	❑
#70554	THE MARRIAGE TICKET by Sharon Brondos	$3.50	❑
#70558	ANOTHER WOMAN by Margot Dalton	$3.50	❑
#70562	WINDSTORM by Connie Bennett	$3.50	❑
#70566	COURAGE, MY LOVE by Lynn Leslie	$3.50	❑
#70570	REUNITED by Evelyn A. Crowe	$3.50	❑
#70574	DOC WYOMING by Sharon Brondos	$3.50	❑

(limited quantities available on certain titles)

TOTAL AMOUNT	$
POSTAGE & HANDLING	$
($1.00 for one book, 50¢ for each additional)	
APPLICABLE TAXES*	$ _____
TOTAL PAYABLE	$ _____
(check or money order—please do not send cash)	

To order, complete this form and send it, along with a check or money order for the
total above, payable to Harlequin Books, to: *In the U.S.*: 3010 Walden Avenue,
P.O. Box 9047, Buffalo, NY 14269-9047; *In Canada*: P.O. Box 613, Fort Erie, Ontario,
L2A 5X3.

Name: _____

Address: _____ City: _____

State/Prov.: _____ Zip/Postal Code: _____

*New York residents remit applicable sales taxes.
 Canadian residents remit applicable GST and provincial taxes.

WWD-FINR

Relive the romance...
Harlequin and Silhouette
are proud to present

A program of collections of three complete novels by the most requested
authors with the most requested themes. Be sure to look for one volume each
month with three complete novels by top name authors.

In January: **WESTERN LOVING**   Susan Fox
                                   JoAnn Ross
                                   Barbara Kaye

Loving a cowboy is easy—taming him isn't!

In February: **LOVER, COME BACK!**   Diana Palmer
                                      Lisa Jackson
                                      Patricia Gardner Evans

It was over so long ago—yet now they're calling, "Lover, Come Back!"

In March: **TEMPERATURE RISING**   JoAnn Ross
                                    Tess Gerritsen
                                    Jacqueline Diamond

Falling in love—just what the doctor ordered!

Available at your favorite retail outlet.

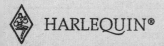

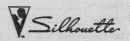

HARLEQUIN®

Don't miss these Harlequin favorites by some of our most distinguished authors!

And now, you can receive a discount by ordering two or more titles!

HT#25409	THE NIGHT IN SHINING ARMOR by JoAnn Ross	$2.99	☐
HT#25471	LOVESTORM by JoAnn Ross	$2.99	☐
HP#11463	THE WEDDING by Emma Darcy	$2.89	☐
HP#11592	THE LAST GRAND PASSION by Emma Darcy	$2.99	☐
HR#03188	DOUBLY DELICIOUS by Emma Goldrick	$2.89	☐
HR#03248	SAFE IN MY HEART by Leigh Michaels	$2.89	☐
HS#70464	CHILDREN OF THE HEART by Sally Garrett	$3.25	☐
HS#70524	STRING OF MIRACLES by Sally Garrett	$3.39	☐
HS#70500	THE SILENCE OF MIDNIGHT by Karen Young	$3.39	☐
HI#22178	SCHOOL FOR SPIES by Vickie York	$2.79	☐
HI#22212	DANGEROUS VINTAGE by Laura Pender	$2.89	☐
HI#22219	TORCH JOB by Patricia Rosemoor	$2.89	☐
HAR#16459	MACKENZIE'S BABY by Anne McAllister	$3.39	☐
HAR#16466	A COWBOY FOR CHRISTMAS by Anne McAllister	$3.39	☐
HAR#16462	THE PIRATE AND HIS LADY by Margaret St. George	$3.39	☐
HAR#16477	THE LAST REAL MAN by Rebecca Flanders	$3.39	☐
HH#28704	A CORNER OF HEAVEN by Theresa Michaels	$3.99	☐
HH#28707	LIGHT ON THE MOUNTAIN by Maura Seger	$3.99	☐

Harlequin Promotional Titles

#83247	YESTERDAY COMES TOMORROW by Rebecca Flanders	$4.99	☐
#83257	MY VALENTINE 1993	$4.99	☐
	(short-story collection featuring Anne Stuart, Judith Arnold, Anne McAllister, Linda Randall Wisdom)		

(limited quantities available on certain titles)

	AMOUNT	$
DEDUCT:	**10% DISCOUNT FOR 2+ BOOKS**	$
ADD:	**POSTAGE & HANDLING**	$
	($1.00 for one book, 50¢ for each additional)	
	APPLICABLE TAXES*	$ _____
	<u>**TOTAL PAYABLE**</u>	$ _____
	(check or money order—please do not send cash)	

To order, complete this form and send it, along with a check or money order for the total above, payable to Harlequin Books, to: **In the U.S.:** 3010 Walden Avenue, P.O. Box 9047, Buffalo, NY 14269-9047; **In Canada:** P.O. Box 613, Fort Erie, Ontario, L2A 5X3.

Name: _____

Address: _____ City: _____

State/Prov.: _____ Zip/Postal Code: _____

*New York residents remit applicable sales taxes.
Canadian residents remit applicable GST and provincial taxes.

HBACK-JM